About the Author

Anthony Guiffreda is a life-long resident of Western New York. He received his bachelor's degree in History from SUNY Brockport and his master's degree in Education from Canisius College. When he isn't working his day job, he and his wife enjoy traveling and spending time with friends and family. This is his first novel.

Facebook and Twitter – @AylaV716

Ayla's War

Anthony Guiffreda

Ayla's War

Olympia Publishers
London

Dedication

I dedicate this book to my parents and to my wife. Thank you for always believing in me.

Chapter 1

Chicago

Ayla's eyes opened wide and she found herself staring at the circular brown water stains that covered the ceiling. Her heart raced as beads of sweat rolled down her olive-colored skin. It was the middle of the night, and another nightmare had jolted her awake. Her light brown hair, which was usually long and silky, was now knotted and tattered. The oversized gray shirt that she had worn to bed was disheveled and damp. The ring of sweat around her neck was as clear as the memories that haunt her almost every night. They're always the same, flashes of her past life that she just can't seem to forget. She pulled herself up and sat on the edge of her bed. She stared at her feet as they formed footprints in the stained beige carpet. For a moment, she drifted off, and imagined her feet were slowly sinking in the sand of a beautiful beach somewhere far away from the city. For a moment, she didn't have nightmares and didn't have to deal with the burden she carried with her every day. The sounds of shouting and shattered glass from an open window brought her back to reality. Once again, her feet were on the ugly carpet and she slowly stood up from her small bed taking care not to wake her roommates.

There were five others who shared the small apartment with her and each had their own unique circumstances that brought them to Chicago, one of the few remaining cities in the United

States. Calling it an apartment was quite generous actually; Ayla viewed it more like a prison cell. She crept toward the bathroom and to her left were Gabe and Zoe, a young married couple who managed to survive together through the war that saturated the country just eight years ago. They were both in their mid-thirties, but like everyone who lived in the harsh environment of postwar Chicago, they appeared older beyond their years. Gabe was an average looking and average sized man with brown hair. Ayla had always thought he was a nice guy, but even she had to admit he was just ordinary. Zoe on the other hand was cheerful and happy, which was an accomplishment for the life they were living. She was almost as tall as her husband with shoulder length dark hair. The apartment was furnished with twin beds but Gabe and Zoe pushed theirs together every night.

Directly across from Ayla slept a boy named Raj, who when the war had just begun, lost his family at the age of seven. Raj was young, no older than sixteen He didn't remember too much of what the country used to be like, so in a way, this life was all he knew. He was a tall, athletically built young man, but was still long and lanky with room to fill out.

Sleeping next to him were two former resistance fighters named Malik and Juliette. Like Gabe and Zoe, they too were in their mid-thirties, although Ayla wasn't sure of their exact ages. They fought together in Texas during the uprising but when the war was over, they were forced to go into hiding. Malik was tall, and looked to be big and strong. Juliette was just the opposite; a small, skinny red head. You would never have guessed by looking at her but, like Malik, she was a brave soldier who saw plenty of action.

Ayla snuck past their beds, which, with the exception of Gabe and Zoe's, were laid out like an orphanage. She made her way to the bathroom door, and slowly closed it behind her as she entered. She flipped the light switch, which caused the fixture above her to slowly flicker before turning on with its normal electric humming sound. Her feet were cold on the tile floor but she was still reeling from her dream, so she welcomed the feeling. She reached down toward the old sink and turned on the cold water. As she placed her hands under the trickling stream from the pitted faucet, she imagined what life was like for the lucky few who lived in the newly relocated capital. Those that were able to enjoy the simple pleasures she used to take for granted, like hot showers. She cupped her hands together and splashed a small amount of water gently on her face. She took a moment to allow the cooling sensation to take effect. She then grabbed the gray washcloth that was hanging near the sink and pressed it against her face. It was at this moment that she saw her reflection in the tarnished mirror. She looked deep into her own eyes and thought about the person she used to be. She questioned if that person was gone or just hiding somewhere within herself. After about a minute of this, she quietly returned to her bed, and eventually fell back asleep.

Sometime later, Ayla felt the warm sun on her face that crept through her partially opened maroon curtains. It was only a sliver of light, but it was enough to wake her. She rolled over and grabbed her mother's old wristwatch that was lying on her nightstand; it read 7.32 a.m. Some of her housemates, as they usually did, had already left for the day: Malik and Juliette, who worked for the CFD, *The Chicago Fishery Department,* and Gabe and Zoe, who were employed by the CHC, *The Chicago Hunting Club.* These agencies were part of a series of programs implemented by the city's appointed Governor, Jeffery Gould. Each city's governor had the freedom to choose how to manage the residents who lived in their jurisdictions. Unfortunately for the dwindling population of Chicago, the programs Gould created did not generate nearly enough food or services to help. To add to the dilemma, governors were appointed now, not elected, so they were stuck with him.

Both the CFD and the CHC were controlled and regulated under Gould's watchful eye. Every fish caught and animal hunted had to be reported and turned over to the agency headquarters for redistribution to the general population. In return for their efforts, employees were given a small wage that mostly went toward paying for the food they helped catch and for rent to live in the government-owned apartments. It was all a corrupt cycle that only benefited Gould and his associates.

Raj was still sleeping. Like many of the young men living in Chicago, he was learning to work for one of the programs created by the governor. Malik was able to get him an apprenticeship working on the docks for the fishery department. Every day, he made his way to the edge of Lake Michigan and was primarily responsible for carting the fish to the agency headquarters. He also had to do jobs such as scrubbing boats, decks, and other general labor duties.

The economy of Chicago wasn't the only thing that had changed; the cityscape was also drastically different from what it was before the war. Gone were most of the skyscrapers, reduced to rubble during the air raids. The remaining few buildings were converted to tenement houses, like the one Ayla lived in. The tall living quarters were surrounded by small shelters and tents used by those who either refused to pay rent or who couldn't afford it. The majority of those who lived in Chicago did so along the canals and rivers the city was once famous for. Not far from Ayla's home was a large open-air market where many did their best to survive.

In fact, a lot of the country had changed significantly; most of the major highways were destroyed along with the bulk of the cars that traveled on them. Although occasionally the average citizen did somehow manage to find a working vehicle, in most cases they were only driven by government employees. The few industries that were around before the war were either now destroyed or closed and many places that were once seen as tourist destinations suffered the same fate as Chicago, or worse.

There were only a few major cities left like Chicago in the United States. New York City, Los Angeles, and Seattle were the only other metropolitan areas that survived the war and each was still heavily populated by post war standards. Seattle was also the home of the new capital and governing body of the United States. The rest of the population outside of the cities lived in small settlements, spread throughout the countryside, usually along rivers and lakes.

Ayla again quietly made her way to the apartment's bathroom to shower and get dressed for the day. She took off her gray shirt which had since dried from her stress-filled sleep. As she waited for the shower to turn from cold to slightly less cold, she again was transported to her past. Her naked reflection was another reminder of a life she had been pretending didn't exist. She took a moment to inspect the small scars that lay across her skin. She ran her fingers over them noting the differences in textures and sensations. She then cautiously entered the tepid water to clean up for another day in the city.

For breakfast, she had bread with some leftover deer meat that Gabe and Zoe snuck home from work. After she finished, Raj was just waking up to start his day. Ayla liked to think he thought of her like a big sister; in reality though, Raj had a little crush on his roommate. "Morning, Ayla," he said with a smile as he sat up in his bed.

"Morning, Raj," she replied. "You better get going; Malik might beat you if you're late again," she said jokingly.

"I know," he said reluctantly as he climbed out of bed and headed toward the bathroom to shower. Ayla smiled because she liked to give him a hard time. He reminded her of her younger brother who was killed during the war.

Since relocating to Chicago, Ayla, like many others, usually spent her days working in the market. She considered herself lucky that she was able to find work with an elderly woman who lived a few floors below her. The woman sold clothes she made from sewing or knitting, and also did repairs. She paid Ayla a small wage to collect and deliver items, which she then put toward food and rent.

Each day, Ayla and her roommates would go about their business trying to survive and avoid conflicts with the city's enforcers. Enforcers were basically policemen hired to keep the population under control and they were authorized to use any means necessary to do their jobs. Each city had their own breed and they operated under the direction of the governor.

Just as Ayla was about to begin another day in the market, she heard a knock at the door. This puzzled her because they never had visitors, and if they did, they normally chose to entertain them somewhere else. She slowly approached the mold speckled door and secured the rusted chain lock. Hesitantly, she unlocked the deadbolt and opened the door. Through the small crack, she saw the familiar face of an old man dressed in drab clothes in his late sixties. His grey hair was neatly shaped into a flattop just like she remembered. She almost didn't recognize him, as Father Time had taken its toll; but the long scar on his cheek was something Ayla would never forget.

"Hello, Major, it's been a long time," the old man said as he stared back at her, grinning through the small crack.

Chapter 2

Martial Law

Ayla was just sixteen years old when the resistance started to fight back. What was once a democracy, the United States suspended the rights of its citizens in 2025 following the emergence of a radical militant group that referred to themselves as Cats. Without any context, it sounded quite silly, but C.A.T. actually stood for *Citizens Against Tyranny*. At first, members of C.A.T. staged peaceful gatherings and rallies that protested numerous issues including the outsourcing of jobs, the end of federally funded programs to help the impoverished, the widening gap between the rich and the poor, and of course, political corruption. At a rally in Boston during the summer of 2023, some of C.A.T.'s members crossed the line when their actions provoked a riot. They flipped cars, looted stores, and even attacked the Boston Police Department. The response from the police and the United States government was to use deadly force. Several major leaders of C.A.T. were killed during the conflict and the movement almost died with them.

From the ashes of the violence, a new leader emerged. His name was Alexander Dumont, a former Navy Seal who was dishonorably discharged following the suspicious deaths of five Marines who were under his command during the Israeli – Iran war of 2016. Dumont took a much different approach to leadership than his departed predecessors. He recruited, trained, and armed civilians who were prepared to go to war over their beliefs. For the next two years, C.A.T. claimed responsibility for over fifty different attacks on the United States government and for the deaths of over one thousand of their fellow Americans.

After several failed attempts to squash the efforts of C.A.T., the United States government implemented martial law in almost every major city. Ordinary citizens were detained, interrogated, tortured, and sometimes even killed for being suspected C.A.T. members. Eventually in 2027, Alexander Dumont and his officers were found and arrested. The United States had beaten C.A.T., but in doing so they alienated more than half of the population. Most people started to see the United States government as the enemy and Alexander Dumont was perceived to be a martyr. In major cities across the country, pockets of resistance formed, and their numbers were more than Dumont could have ever imagined.

By 2029, the resistance was armed, highly organized, and was present in every corner of the country. They strategically attacked the United States by first taking over National Guard armories which gave them access to military vehicles and weapons. They then secured multiple locations where the United States had been storing nuclear weapons. What ensued was a bloody civil war of epic proportions which saw both sides using weapons of mass destruction, massive ground and aerial battles, and chemical warfare. This resulted in the deaths of millions of Americans from both the resistance and for those fighting for the government. After ten years of war, the military power of the United States proved to be too strong for the resistance. The country suffered greatly as nearly half of the population had been killed, most American cities were abandoned or destroyed, and the remaining leaders of the resistance had scattered across the country in an attempt to escape a public execution

It was now the year 2047; it had been eight years since the resistance was crushed by the United States. Many people were much like Ayla's roommates, Gabe and Zoe, simple folks who struggled to survive on a daily basis. Those that served the United States Government lived a much better life either in the capital area or within the governors' residential neighborhoods. After Washington D.C. was destroyed, the government chose Seattle to be the new capital because it was untouched during the war and was far from the general population that remained alive.

When martial law was instituted to destroy C.A.T., Ayla was only twelve years old. She was living in a suburb outside of Buffalo, New York called Orchard Park. Her mother and father were both working as defense attorneys at a firm downtown while she and her brother attended the local school. As more and more innocent people were being detained and interrogated by the government, Ayla's parents became increasingly involved in the discussions surrounding the injustices that were happening to their fellow citizens. They started defending people who had been targeted by the government and as their client list grew, so did their hatred for what was happening to their country. Not only did Ayla's parents represent their clients for free, but they also publicly denounced the actions of the government. In the eyes of the United States, her parents had become a threat and had potential connections to C.A.T.

One weekend in the summer of 2026 at the peak of unrest in the country, Ayla and her brother were playing outside when three green army Humvees arrived at their home. Ayla was young, but still somewhat aware of current events. She grabbed her brother and they both hid behind a neighbor's above ground pool. While shielding her brother's eyes, she watched as the men in army uniforms who proudly displayed the stars and stripes, dragged her parents outside, placed them on their knees, and executed them in their front yard. The soldiers left their bodies in the street as a message to any C.A.T. sympathizers in the area.

Distraught, confused, and saddened, Ayla now had to protect her younger brother. She knew she couldn't use her cell phone because the government was probably monitoring their calls, she couldn't go to a relative's house because if you were thought of as a C.A.T. supporter then so was the rest of your family. She went to the only person that seemed logical to approach. A neighbor several houses down that her parents often talked to, especially near the end. He shared their displeasure with the atrocities the government imposed on its citizens. At the time she didn't know him very well, and the only reason she thought to go to him was because her dad had told her stories about how he was a real life hero.

Chapter 3

The Man at the Door

Ayla was looking at a face she had not seen for nearly twelve years. For a moment, she thought she was having another nightmare, but she quickly realized that this was real and her commanding officer, and her friend, was somehow at her door. His name was Colonel Miles Lang. He was the neighbor that sheltered Ayla and her brother during their darkest hours. He was the father figure in both their lives, who raised them to be brave soldiers who fought for a belief rather than a paycheck. He was the veteran of three wars in Iraq, Afghanistan, and Iran. He was the winner of several medals and military honors for his bravery and dedication to the United States Marine Corp. He was also the head of the entire Northeastern resistance movement during the war.

Face to face with him once again, many emotions and questions flooded her mind. She was happy to see him but she knew this encounter meant her secret life in Chicago may have run its course. Ayla had felt confident in her anonymity, having fooled the two resistance fighters that she was living with. As far as they knew, she was simply a survivor looking to find her way.

"Aren't you going to invite me in?" he asked, as Ayla stood in the doorway, speechless.

"What are you doing here Miles?" Ayla whispered anxiously but before he had a chance to answer her, she shut the door, unlocked the chain and let him in. The two old friends and veterans shared an emotional but brief hug.

"Hey Ayla," he said as she let him go.

"So, I guess you're not dead then," she said smiling.

"Alive and well," he said.

"You're not here just to visit, are you?" she asked even though she already knew the answer.

"Something's come up," he said.

She could see his serious demeanor and knew he hadn't come to tell her how retirement was going. Not knowing where the conversation would lead, she thought it best to have it take place somewhere other than her doorway.

"Raj, I'm leaving, don't be late!" she yelled toward the bathroom as she grabbed her coat.

She locked the door on her way out and they made their way toward the elevators at the end of the long hallway. The hall was dimly lit, and some of the overhead lights flickered much like the one in Ayla's bathroom. The walls were painted a creamy, yellow color and the years of neglect were evident in the peeling paint, stains, and graffiti. Typically, when Ayla walked down the hallway, she kept her head down and stared at the linoleum floor, focusing her attention on the cracked tiles, trying not to draw attention to herself. This time, however, she kept her head held high and walked with the same bravado that she used to back when she and Miles were leading men and women into battle. It was no surprise that being with him again gave her confidence; despite losing the war, when the two were commanding forces on the ground, they accomplished many great things together.

The walk to the elevator seemed longer than normal. Several thoughts raced through her mind. Would she ever come back here? Did she want to come back here? What about her

21

roommates? Were they in danger? She imagined the worst-case scenarios and started to become quite anxious. That anxiety turned into anger toward Miles. She started to ask herself why he came to her apartment in the first place. Why not meet her in the market; surely, he knew she worked there if he was able to find out where she lived.

As they arrived at the elevator, she pushed the down button and after a few moments, the metal doors opened slowly and they entered. Once the doors closed, Miles pushed the button labeled *L*.

"What the hell is happening?" Ayla asked impatiently.

"Nothing's happening, nothing yet; just two old friends having a chat," he said.

"Nothing yet," she shot back sarcastically. There was a brief silence before the anger that built up in the hallway came out. "Why did you show up here? You had to come to my apartment? My life isn't great, but I swear if you mess this up." She didn't finish her thought and didn't need to, as Miles knew what she was implying. He figured that showing up out of nowhere might be a shock for her but he was still surprised at her sudden outburst. Ayla, on the other hand, was starting to realize that the life she had created in Chicago was most likely about to be upended.

Before he could respond, the elevator doors opened and for a second time they reverted to silence. The lobby of her building was actually quite nice compared to the rest of it; at least it probably was at some point. There were two old couches that were situated around an unused, ash-filled fireplace which was surrounded by stone. There was even an old television mounted on the wall, although now it only collected dust. They continued through the lobby, toward the set of glass doors that led to the street. As they approached the exit, she could feel the warmth from the sun coming through the glass: a rare sunny day for the end of autumn.

As Miles pushed open the doors, the brisk air hit them and the smell of the streets filled their noses. One unfortunate result of the war was that the city's sanitation workers weren't as proficient as they once were, and that's putting it nicely. Miles and Ayla made their way through the crowded market that was just outside of her building. The people were busy buying, selling, and negotiating. No one seemed to notice the two old friends, as they casually walked to an abandoned building toward the end of the long line of shops and stands. The old brick structure was aged and had four floors and as she got closer, Ayla looked up and noticed most of the windows were broken or covered with black soot.

Miles led her to a door on the side of the building; he let her in and took one last look around to ensure no one had followed them. Once inside, she took a moment to take in her surroundings of the long-abandoned building. The air was stale and there was an unusual amount of mirrors and display cases that were broken and had been left to age in the forgotten structure. It was a jewelry store, she thought to herself. She turned to Miles, who had been watching her make her observations.

"Still thinking like military, I see," he said as he watched her canvass the room. She didn't respond to his small talk. She instead walked away from him, streaking her finger through the accumulated dust on top of the old display cases. He sarcastically tried again, "Hey Miles, Nice to see you, I miss you...Any of those things would be nice to hear."

Ayla finally directed her attention back to him. "Sorry; it is great seeing you again," she said as she walked back toward him and hugged him again, this time for longer and with a bit more feeling. "I just know that you showing up here out of the blue is probably not a good thing," she said as he hung his head briefly admitting that her theory was correct. "Where have you been?" she asked with genuine concern.

"Do you remember the last time we were together fighting out in Philly?" he asked her.

"I'll never forget it," she said.

"That was the worst day of my life. I've never told anybody this but we lost contact with HQ and never got word to fall back. We were surrounded, and it was either fight and die or surrender. So, I ordered my men to put their weapons down. I hoped they would only kill me." He paused to regain his speech; he felt that lump in his throat start to rise. "They killed them... all of them. They made me watch." Again, he paused and Ayla put her hand on his shoulder giving him the courage to continue. "They didn't even ask me any questions until after they were all dead," he said wiping his eyes before a tear could fall.

Ayla did her best to console him, but she knew her words wouldn't help and it was just something he needed to get off his chest. "There was nothing you could do, it wasn't your fault," she said to him as he nodded appreciating her efforts. "What happened next?"

"They took me to Seattle, tortured me for about three months looking for answers." He continued on, "After they realized I wasn't talking, they transferred me to a work camp somewhere in North Dakota."

"North Dakota?" she asked surprisingly. "I never knew they had camps up there."

"I think that was the point," he said. "If we didn't know where the camps were, how could we set our people free?"

"So how did you get out?" she asked him.

"A good old-fashioned prison break," he said with a smile.

"A prison break?" she asked skeptically.

"Yea, can you believe it?" he asked her. Ayla was still looking thrown, which prompted him to go into further detail. "As time dragged on, the number of guards at the camp dwindled. Looking back at it now, they probably just didn't have the manpower any more to keep up." He continued, "Anyways, myself and the other officers detained there began to organize and observe, see if there were any weaknesses we could exploit. Our only chance was when we were in the mess hall. It was the only time we were all together. Any other time they kept us in cabins that held about six people. So, when the time came we acted. We lost a few, but we were able to overtake them, steal their weapons, and escape."

After hearing this unbelievable story, it only created more questions for her. "Where did you go? How come I never heard from you?"

"I left, I was done. All of us there felt like we had given enough. You don't know misery and despair until you lived in a prison camp during a North Dakota winter."

"So you just quit? Disappeared?" Now Ayla's feelings were changing from curiosity and sympathy to anger and betrayal. "We were still fighting! What about us? We needed you out there…I needed you." Her voice trembled with anger.

Miles looked at her and said simply, "We all make decisions we regret, Ayla. That's one of them for me and I'm sorry for that."

"So am I," she said sarcastically. "I'm sorry I ever cried about losing you. I thought you were dead, I thought you died for a cause. A cause I was still fighting for!" She paused for a moment, never being the one to choose her words carefully, she added, "You're a coward."

The reunion of two old friends quickly turned into an argument. Miles responded to her with sternness in his voice, "Maybe you're right, maybe I was a coward. But I'm here now, and you can either choose to listen to me, or go on home and sell sweaters or whatever the hell you're doing." She flashed him a displeasing look but waited for him to continue. "I am here for a reason; I didn't come here just to say hi."

"Well, go on with it," she demanded.

"Look around you Ayla," he said as he held his arms out. "Is this the America you envisioned would rise up after the war?" Ayla looked at him as if he had asked a question he already knew the answer to. "I've been in Los Angeles since I left the camp. Just like you, I was pretending to be somebody I wasn't. I was a baker…making bread." He laughed and for a brief moment Ayla also cracked a smile. Miles continued, "One day, about three months ago, a man came into the store asking about Zion."

Ayla immediately looked at him with a surprised but focused intensity and repeated the name, "Zion, as in resistance headquarters Zion?"

"Yep," he replied and asked her another question, "Does the name Alexander Dumont mean anything to you?"

Chapter 4

The Road to Zion

As she stood in the abandoned jewelry store, Ayla was surrounded by reminders of what is and what used to be. When Miles mentioned the name Alexander Dumont, all of the burdens of her new life disappeared. She forgot that she lived in a tenement house with five people, she forgot about the cold showers, the twin mattress she slept on, she forgot the fact that she sells homemade clothing so she can feed herself. At this moment, she was engrossed by the fact that Colonel Miles Lang was talking to her about meeting Alexander Dumont. She repeated the name aloud, "Alexander Dumont? The Alexander Dumont was in your bakery?"

"Yes!" Miles replied with a determined yet happy expression on his face.

"C.A.T.'s Alexander Dumont?" she again questioned his statement. Miles again nodded to affirm his previous claim. "How is that even possible?" she asked and, without waiting for an answer, continued, "He was arrested before the war. How is he even alive? Isn't he like ninety?"

"He was arrested before the justice system went to hell." Before he continued, Miles motioned for Ayla to follow him. They carefully stepped around the broken shards of glass, leaving footprints on the dusty floor behind them. He found a couple of old chairs and set them in what appeared to be a storage room of some sorts. The room was small, probably half the size of Ayla's communal bedroom. She knew the conversation was about to become serious if he was going to this much trouble to keep them out of sight.

They were sitting now, face to face and Ayla was ready to hear the rest of Miles' story. He picked up where he left off from before.

"When Dumont was arrested, everyone still had a right to a trial, to be judged by a jury of your peers."

Ayla had learned about all of this when she was still in school but for all of her adult life, most law breakers had been simply murdered by the enforcers or thrown in jail without any due process.

Miles continued on, "Dumont was so smart that he carried out the attacks by C.A.T. through cells he had positioned in several cities across the country. When he was caught, he went to trial. They couldn't pin the deaths of all those people on him directly. He was found guilty of multiple counts of conspiracy, but that's it."

As Miles told the story, Ayla listened intensely.

"They locked him up in some prison in Louisiana and he was forgotten about."

"I don't understand," she said. "So what, twenty years go by and they just let him out?"

"See that's the thing that I questioned too," he added, "Apparently, when they put him away the entire infrastructure was still intact; phones, the internet, and electronic databases that housed records, including prison records, all still operational. But after the bombs dropped, all of that changed. Not only were the electronic databases destroyed, but Louisiana was completely cut off. The prison became its own enterprise; sort of a family business. They took in criminals and collected small fees from settlements that needed bad men to go away. But they also released prisoners who served out their sentences and who behaved themselves. Guess who behaved himself just well enough to get released?"

Ayla smiled as she replied, "Alexander Dumont."

"Alexander Dumont," he confirmed with a nod.

Ayla still had so many questions. "So why did he come find you?" She shifted her position and leaned back in her chair a bit more relaxed and fired another question, "How does he even know who you are?"

"Apparently there were a lot of Dumont fans in the south during the war," he replied as he folded his arms across his chest. "They would come and visit him, bring him gifts and what not. He would talk to certain people and eventually he developed a kind of communication network that kept him up to date on everything and everyone involved, including us."

"And he told you all this?" she asked skeptically.

"Yep, right in the basement of the bakery," he confirmed.

"So, what's going on now? You still haven't told me exactly why you're here." Ayla, clearly immersed in the entire situation, couldn't help herself from wanting to know more.

He nodded and leaned in closer to her. "Dumont specifically requested I find you and bring you in."

With a curious expression, Ayla asked, "Bring me in where?"

Miles smiled, and paused for a moment. He looked her in the eyes and said, "To the Revolution."

Chapter 5

To Be or Not To Be

Ayla and Miles sat quietly in the small storage room of the abandoned jewelry store. After several seconds, he finally broke the silence. "Aren't you going to say anything?" He paused and waited for a response but she was deep in thought. "Ayla!" he said louder. She looked at him. "This is our chance. All I'm asking is that you come with me and meet him. Listen to his plan; hear what he has to say." She heard him, but was still lost in her own thoughts.

"Listen, I'm leaving tomorrow morning. I'm catching a ferry that leaves at eight am. That ferry is going to take me to the old docks in Green Bay. If you want in, be there." He stood from his seat, leaned in, and kissed her softly on the forehead. "I've got to go," he said. "I hope to see you tomorrow." She watched as he walked through the dusty jewelry store and out the door.

She sat and thought a little while longer but eventually she decided to head home. As she exited the jewelry store, she noticed that it was much colder outside. The sun had been completely covered by clouds and the wind was picking up. Most of the traders and vendors had retired for the day due to the change in weather and the few remaining were closing up. Lost in her own thoughts, she hardly realized the chill in the air. As she slowly walked back through the market, her mind was racing with questions and imagined scenarios of what would happen if she left or if she stayed. When she was a girl, she really didn't have a choice; she went to Miles and he raised her to be a soldier and a leader. Now, all these years later, she had a choice. She looked around at the crumbling remains of Chicago and the sorry excuse for a city that it had become. As she approached the entrance to her tenement building, she paused just outside the door.

She needed a moment to think about what Miles had just told her. She replayed them in her mind, "Is this the America you envisioned?" She looked at the garbage on the streets, streets that were overgrown with weeds escaping through the cracks in the asphalt. She watched the people trying to insulate their haphazardly constructed shanties where many will more than likely freeze to death in the upcoming winter. Every day, she saw the hard work of these ordinary people benefit no one except the city's governor. She realized that she didn't have a choice this time either. It was her duty to once again, join the revolution.

When she settled in Chicago, Ayla thought there was a chance she might never be able to fully escape her past. Instead of entering her building, she walked around to the back where there were piles of garbage and a dilapidated playground nestled into an unkempt lawn. She returned to the same spot where she went when she first arrived after the war. She found a rusty old gardening spade leaning against a decaying plastic bucket and she started to dig.

After unearthing a few inches of dirt, she extracted a muddy old tin container. Her eyes were now fixed on the rectangular box; she softly brushed away the loose dirt particles and opened it. The smell of her past filled her spirit with warmth. Inside and unblemished were the memories she had kept hidden from her new life. Her black arm band with the symbol of the resistance was still finely sewn, preserved perfectly in the air tight bin. She looked down at the insignia she so proudly represented during the war. The symbol was a coiled snake, ready to strike, similar to the snake the founding fathers displayed during the birth of the nation. The snake was yellow, which represented intelligence and intellect. It was set in a red background to represent power and the willingness to take action. The background itself was in the shape of a shield because the resistance believed that it was their duty to protect the ideals of democracy.

She set the arm band in her coat pocket to protect it from the elements and to keep it out of sight. Underneath her arm band were more important items, her 9mm pistol, three extra clips, and a case of ammo. She picked up the gun and inspected it like she was trained to do. She checked the sites and the frame for damage, cocked the hammer and pulled the trigger; a dry fire to make sure all was in order. She loaded a clip into the chamber and holstered the gun into the back of her pants, concealed by her long coat.

To her surprise, there was one more thing settled in the bottom of the box, an envelope, unsealed. She opened it and as she pulled out the item inside, she remembered what she had concealed away. It was a picture of her family; all dressed up in blue and gold on their way to a hockey game. She studied the picture for a moment and the unexpected glimpse into her past caused a single tear to fall down her cheek. It was at this moment she remembered why she was actually fighting. This was why she joined the resistance, not because Miles raised her to be a soldier, but because it was the only way she knew she would find peace. She wanted to make sure that what happened to her family would never again happen to anyone's family. She thought to herself, maybe my nightmares happen because I haven't fulfilled my promise, not because I'm afraid of my past, but because I dread my present.

She regained her composure, returned the photo to the envelope, and placed it in her pocket. She then filled the empty hole in the ground, and tossed the metal bin onto the already heaping pile of garbage. Feeling refreshed and motivated, she returned to the front and entered. She walked through the lobby and continued to the silver elevator doors and pressed the up button. Riding the elevator to the seventh floor, she thought of her five roommates. She started to think about what she would tell them; would she tell them the truth? Recruit them even? Or would she lie to try and protect them? She would have to make a decision soon, as the ascending elevator was nearing her floor.

Moments later, the doors opened and she again found herself in the long yellow hallway. She made her way toward her apartment taking note of the peeling paint, and admiring the graffiti. For the first time, she saw it as a creative expression and she imagined that whoever was responsible must have had some artistic talent.

As she approached her door, she could see the flickering light from her bathroom spill out onto the linoleum hallway. The sight of this froze her. No one ever left the door open. For a brief moment, she forgot what to do. She forgot she was a trained military officer. She forgot that she wasn't Ayla the clothing vendor. The fear seemed so genuine, but it only lasted for a second and her training came back to her. Now her back was pressed against the wall, and her heavy breathing subsided.

She quietly pulled out her pistol and turned the safety off. She entered as she was taught, ready for anything. She checked the corners and then the bathroom. Stealthily, she headed toward the sleeping area. Before she turned the corner, her fears came to fruition as she spotted a pool of blood creeping into the hallway. She approached and peered around the corner and saw the bodies of Malik and Juliette, the two ex-resistance fighters from Texas. They had been executed, shot in the back of the head. Once she was confident she was alone, she holstered her weapon and she tended to the bodies of her fallen roommates. She knelt down and confirmed they had passed.

Before she had a chance to feel sad for the departed, Raj sprinted into the apartment, recklessly slamming the door against the wall. Frightened, Ayla turned around and took aim ready to shoot first and ask questions later. Raj shouted at her with his hands up, "Whoa, Ayla! Stop!"

"Raj! Are you trying to get shot?" she shouted back at him. "Where are Gabe and Zoe?" she asked him frantically.

Raj, in shock from what he was seeing didn't answer. "Wh. Wh…what happened?" he stuttered. "Why are they dead?" and in an even more shaky voice he asked, "Why do you have a gun?"

Ayla, realizing he might have the wrong idea, returned the gun to the back of her pants and calmly looked him in the eye. She could tell he was afraid, she had seen it before on the young men and women she trained for battle. "Raj, listen to me, did you see who did this?" she asked him. He was frozen in fear. She tried again. "Raj!" she shouted with both hands on his shoulders. "We need to leave now. Grab your coat and boots!" Raj didn't verbally respond to her but he did as he was told and they soon left the building.

Ayla, unaware of where Miles was staying for the night, brought Raj to the only place she knew was safe: the abandoned jewelry store. Raj still hadn't spoken, but she directed him to the storage room where she learned all about Alexander Dumont. This is where they would stay for the rest of the night. Raj fell asleep rather quickly; Ayla assumed it was an adrenaline crash from the unsettling events he witnessed earlier. She, on the other hand, did not find sleep as easy. The cold concrete combined with many looming questions kept her awake. Her thoughts centered on one question: who else did Miles tell about her? That was the only plausible explanation as to why two of her roommates were dead, two others were missing, and the fourth was probably in shock. After a while, she eventually managed to get some sleep.

Chapter 6

The Letter

The next morning, the sound of her wristwatch alarm woke her from her sleep. It took her a moment to realize where she was and how she got there. The confusion lasted only a second and once it subsided, she sat up quickly and looked to her left. Raj was nowhere to be seen. She sprang to her feet and hastily examined the store, searching for any signs of him. By now, there were too many footprints on the dusty floor to distinguish between the three people who had been walking around. As she paced wondering what to do next, she remained vigilant with her hand clutching her pistol. One thing she was certain of: standing around in the empty building was not an option. It was daylight, though, and she couldn't be seen walking the streets of Chicago yielding a handgun, so she holstered it before exiting the building. She stepped outside onto the cracked and uneven sidewalk that ran parallel to the store front. Normally, there weren't many people out and about this early. If Raj was around, she was hoping she'd spot him out in the market area.

As she stood aimlessly on the sidewalk trying to think of her next move, she slid her hand into her other pocket and felt something that wasn't there before. It was paper, folded into fourths, with a familiar texture. Once she retrieved it, she realized it was paper from Raj's sketch pad. It was a letter he had penned after she had fallen asleep. She read it quietly to herself.

Ayla,

Not sure what I walked in on there. Zoe said enforcers had Malik and Julie. Then I saw you with a gun and they were dead. I freaked. We are leaving town tonight. Find us at the old bridge. Please don't kill me.

-Raj

Ayla chuckled at Raj's humor but even she had to admit that him walking in on her holding a gun over two dead bodies was probably pretty shocking, maybe even suspicious. After all, there were stranger things that had happened in postwar Chicago besides someone going crazy and killing people. She was concerned that her housemates were out there on their own and afraid, but on the other hand, she was also worried that whoever killed Malik and Juliette might be after them too, or use them to get to her. She ultimately decided that her best course of action would be to meet Miles like he arranged and ask him to help her track them down before they leave.

She found him exactly where he said he would be, near the ferry landing ready to embark on the long journey across the country to Los Angeles. Happy that she decided to come, Miles was smiling from ear to ear. However, this time the smile was not returned from Ayla and as soon as he saw her face, he knew that something wasn't right. "We've got a problem," she said to him slightly out of breath.

"I can see that," he replied. "What's happening?"

"Someone knows we're here," she told him. "They killed two of my roommates; the other three are waiting for me to leave with them. Something's going on." As she finished her explanation, she grabbed his hand and placed the letter from Raj in his open palm.

"What's this?" he asked.

"That's the letter I found in my pocket this morning, after I slept all night in that stupid store," she said theatrically to him. She continued to explain the events that took place after their meeting. She urged him to consider how someone must have been following him or someone he trusts must have betrayed him. "Nobody knew I was here Miles. Eight years I lived in that stupid apartment and nothing happened. You show up, and two people die. What are you not telling me?" she asked with concern in her voice.

He searched for anything that could explain their predicament and came up with one theory. "When I left Los Angeles, Dumont sent another guy with me. I thought he was headed to New York. We were together the whole trip until we got to the Mississippi. I went north and he supposedly kept going east," he said.

"Could he be a spy?" she asked.

"I don't know, maybe…All I'm saying is that he knew where I was going and who I was coming to see, so maybe," Miles said, not quite ready to accept the fact that there could have been spies infiltrating the resistance before it even began.

"What's his name?" she asked out of curiosity.

As he tried to remember, Miles paused for a moment. Eventually, he said, "All he told me was that his name was Ryan and he never went into any more detail than that."

"Well you spent a lot of time with him. Did you lose your touch?" she asked sarcastically.

Miles scoffed, "No way! If he's a spy, then he's a good actor. The way he was carrying on about the oppressive government was pretty convincing." He offered a suggestion hoping to end their bickering, "I think the next thing we need to do is to find your friends."

As they made the short journey to where Raj had asked them to meet, they reminisced about their shared history. They laughed and joked about the good times and they remembered the bad times. Once they were closer to the arranged location, they decided that Ayla would approach the meeting on her own while Miles would remain hidden to provide her with any cover she may need. The old bridge was Chicago's once famous Canal Street railroad bridge, which was about a mile away from the ferry landing. It had since become overrun by nature from the years of neglect. In an attempt to delay supply lines to their enemy, the long-standing railroad ties had been removed by the resistance during the war.

They found an elevated spot for Miles to take cover and watch from a distance, aiming with his pistol in case the situation became dangerous. As he watched, she made her way toward the base of the bridge where she could see people huddled together around a fire keeping warm in the chilly fall morning. She walked toward the group and as the distance between her and her destination dwindled, she realized that there were not three people like she expected but five. The group saw Ayla on her approach and as Zoe and Gabe rose to their feet, Raj excitedly ran toward her yelling back to them, "Hey, it's Ayla, she came."

"Hey Raj," Ayla replied calmly. "You okay? How are the roomies?"

"We're doing okay. Not sure what's going on, but we're fine," he responded in a convincing manner.

"Who are those two men with you?" she asked him.

"You better just come listen for yourself," he said.

Ayla and Raj walked back toward Gabe, Zoe, and the two mystery guests. Ayla, not taking any chances, had her hand in her pocket grasping her 9mm firmly as the three friends greeted each other briefly. Before acknowledging the two gentlemen she had not yet met, she told Gabe and Zoe she was glad they were safe.

She then directed her attention to the two men who accompanied her housemates. As she took in their appearances, she asked, "Who are your friends?" The man on her left was taller than his partner. The first thing Ayla noticed about him was his perfectly groomed beard. His hair was receding but was dyed black, matching his facial hair. He was well dressed and most likely did not reside in one of Chicago's tenement houses. His shoes were polished and he had a nice warm coat. His counterpart, the man on Ayla's right, was much more disheveled. He was obviously younger and more athletic-looking than the other stranger. He had dirty clothes on that were worn, a scruffy five o'clock shadow, and though he had a full head of dirty blonde hair, it was matted and appeared he wasn't too keen on washing it.

The older, cleaner gentleman extended his hand and said, "Hello, I'm Jeffery Gould, and this is my brother Ryan."

Chapter 7

The Meeting

Ayla had never met the governor of Chicago but she knew the name Jeffery Gould very well. With her hand confidently grasping the pistol concealed in her pocket, her first thought was to draw her weapon and pull the trigger. She was too smart for that though. She also questioned why they were here with her friends, and if they hadn't arrested her yet, maybe they didn't know who she was. She knew that she hadn't exactly been truthful with her roommates when it concerned her involvement in the resistance, so there was a chance her cover wasn't blown. With Miles looking on from a distance, she casually extended her hand and said, "Ayla, nice to meet you."

"Ayla Vural, I assume?" asked Jeffery.

Ayla instantly grew nervous. She hadn't used her real last name since the day she enlisted. Although both her parents were born and raised in the United States, a long time ago her father's family emigrated from Turkey. Ayla, the name they chose for her, meant moonlight halo. Her mother chose the name because she loved the poem titled *The Moon*, by Robert Louis Stevenson. Now, in her late-thirties, the poem seemed perfect to be attached to her name. *The moon has a face like the clock in the hall; she shines on thieves on the garden wall.* Much like the moon, Ayla wanted to shine her light on the government, exposing them like the thieves that they were.

"You know who I am?" she asked the men with a puzzled look and a suspicious tone. In her pocket, she turned off the safety on her gun.

"I know all about you thanks to my younger brother here," he said.

She couldn't keep a calm demeanor any longer, she drew her weapon and before Ryan Gould had a chance to react, she aimed the barrel at Chicago's governor. At this point, Miles rushed in from his hidden observation post but not before she heatedly asked the governor, "Was it you? Did you kill them?" She of course was referring to her fallen roommates.

"Take it easy, Ayla," Miles said, trying to talk her down after recognizing his traveling partner Ryan.

Zoe, who had never seen Ayla with a gun, let alone aiming it at someone's head, asked in a frightened tone, "What are you doing, Ayla?"

"He killed them, Malik and Juliette," Ayla said without taking her eyes off her target. "On your knees!" she ordered them.

As Jeffery slowly got down on his knees with his hands raised in the air, he began to speak, "Let me ex…"

Ayla interrupted him, "Shut up!"

Jeffery, still on his knees, tried again in a stern but shaky voice, "Please just let me explain, you don't want to kill a city governor." As he was speaking, Ayla pressed the barrel to his forehead. Hoping to finish his sentence before she decided to pull the trigger, Jeffery quickly continued, "Especially one who works for Dumont!"

She slowly lowered her gun, but she was so taken aback by his statement that she waited for him to continue. "Now listen, we are on the same side," he said as he cautiously rose to his feet with his hands still raised and dirt marks around the knees of his pleated dress pants. His eyes were fixed on Ayla's and he continued, "I have been working with Dumont for the past three years."

She cut him off again and as she pointed the weapon back at his head, she exclaimed, "That's a lie! He's been in prison."

"Yea, I know. Down in Louisiana, right?" he asked her pretentiously. "Well, my brother here just so happens to be a former prison guard there. He's been my contact."

Ayla lowered her weapon and asked, "Why are they dead?" She could tell he knew something about her deceased roommates, so she pressed him.

"They were a casualty of war, I'm sorry." He paused, but Ayla gave him a look that implied she wanted to hear more, so he continued, "One of Ryan's runners was carrying a message from me to Dumont; it had information in there, about them. I thought he would want to bring them in considering their history. The letter was intercepted by my enforcers and brought to me. I had to make the call or risk blowing my cover. We're just lucky your other roommates weren't home."

"So you killed them…" she said as she looked to the sky, wondering it was all worth it.

"We have rules, Ms. Vural; Seattle has a long-standing policy to execute any known members of the resistance on site," Jeffery said, implying his need to keep up appearances.

She looked toward Miles, who was standing beside her and asked him, "Did you know about this?"

Miles, knowing full well his response would not be pleasing to Ayla, reluctantly answered the question, "I had orders, Ayla. I wasn't to tell you anything other than what I did."

With a disgusted look on her face, she swiftly turned toward Miles and before he had time to react, she threw a straight jab which landed squarely on his nose. He fell backwards and hit the ground. A plume of dust and dirt swirled around him. He rubbed his nose and smeared a trickle of blood across his upper lip. He looked up at her in shock. In an angry voice he asked, "What the hell was that for?"

"That's for lying to me, and don't act like you didn't deserve it," she said, as she extended her hand and helped him to his feet.

"You didn't have to punch me," he said unhappily as he tilted his head upwards in an attempt to stop his nose from bleeding.

Ayla asked, "You knew the entire time that Jeffery Gould was working with Dumont?" Miles nodded his head while still attempting to quell his bloody nose. "Unbelievable." She said to herself as she turned her back to the rest of the group placing her hand on her forehead in disbelief. Meanwhile, Zoe, Gabe, and Raj who had been watching the entire chain of events unfold, were looking dumbfounded.

Gabe finally spoke up, "Does anyone want to fill us in on what the heck is happening here?"

Miles sarcastically responded to his inquiry while still clutching his nose, "Your roommate here was a high-ranking officer in the resistance and has been hiding in Chicago masquerading as a lowly store vendor whose superior officer, that'd be me, has recently contacted her in an attempt to convince her to team up again."

After a short pause, Gabe not knowing what to say simply responded with, "Oh, okay." He looked to his wife Zoe and their friend Raj, who were equally stunned by the short narrative provided by Miles.

Ayla, feeling guilty about having lied, turned to her roommates and said, "I can explain, but not now." She directed her attention back to Jeffery and Ryan. "So what happens now…

Governor?" she asked mockingly.

Jeffery responded, "I'll stay here in Chicago and keep up appearances. I'll eventually have to send a search party to try and catch you. Malik and Juliette weren't the only people mentioned in that letter I told you about. As of now, you and your friends here are all wanted by the United States government for treason."

"Oh, that's just great," Gabe said cynically as Zoe and Raj expressed similar displeasure.

Jeffery continued, "Like it or not, the three of you are now part of this too."

Raj, being young and uninformed blurted out, "Why? Why can't we just hide?"

"They'll find you, Raj, and what happens after that you won't like," Ayla said to him sympathetically. Addressing all three of her roommates she said, "I'm sorry I got you all into this." They weren't pleased but they accepted the fact that they didn't have a choice and must now follow Ayla wherever she might be going next.

"What are we supposed to do?" Ayla asked openly to Miles and the Gould brothers.

"The six of us will travel to Los Angeles as refugees." Ryan said.

Surprised that he actually spoke up, Ayla asked, "Refugees from where?"

"There was a settlement just north of here that was attacked by bandits a couple days ago. Most of the people were killed but some escaped. We should be able to make our way without any problems."

Just like there were sporadic settlements of people living outside the cities, there were also organized groups of thieves and criminals that preyed upon the unprotected communities.

Because these people chose to live on their own, the government had made it their policy that the settlements would be responsible for their own security and safety.

Jeffery chimed in, "I need to go; I've been gone too long already. You all gather your things and get to that ferry. By the time you get to Los Angeles, Dumont will be ready to tell you your next assignment. If you're caught, we've never met, this meeting never took place, and I would get rid of that resistance arm band in your pocket Ayla." She looked down toward her coat pocket and saw that during the commotion of their impromptu rendezvous, the yellow and red symbol of the resistance had made its presence known. Jeffery looked toward Ayla's roommates and said, "Good luck, and don't worry, you'll get used to it." He then gave Ayla an irritated look as he dusted off his knees followed by an awkward hug with his brother. Before he turned and made his way back to the city, he directed his attention toward Ayla and Miles. He saluted them and said, "Generals, I trust you will do your duties."

Chapter 8

Lake Michigan

"General Vural," Miles said as he approached Ayla on the ferry. "Has a nice ring to it, doesn't it?"

Ayla, who was sitting on a bench near the front of the forty-foot ferry, raised her eyes and looked at Miles with a smirk and said, "Yea, I like it." He sat down next to her and put his arm around her. For a brief period of time, they just sat together in silence as the ferry traveled north along Lake Michigan. As the boat bobbed slightly up and down from the choppy water of the great lake, they both felt comfort and peace for the first time since being reunited. In this short-lived period of calmness, Ayla enjoyed the sunset with the closest thing to a father she had since losing her own. Miles, with no family of his own, saw Ayla as the daughter he never had.

Knowing the moment couldn't last long, Ayla broke the silence with a question. "Miles, why do you trust Dumont? I mean, I'm glad we're doing this, but the guy was a mad man back in the day."

"I was wondering when you were going to ask me that," he said as the two pulled away from each other. "Alexander Dumont was a young man during his C.A.T. days. He was forty-five years old when he was arrested. Did you know I served with him in Iran?" he asked her.

"No, you never told me that," she said astonished as she

stood from the bench to stretch her legs.

"We were stationed at the same base, but we never really crossed paths," he said casually. "But we knew each other." He added, "Anyways, in his younger days he was pretty extreme obviously, doing all those things, but his motivation was in the right place."

"Is he any less crazy now?" she asked.

"I wondered the exact same thing when he showed up in Los Angeles. Apparently, that prison he was at had a pretty extensive library." He said to her as she looked at him wanting to know more. "He told me that he had plenty of time to read and think about his methods. He said he read books like *The Art of War,* books about the first American Revolution, the French Revolution, the Haitian Revolution, he went on and on. Now he's seventy-something years old, he's smarter, he's more motivated than ever, and he was very convincing." Ayla nodded in silence confirming that she understood why Miles had put so much faith in him. He continued, "Remember when we talked in the jewelry store and I told you to come with me and just listen to his plan?"

She jokingly responded, "No, I forgot all about it."

He laughed and said, "I think you're going to like what he has to say."

By the end of their conversation the sun had set. Miles bid Ayla goodnight and retreated to his quarters. It wasn't too late and Ayla felt it necessary to find her friends who had been forced to join her in the cross-country voyage. They were sharing a four-person cabin. Ayla approached their door with a tender knock and without waiting for a response, she entered. Zoe and Gabe were sharing a bunk, wrapped in each other's arms. Raj was positioned to her right with a pad and pencil sketching a drawing of her. He was still secretly enamored with her, maybe even more so with his new perspective.

As she took a seat next to him, Zoe and Gabe sat up in their bunk anticipating further explanation from their roommate. Ayla looked at Raj's drawing of her, which to her amazement was an unexpectedly realistic depiction of her pointing a gun at Jeffery Gould. She asked with a smile, "Is that me?"

Raj looked at her and said, "Yea, do you like it?"

Hoping to make him laugh she said, "I think you made me too much of badass." He smiled and continued to draw.

Gabe took the lead on the next topic of conversation. Sitting next to his wife he stated, "So I think, we think, it's time you told us who you really are, Ayla."

"I know I owe you an explanation and an apology," she said with her eyes to the floor. She then leaned back, and opened up to them. "Believe me, if I would've ever had the slightest idea that this would happen I never would've even looked for roommates. I would have just found a place where I would have been alone." The three friends eagerly waited to hear more. "When we lost the war, I was beaten. I thought I had lost Miles, I had lost my entire family, and the worst part was that we lost the war." The passion in her tone intensified, "I ran, and I hid just like everybody else. I came to Chicago because I had never been there before; I figured no one would recognize me." At this point, Ayla was standing in the small ferry cabin and began to pace toward the door. Facing away from her friends, she continued, "I didn't count on finding a new family." She turned and looked at them.

Ayla returned to her seat next to Raj who had stopped drawing and was listening intently. Zoe spoke up first, "Ayla, I know we're fleeing for our lives right now, but you rescued us." Her husband looked at her with confusion as Zoe continued,

"Sure we were alive, but we weren't living, we were surviving. At least now, we are doing something about it." She paused and allowed Gabe and Raj to soak in what she was saying. "I have decided I want to help, what the hell is the point of living if you are afraid of tomorrow?"

Ayla looked at her, smiled, and said, "Thanks, but I'm sure Dumont can arrange a safe hiding place for you in Los Angeles."

Gabe looked at his wife and then turned to Ayla, "No, I don't want to hide, and I don't want to go on wondering if we're going to be able to eat tomorrow. We're in, we want to help." Gabe then looked at the youngest of the group and said, "What do you say Raj? Do you want to be a dockworker forever?"

Raj paused for a moment and looked down at his drawing. He saw the sketch of Ayla and the details of her revolutionary arm band which he drew protruding out of her coat pocket. He always had a crush on Ayla but now he also thought she was a badass as she put it. The three people in the small ferry cabin were the only family he knew. He set the pad of paper down beside himself and fixed his gaze on them and said, "Well, I got fired a week ago and never told you guys anyways." They all laughed in astonishment at his admission.

After their emotional conversation and realizations of their inevitable futures, Ayla said goodnight and made her way to her cabin. They all needed their rest; tomorrow they would be embarking on the long journey in the cold fall weather of the northern mid-west.

Chapter 9

The Plan

As the old ferry approached the abandoned docks in what used to be the city of Green Bay, Miles gathered everyone to discuss what the plan would be moving forward. "All right, people," he said to them as they stood close to one another on the bow of the boat. "This boat is about to dock in Green Bay, far enough away from Chicago to put some distance between us and that search party that Gould will most likely dispatch this morning." Ayla couldn't help herself from thinking how funny it was that Miles was addressing the small group like they were battletested Marines. He continued, "From Green Bay, we will rendezvous with Ryan's contact in Pikesville, a small settlement on the Wisconsin River. He will provide us with horses and a wagon. Now how many he has, I don't know. Our information is going to be a bit murky from here on out. Bad news is that we'll have to walk there; if we get a solid ten hours of walking each day, it should take about three days."

Out of the three new resistance recruits, Raj was the one who had the courage to speak up first. "So you're telling me we're riding horses, all the way to Los Angeles?" he asked halfheartedly.

"Yep, with a few stops along the way. Any other questions?" Miles asked, pausing for a moment, and after giving ample opportunity for questions he continued on, "Once we get our horses and supplies in Pikesville, we'll travel southwest to Nebraska and visit a town named Elsie. There's a small gun store there that supplied the resistance before the end of the war and our intelligence suggests that it's not completely destroyed. We're to go investigate and salvage anything that may be useful, including guns, ammunition, knives, anything that will help us on the ground. From Pikesville to Elsie, we're looking at almost a month of traveling depending on the condition of the horses and the weather."

"A month?" Raj exclaimed, while Zoe and Gabe both displayed similar expressions of frustrations.

Ayla decided it was time for her to chime in and try and reassure her friends, "Listen, we'll be fine, it's no worse than being back in the city. We've got two great hunters and a fisherman who can feed us, and three people who are fully capable of protecting us and know how to survive out in the elements. Heck, we'll probably live better than we ever did while we were in Chicago." She hoped to ease their apprehension by having them focus on how they could contribute rather than the unpredictable month-long journey from Wisconsin to Nebraska.

Ayla, on the other hand, couldn't wait to get started. For her, living and surviving in the bush was like second nature. In the days of the resistance, she and Miles had spent most of their time traveling long distances between resistance outposts. By comforting her friends, she inadvertently reminded herself that this lifestyle was something she had been missing for the past eight years. The ferry hadn't even docked yet and she was already looking forward to trudging across the country and being completely immersed in the outdoors.

After Ayla finished her attempt to calm her friends, Miles continued on with the details of their adventure, "From Elsie we'll continue southwest on a straight path and hit Vegas.

Dumont has arranged so that we can dump our cargo with a small resistance outpost stationed there and then the last stop is Los Angeles."

"What'll happen to the weapons when we drop them off?" Ayla asked as she was usually the one questioning her superiors, even though now they were technically equals in terms of their ranks.

"Whatever Dumont wants to happen will happen, and we'll be informed when necessary." Since he was accustomed to her inquiring mind, his response was almost robotic. She just rolled her eyes at him and decided not to press him for now. "So here's where it gets risky for us." He continued, "Between Elsie and Vegas, our cover story will not fly. Most refugees don't travel with a wagon that we hope will be stashed with weapons. If something happens, we'll have to make a call depending on what and who we come across. If it's a small patrol, we could dispose of them but anything larger than a four-man team we'll have to improvise." As unlikely as it was, the Army did have random patrols that were sent out to address a multitude of different issues that concerned the capital. They were few and far between though.

"What do you mean by 'dispose of'?" Zoe asked reluctantly even though she already knew the answer.

"We'll have to kill them. Let's not forget that we are trying to start a war here. We can even pull it off considering most of the army's toys are obsolete," Miles said as Zoe started to realize just what she was getting herself into.

"Toys?" Raj asked simply.

Miles responded by saying, "Jets, tanks, helicopters, even those fancy drones we used back in my days of service. Those are all gone now." After the rest of the world witnessed the demise of the United States and their cruelty they showed their own citizens, most countries placed an embargo on the United

States, which essentially isolated it entirely. This also eliminated all imports including foreign oil products, making anything that ran on gas irrelevant. It is worth mentioning that the resistance had also destroyed most of the country's reserve supplies during the war. The few cars that existed were long ago converted to operate using some alternative fuel source, like recycled vegetable oil or solar power. In a last-ditch effort to procure funds for the ongoing war, the president sold off large portions of the Navy and Air Force. In his eyes, there would be no need for those things if they were defeated and besides, his enemy was right in front of him. It was just one of many poor decisions by the government that got them to where they were today.

Having not finished the details of the plan, Miles picked up where he left off, "When and if we get to Vegas, we will drop the weapons and make our way to Los Angeles back under the guise of refugees looking to find work. When we get in, we'll rendezvous with Dumont and receive new orders, any questions?" Gabe, Zoe, and Raj all appeared to be overwhelmed with the information and they remained silent.

Shortly after laying out the details of the plan, the ferry arrived at the docks in Green Bay. The motley crew composing of two generals, the hunting husband and wife, the young dock worker, and Ryan Gould, who no one knew anything about, all exited the boat and stepped onto the aged dock. It at one point must have been painted white as there were spots where its original coat had survived the years of weathering. In a single file line, they trudged down the creaking dock and made their way to dry land. The ferry boat captain turned his ship around to make the lonely trip back to the ports of Chicago.

Chapter 10

Into the Great Wide Open

The city of Green Bay was now mostly overrun with forests. The resistance picked Green Bay as an outpost to train and recruit people from the surrounding areas during the war. Word quickly spread that it was not only a place to gather and train resistance fighters, but also a safe haven for those looking to free themselves from oppression. Early in the conflict, the president had learned that the entire city was full of revolutionaries and their families and they naturally viewed it as a threat. Instead of wasting valuable manpower by sending in troops, they unfortunately decided it would be easier to fire missiles into the heart of the city. Almost two hundred thousand lives were taken in a matter of minutes including women and children. The city had since been abandoned; the only reminders of human civilization came in the form of roads and highways infused with grasses and crumbled pavement. Every other structure or vehicle was destroyed by the explosions and their remains were hidden by the ever-increasing vegetation.

The ferry had docked near the mouth of the Fox River, which passed directly through the center of the city's remains. Ayla and the rest of her small team decided to follow an abandoned rail line that ran parallel to the river. There was not much conversation on their first leg of the journey. Ayla's roommates were still stunned that they were actually participating and the others were making internal observations on how quickly Mother Nature had reclaimed the city. They followed this path until they reached what used to be a highway. "Okay," Miles said. "This road here used to be Highway 29; it will take us directly to Pikesville. We'll follow it by day and camp in the woods at night."

"Why do we have to sleep in the woods?" Raj asked. Having lived in Chicago his whole life, he wasn't too sure about the whole camping thing.

Miles tried not to sound too alarming when he answered him. "Well, soldier, fires are a dead giveaway. So, at night we'll steer clear of the road and sleep in the woods. If anybody's out there looking for us, they'd see those flames a mile away." Raj nodded his head as he obviously preferred to venture into the woods rather than encounter anyone wishing to do them harm.

In a formation that Miles organized, the crew started their journey along the abandoned highway. Miles led them by taking point and making sure no one approached from the direction they were walking. Following him were Gabe and Zoe. Ayla was behind the couple, keeping an eye out for any threats to their left or to their right; Raj accompanied her and walked by her side. Ryan Gould took the rear and was responsible for identifying any threats that may be following them. Ayla instructed Gabe, Zoe, and Raj to all keep an eye out for anything unusual, but ultimately the others knew they shouldn't be depending on them.

After a couple of hours of traveling on the desolate highway, which was surrounded by trees and overgrown grasses, Ayla could see her roommates were ready for a break. "Miles!" she called to him as her breath could be seen in the cooling fall temperatures, "Time to take a break, and get some lunch." Miles nodded in agreement and led the group off the highway and into the forest, which had begun to shed its autumn leaves. They walked for about ten more minutes until they approached a clearing in the woods where a few large trees had created a natural canopy. The forest floor was almost covered from the falling leaves but there was still plenty attached above their heads. As the rest of the crew looked for a place to rest, Gabe reached into his bag and handed out the remaining deer meat and bread he and Zoe had saved from their last hunt in Chicago. As Ayla ate her portion of the rations, she admired the gold-colored forest floor, a sight she hadn't seen since moving into that depressing tenement house in the city.

After a few moments, Ayla gathered the few canteens the group had brought with them and ordered Raj to fill them from a nearby creek. Raj, not entirely educated on how a military unit is organized, protested, "Why do I have to go fill them?"

"Because I'm your commanding officer, and I have a gun," she said as she pushed the canteens in his chest and gave him a smile. "And hurry up, I'm thirsty," she added. Raj returned the smile and made the short walk to fill up the canteens as the rest of the crew gathered their things in preparation to hit the road once again.

He returned and set the three canteens on the ground. Ayla dripped a few iodine droplets into each, making the water safe to drink. The team then made their way back to the highway and in the same staggered formation from before, they continued on. The weather had changed since their lunch break from being cloudy and cool to a light misty rain, making it even colder than before. The wind had also picked up and slowed the group's progress slightly. After a few hours of this, the rain intensified and the group decided to make camp about thirteen miles from where they had started in Green Bay.

They made camp a few hundred yards from the highway. Miles addressed them again, "All right, we made pretty good progress today, and by my count we're just a little over our ten miles per day goal we made for ourselves, so good job everyone. Now it's important for us to work as a team here tonight. Each of us will have a job, and like Ayla said earlier, you're all good at something so we will try to take advantage of that."

After Miles delegated the responsibilities to the five other travelers, he walked back toward the road for the first lookout duty. Ayla and Raj's job was to provide warmth for the team so they began to search the partially covered forest floor for any dry fire building materials. It was the most important task because the weather felt like it was getting colder by the minute and without a fire they would risk getting hypothermia. Ryan was tasked with building a simple shelter to help keep his companions dry throughout the night. The hunters, Gabe and Zoe, set off deeper in the woods yielding Ayla's pistol with Miles's silencer attachment. Luckily, he had brought it with him expecting this type of situation. It would be very dangerous to recklessly shoot a gun without knowing what people, if any, were around to hear.

With the shelter built and the fire roaring, Ayla, Raj, and Ryan took their outer layer of clothes off and placed them near the flames in an attempt to dry them from the rainy afternoon they endured. The light of the day was dissipating as Zoe and Gabe returned with two large beavers, already cleaned and ready for the fire. "Wow awesome job you guys!" Ayla proclaimed as Ryan and Raj both climbed to their feet in excitement. "We can cook one of those tonight and eat pretty well. We'll smoke the other and bring it with us during the day tomorrow." Ryan Gould created a makeshift fire spit to cook the meat as the hunters took note of the drying clothes and followed suite.

As they ate their dinner and sat around the warm fire, Ayla told her roommates stories from her previous life. She retold exciting moments that had them sitting on the edge of the fallen tree they claimed as their seats. It was still unbelievable to them to hear of such amazing stories of conquest and adventure from someone they believed to have been a lowly clothing seller in the slums of Chicago.

After they ate, Ayla said to them, "You three better get some rest, I'm going to relieve Miles so he can eat and get some sleep. Ryan, come and switch with me in a few hours."

"No problem, General," Ryan said to her.

Armed once again with her pistol, Ayla made her way to Miles with a smile on her face. It felt refreshing to her to be candid with her roommates, more than she had ever been previously. Not really knowing how she felt when they started this journey, she was now glad they were here with her but of course, she still worried about their safety. She made her way toward the more open landscape near the road and whistled out for Miles. She waited and heard his whistle back to her and he stood up by a tree near the road. "Why do you look so happy?" he asked her.

"I look happy?" she asked, amused.

"Yea, you do actually," he said.

"I don't know, it just feels good to be back out here again, to be a part of something," she said meaning both the resistance and being a part of her tenement house family as herself. He nodded, knowing full well what she meant; he too had felt the emptiness before he embarked on his long journey from Los Angeles.

"A tiger can't change his stripes," he said to her with a grin.

She returned the smile and said humorously, "Also beaver is my favorite, so that could be it too."

The pair shared a laugh as Miles continued the joke, "What kind of sides are there?"

"Tree bark, paired with creek water," she said.

Before he left, he turned back and said jokingly, "Don't go falling asleep on us now." She smirked as he disappeared into the darkness of the forest.

The rain was steady but nothing overwhelming as she made herself comfortable against the same tree her fellow general had occupied. It was a good vantage point, she could see well enough that if someone was traveling down either end of the road she would have plenty of time to return to camp, extinguish the fire, and warn the others.

It was the first time she was alone since waking up in the abandoned jewelry store in Chicago. She thought about how much had changed in such a short period of time. Although she thought one day someone might find her, she never expected that it would be Alexander Dumont or Chicago's governor, Jeffery Gould. She certainly never expected to be sitting around a campfire with Gabe, Zoe, and Raj somewhere in the wilderness of Wisconsin embarking on a cross country voyage to Los Angeles. After a few hours of reflection and watching for potential threats, she heard Ryan's whistle and made her return call. He found her and after a brief exchange, she made her way back to camp to get a few hours of rest before the next day of walking commenced.

Chapter 11

Highway 29

After her brief period of rest, Ayla awoke to the sight of the smoke from their smoldering campfire rising up through the morning sun rays that were making their way through the forest canopy. It was still early, and it appeared to her that Miles had gone back and taken watch duty sometime during the early morning hours because it was Ryan Gould who was sleeping near the fire. He was startled when she gave him a soft kick in the leg to wake him. "Go switch with Miles, and take some breakfast with you," she said to him.

"Good morning to you too, General," he said with a sleepy voice as he pulled himself to his feet.

She looked back at him and smiled and said in a British accent, "Good morning Mr. Gould, would you like some tea for breakfast?"

"Was that a joke? I never knew you had a sense of humor," he said bluntly.

"I don't, just trying to motivate the unmotivated," she said to him as he gathered his supplies and placed them back in his pack. She handed him his dried beaver breakfast and he made his way to Miles.

Ayla knelt down and woke her roommates who had been sleeping close together in a row. "I'm going to fill the canteens; you guys get yourselves some breakfast and gather up your stuff.

I'll be back in a few minutes," she said to them as they slowly came to from the uncomfortable night of sleeping on the ground.

Ayla trudged down the sloped embankment and approached the small creek that was luckily within walking distance from where they were camping. She knelt down and unscrewed the cap from the first canteen. As she placed the opening in the stream she could feel the cold water rush over her hands. One by one, she filled them up with the hope that they would last until their next break. Just as she did the night before, she placed the iodine in the collected drinking water in order to purify any toxins that may have been lurking.

By the time she returned, Gabe, Zoe, and Raj were eating their breakfast on the same fallen tree they were sitting on last night. Their bags were packed and they looked ready for another day of walking toward Pikesville. Miles had returned from the watch post and was also eating. He looked at Ayla and asked, "Where's the coffee?"

"River water will have to do, I guess," she said as she tossed him a canteen.

After a few minutes of eating, the team gathered their remaining supplies and met Ryan out by the road. Miles extended his hand and helped Ryan to his feet and the team made their way back to Highway 29. They again walked in the staggered formation with Miles taking point and Ryan watching the rear. Miles turned and as he was walking backwards along the road, he addressed everyone, "Okay, if we have another day like yesterday we should be on track to get to Pikesville tomorrow afternoon. If you see anything out of the ordinary, don't be shy, speak up." This was mainly for the three inexperienced travelers as Ryan and Ayla were well aware of the dangers that may be hiding along the roads near settlements.

"So, are you going to teach me to use a gun?" Raj asked Ayla as he looked down at the pistol she was holding in her right hand. She looked down at her gun and realized that he was right. Soon enough, Ayla would have to train and arm Gabe, Zoe, and Raj. Gabe and Zoe were obviously pretty good with a gun already but that was about the extent of their abilities.

"Now that you mention it, I guess I'll have to teach you a thing or two about being a soldier at some point, huh?" she said.

"Really?" he asked excitedly.

"Well yea, how do you expect to be a soldier if you can't shoot a gun?" Raj didn't reply; he just looked straight ahead with a smile on his face envisioning himself as a gun-toting military man. Ayla smiled as well, she could tell he was excited to learn, as most teenage boys would be. "You know, I was about your age when I first started training," she said to him.

"You were?" he asked wide-eyed.

She nodded and said, "Yea, around there."

"Why were you so young?" he asked.

"It's a long story," she told him not really wanting to get into it all.

"It's a long walk," he said trying to entice her to tell him.

She gave him a small grin and said, "Maybe later." Raj picked up her hesitation and realized it was something she would rather not talk about and the two continued on in silence while he thought of the next thing he could ask her.

After a few uneventful hours of traveling and small talk, Miles stopped and put his fist in the air, ordering the others to stop their movements. Raj turned to Ayla but before he could speak she covered his mouth and put her finger to her lip, signaling him to be quiet. With their eyes fixed on Miles, he motioned for them to move off the highway. The traveling group ran off and took cover a few feet from the road and ducked down into a wet ditch. They all looked toward the road in anxious anticipation hoping to not be seen. Ayla made eye contact with Miles and mouthed the words, "What is it." Miles responded by taking out his pistol and aiming it toward the road. Ayla followed his lead and did the same. She turned to Ryan and he too had his weapon ready.

The team waited in silence when eventually the sound of an engine approached their position from the same direction they were walking. As the sound grew louder, Ayla tried to identify what it was based on the tone and pitch of its rumbling, but all she could determine was that it was something big and slow.

As the engine roared closer toward their location, Ayla looked to Raj who appeared to be a little nervous, as did Gabe and Zoe. She chose to ignore them, hoping they would stay quiet. Eventually, the front end of a big old farm tractor crept into their field of vision. The tractor was pulling a trailer that Ayla recognized from her childhood. It was the type of trailer that landscapers used, the type that would be out in front of so many of her neighbors' homes once a week during the summer months. The driver was middle-aged and appeared to be quite filthy; he was armed with a machete tied to his waist. In the trailer there were eight other men who were similar in their appearances and they were all armed with some sort of blade. Some had knives and others had large chopping type weapons. Each of them, including the driver, was wearing black, tattered clothing and had facial hair that clearly lacked any form of grooming.

As the tractor slowly rolled by them, Ayla took a closer look at the driver. Around his neck, he wore a chain sporting what looked like several large diamond rings. Bandits, she thought to herself. One of the bandits slung his arm over the side of the trailer and tossed several glass bottles that shattered on the road. It must have caught Zoe off guard, as she let out a small audible gasp. The tractor suddenly stopped as the driver stood from his seat and studied the tree line just beyond where the team was hiding. The eight passengers in the trailer had stopped drinking and carrying on and also took notice.

With her heart thumping, Ayla prepared to fire her weapon. Just as she pulled the hammer back, the driver returned to his position and the tractor pulled away. The team remained in hiding until the sound of the engine dissipated. Ayla was the first to stand and she motioned to the rest of the team to remain in position. She approached the road to ensure the roving bandits were out of sight and no longer a threat. She signaled for the rest of the team to join her along the side of the road in order to regroup and evaluate.

"Where do you think they came from?" she asked Miles as she wiped mud from her forehead.

"Unless there's another settlement on this road that we don't know about, I'd guess Pikesville," Miles replied.

Ayla turned to Ryan Gould and asked, "Did you guys have a backup plan in case something went wrong?"

"Yea, a place just south of Pikesville, Stevens Point, but we have no way of knowing if he left unless we go there anyways," Ryan replied.

"Right," Miles said. "It's too risky to go to the backup option without knowing for sure if he left."

"All right, let's take a break and eat some lunch. I think we could all use a timeout," Ayla said mostly referring to her shaken housemates who all welcomed a chance to catch their breath. The group found a nice location deeper in the woods away from the road. They drank their purified water and chewed on some smoked beaver while they rested their weary legs. Although Ayla convinced herself that she was excited to be out in the wild again, she too was feeling the effects of the sedentary lifestyle she had become accustomed to while living in Chicago.

After they ate, Ayla decided it was time to show Raj some basic gun safety. Plus, she thought it would be a good distraction from the earlier excitement. With Gabe and Zoe looking on, she went through the basics with him as an introduction. She told him all the proper terms and what each piece of the gun was responsible for. She showed him how to handle it correctly and the procedure that should be followed when preparing to fire. Removing the clip and emptying the chamber, she turned to him and said, "Okay, show me what you've learned." Raj loaded an empty clip and held the gun with both hands. As he aimed down its sights, he turned off the safety, exhaled, and pulled the trigger, which prompted a clicking sound. "Nice job," she said to him confidently.

"Okay, how about a real one this time?" he asked her.

"Not just yet, we should get going; we don't have bullets to spare anyways. Also, side note, guns are loud, we want to stay sneaky," she said to him, to which he nodded as he remembered they were trying to not be seen or heard.

Miles rallied the troops once again, "Okay, let's get this show on the road. We only have a few hours before we start losing daylight and have to make camp again."

Ryan was the first to reach the highway, and as he stepped onto the road he turned back around to check the progress of the others. As soon as Ayla made eye contact with him, the sound of rifle fire reverberated through the forest. A loud thump could be heard as the bullet struck Ryan through his thick coat. He dropped to his knees before falling backwards onto the deteriorated highway.

"Get down!" she yelled to the rest of the group. Zoe, Gabe, and Raj all jumped back down into the same ditch as before. Ayla did her best to stay low as she ran to her fallen comrade who was struggling to breathe. She finally reached him, and as she dragged him to the side of the road into the grass, she looked toward the direction of where the gunshot came from. In the distance, she saw the same group of bandits who had passed them earlier. As Miles quickly made his way to the edge of the road to investigate for himself, Ayla removed her coat and used it to apply pressure to the bullet hole in Ryan's rib cage. "Raj, hold this right here! Hard!" She instructed him and he fearfully did as he was told.

She made her way back to Miles and the two of them were concealed as the group of Bandits ran toward their position. "They must have doubled back on us," he said in a calm manner.

"I count seven. Where are eight and nine?" she asked.

"Going to have to figure that out later, you ready?" he asked her as he aimed toward the sprinting bandits who were now less than a hundred yards away, yelling with their blades held high.

"Yep, I'll take the four on the left; you take the three on the right," she said to him as he nodded in agreement. "Let's go," she said calmly as the two combat veterans both rose to their feet and walked down the road with their weapons aimed at the armed bandits. In an instant and without hesitation, Ayla fired four rounds hitting each of her targets dead on, while Miles needed five shots to kill his three bandits. They were successful but Ayla noticed Miles' missed shots, which he never used to do.

They holstered their weapons and immediately returned to Ryan Gould who was being tended to by the others. He lay gasping for air as blood filled his lungs. Ayla knew it was too late and there was nothing that could be done.

In a last ditch effort she looked him in the eyes and asked him, "What's your contact's name, Ryan?" She paused a moment while he struggled to speak. "His name, Ryan! What's his name?" It was too late, his labored breathing slowly stopped and Ryan's body went limp. Ayla stood quickly and turned away in frustration as Miles dragged his hand across Ryan's face and closed his eyes.

"Let's go," she said to Miles. "You three stay here, get rid of his body."

"Get rid of his body?" Zoe asked shocked.

"Go hide it in the woods," Ayla demanded.

"Don't you think...?" Zoe said, feeling like they owed him more, but was cut off by Ayla.

"We don't have time for anything else. Get rid of his body, we'll be right back. Empty his pockets too!" she said commanding her three friends who were all taken aback equally by both her confidence and decisiveness, but also her lack of compassion.

Ayla and Miles made their way toward the seven dead bandits by running through the woods parallel to the road. The rifle, which they presumed to be the one that killed Ryan Gould, was next to one of the fallen aggressors. Knowing the danger of an incoming shot had most likely passed. They searched each body and dragged them to the side of the road to avoid any unwanted attention. They picked up the rifle, and ran back toward where Ryan was killed.

The team was back together once again minus one. They were kneeling in a circle just to the left of where most of Ryan's blood had left his body. "Did Gould have anything useful on him?" Ayla asked Zoe as she caught her breath.

"This is all he had," Zoe said as her blood-stained and

shaking hand gave Ayla Gould's pistol, a case of bullets, and a small leather-bound booklet.

"I doubt the other two are going to come back but I can pretty much bet that they're part of a larger clan," Miles said to the remaining team.

"Okay, for the rest of the day we should stay under the cover of the woods and stay away from the road, but we definitely need to get out of here. Who knows who heard those gunshots," Ayla told them.

"I agree if anybody starts poking around here, it won't take long for them to figure out what happened," Miles said.

With a quickened pace, the now six revolutionaries continued on through the forest until it was too dark to see. After a day that would stay with them for quite some time, they traveled even deeper into the woods to make camp for the night. Due to the somewhat favorable weather that evening and to avoid the risk of being exposed, they decided to forgo a fire for the night. Instead they all ate the rest of the dried beaver in the dark without many words being spoken.

Later on, as her companions slept, Ayla used the bright moonlight to examine the booklet that Zoe found on the body of Ryan Gould. The cover was made of what looked like leather but Ayla didn't know if it was real or not. It was about the same size as a diary would be. She ran her fingers across the front, swiping away some dirt that was stuck to the blood-speckled cover. She opened the book and began to examine its contents. Inside were locations listed in alphabetical order, accompanied by one or two names. On a hunch, she flipped to P and scrolled down the page until she found the word "Pikesville." Next to Pikesville there were two names written. The first name she read was "Johnathan Morris" and the second was "Evan Vural".

Ayla, who had been lying down with her head resting on her pack was stunned when she saw the name. She sat up quickly and on her hands and knees, she crawled the few feet to get to Miles. "Miles, wake up," she whispered intensely as she grabbed his shoulder and shook him.

"What?" Miles asked in a surprised tone as he came to.

Ayla looked at him and with anger in her voice she asked, "Why is my brother's name in this book?"

Gabe, Zoe, and Raj all awoke to the sounds of Ayla yelling at Miles as they stood face to face in the moonlight. "Did you lie about him too, Miles! Is he alive?"

Miles tried to answer, "I don't know any—"

She didn't allow him to finish his thought and as her face turned redder, she continued on. "Don't lie to me, Miles! Don't do that to me." Before she finished her sentence, her eyes started to well up as she frantically threw punches at him. Gabe sprang to his feet, wrapped his arms around her waist, and pulled her away as she attempted a few last-minute kicks. They both tumbled to the ground and as Gabe climbed to his feet, Ayla stayed down, emotionally drained and confused. She managed to get to her knees and sat there for a moment.

"I swear, Ayla; I don't know what you're talking about." Miles said in an attempt to calm her down. She looked up to him from her kneeling position and shot him a look of anger. From there, she climbed to her feet and without saying anything to anyone, she grabbed her pack and walked deeper into the forest.

"Where are you going?" Raj asked her as he tried to chase after her.

"Whoa," Miles said as he grabbed him by his shirt to stop him from following her. "Just give her some space, she'll be back."

"What happened?" Zoe asked.

"She was looking through that book and her brother's name was there, next to Pikesville. Then she lost it," Miles said.

"Why?" Zoe inquired.

"Her brother is supposed to be dead; about ten years ago now." Miles said, "Right before I got captured, we got word in Pittsburgh that he had been killed down in Georgia. So this is either a different Evan Vural or there's more to the story than we were told."

"Shouldn't someone go after her?" Gabe asked Miles.

"I'll go. You three try to get some sleep; it'll be morning soon," Miles said.

Miles started walking in the direction she took off in and soon spotted her sitting on the ground with her arms around her knees, tucked into her chest. Miles wrapped his coat around her, sat down next to her, and said, "You know, I think you forget sometimes that you're like a daughter to me." She heard him but remained looking straight ahead. He continued, "And Evan was like a son to me." As she turned to look at him, he could see where the tears had streamed down her face and left a trail in the dirt that had accumulated from their eventful day. "I honestly don't know why his name is there. Maybe he's dead, maybe he isn't, all I know is that we have a mission to complete and I need you by my side. In fact, I want you to take the lead here."

"I did notice you miss those two shots earlier," she said teasingly.

"Come on now, I'm getting old. You'll hurt my feelings," he said, to which she chuckled slightly. "We'll figure out this Evan thing when we get to Pikesville." She nodded and wiped the remnants of her tears away.

"I'm sorry I punched you again," she said to him.

"It's all right, I can take a beating here and there," he said as he put his arm around her in a rare show of affection between the two.

"Why didn't Gould say anything to me about him?" she wondered out loud.

"I don't know, but we'll find out soon enough," he added as the two climbed to their feet and returned to the campsite where the others had fallen back asleep. They were a good distance from the road so there was no need for anyone to stand guard; both Ayla and Miles returned to where they had been sitting before.

As she stared up at the few stars she could see through the trees, she thought about her brother and the last time she had seen him. They were both stationed near Pittsburgh in a revolutionary stronghold named Fort Canonsburg and there was a need for immediate detail in Georgia. Ayla pleaded with him to stay and remain under her command, but Evan was adamant he must go and reinforce the troops on the ground in Atlanta. A few weeks later, Ayla and Miles had received word that the assault was a massive failure and the Revolutionaries had suffered devastating casualties, including her brother Evan.

As she imagined the possibilities of her brother's fate, insomnia once again took hold of her. She found herself just lying there, staring at the old family picture she brought with her from Chicago. Occasionally wiping a tear, she thought about the life he may have had in the last ten years. She thought about the day that Miles took them in, the days he spent training them to be soldiers, and the day Evan left her in Pittsburgh. She questioned herself much like she did the day she received word he had been killed. Should she have gone and looked for him? Was she a bad sister for not going after him? Logic eventually took hold and she remembered that there was a bigger goal besides her and her brother surviving. Eventually, her adrenaline wore off and she slowly drifted away, sleeping until Raj woke her the next morning.

Chapter 12

Reaching Pikesville

"Where are those two?" Ayla asked as she motioned toward Gabe and Zoe's abandoned sleeping area.

"They left earlier to go hunting," Miles answered as he stirred up a small fire.

"I hope they find something, I'm starving," Raj groaned.

"Don't get your hopes up, I think we got lucky last time," Ayla said to him as she stood and stretched away the discomfort from sleeping on the ground, "Any signs of life out there?" she asked Miles.

With a concerned tone he answered, "Yea, there is, not good unfortunately."

"What do you mean?" she asked.

"I think we know for sure now where those bandits came from yesterday. You can see smoke, a lot of smoke. It's about a day's walk from here," Miles said, implying the smoke was coming from whatever remained of Pikesville.

"That's not good," she said.

Just as Ayla stopped talking, she heard a branch behind her break and in an instant, she drew her weapon and aimed. She breathed a sigh of relief and lowered the pistol as she saw Gabe and Zoe standing still, holding three decently sized squirrels. "Breakfast?" Gabe asked while his hands were in the air.

"Still hungry, Raj?" Ayla asked him as she put her gun away.

Raj just stood there with a grimace on his face, staring at the fresh catch.

"They're actually pretty tasty, man." Gabe said as he walked past him.

They ate breakfast around the small fire as Miles described their plan for the day, "We'll get to Pikesville today but we don't know what we're getting into. They were supposed to be meeting Ryan so we'll have to figure that out on the way. Barring any setbacks, we should get there around sunset."

"Are we going to travel on the road?" Zoe asked.

Excited that she was getting involved, Miles answered her. "Great question, we'll travel on the road until around noon-ish. Then we'll hit the woods when we get closer."

The team took another half an hour to finish cooking and eating their squirrel breakfast. Other than a few more questions about the day, not much else was said for a while. After several moments of listening to the others chew their food, Gabe couldn't take the silence any more. "So Miles, where ya from?" he asked awkwardly.

Miles gave him a look and took it as a cue to start wrapping things up. "Everybody good to go?" he asked ignoring Gabe's attempt at small talk.

They all climbed to their feet and Zoe looked at Gabe mocking him, "Where ya from? Really?"

"What?" he asked as he saw nothing wrong with what he did.

Just before they stepped out onto the road, Ayla turned to Gabe and handed him Gould's pistol and said, "You'll have to take the middle now, I'll take the rear." As she handed him the gun, he looked at her and Ayla gave him one last piece of advice, "If the time comes, don't hesitate." He looked at the pistol differently than he had this morning. He was now being asked to use it to possibly take another person's life. Ayla could see him processing the situation as he held the gun in his hands. "Are you up for this?" she asked.

"I got it," he said somewhat confidently as he cocked the gun putting a bullet in the chamber. He then placed it in his pocket.

Making sure to check both ways this time, they stepped back onto Highway 29 for the first time since losing Ryan Gould. Miles was still on point while Gabe and Zoe took the middle, and Raj and Ayla took the rear. The weather again was overcast with a slight drizzle, which, with the cooler fall temperatures, was enough to cause concern about warmth.

"Make sure you're wiggling your fingers and toes; keeps the blood flowing," Miles said to the team from the point.

After an uneventful morning, the team inched closer to the billowing smoke in the distance. Ayla looked over at Raj who was visibly cold. "Let's take a break, Miles!" she yelled to him from the rear.

They moved off the road to a safe distance in the woods. Ayla made a fire, and Gabe and Zoe again retreated deeper into the forest to find lunch. Miles, Raj, and Ayla all took off their coats and placed them near the fire in hopes to dry the dampness accrued from the morning trek.

"I think we should stick to the woods from here on out. Can't be too careful and it might give us some cover from this weather," Ayla suggested to Miles.

"Sounds good General," he said to her with confidence.

Raj pulled out his sketch pad and began to illustrate another event he'd experienced on their journey. Meanwhile, Ayla and Miles engaged in a lighthearted conversation. "Do you remember that kid, Paul Peterson?" Miles asked as he laughed.

"The guy everybody called P.P.?" Ayla asked as she too started to laugh. Miles nodded his head with a large grin. "I remember him," she said.

"He had the dumbest—" but before Miles could finish Ayla placed her hand on his arm and motioned for him to stop talking. "What is it?" he whispered. After a brief period of silence, the sound of another engine could be heard in the distance. They both jumped to their feet and began to stomp out the small campfire they had just built. Ayla threw her wet coat over the smoldering embers in hopes to limit the sight and smell of the smoke. The three of them were now flat on their stomachs looking through the small opening of trees which provided a sightline to the road. This time the engines were much louder and approached much faster. Ayla and Miles both pulled out their weapons and readied them in case the situation called for deadly force.

Moments later, three aged and rusty looking Army Humvees passed quickly without slowing their pace. As they passed, the green vehicles were almost a blur indicating their high speed. Eventually, the engine sound faded as the patrol sped away from the teams resting spot. "Where are they going?" Raj asked.

"They're going somewhere specific. If they were random patrols, they wouldn't be moving so quickly. They're going to Pikesville," Miles said.

"It's probably Jeffery's search party," Ayla chimed in.

"Why would he send them right where we're going?" Raj asked. "I thought he was on our side?"

Ayla answered him, "He probably didn't have a choice. Either way that changes things for us."

"Why are you guys on the ground?" Gabe asked as the three lying in the dirt jerked their heads around from being startled by him.

"Military, three Humvees headed toward Pikesville," Miles said.

"Oh great," Gabe said sarcastically.

"Correct," Miles replied.

"We caught a rabbit if that makes anyone feel better," Zoe added.

"It makes me feel better. I'm super hungry," Raj said almost as if the severity of what just transpired didn't register with him.

Raj handed Ayla her coat back, which suffered minimal damage from being tossed on the hot coals. They rebuilt the fire and as the rabbit cooked over the rekindled flames, Miles and Ayla discussed what would happen next.

As Ayla suggested, after they finished eating, the team walked through the forest. They stopped about a mile outside of Pikesville. With the settlement in sight, the five revolutionaries did their best to recon the area. From the looks of it, the town had been decimated by the bandits. The black plume of smoke was so thick and dark now, that as it rose in the setting sunlight, it cast a shadow over the small community. From a distance, the team could see that many of the makeshift homes and communal areas, which the people of Pikesville constructed themselves, were either destroyed or damaged heavily. The three Humvees were parked at the main entrance of the settlement and the officers who arrived there were now walking around the town, conversing with the locals. Ayla assumed they were either asking about the bandit attack or probing to see if anyone had seen her or her traveling companions.

"I count fifteen of them," Ayla said aloud with Miles confirming her statement. The soldiers were dressed in the standard army patrol uniform. Each of them was covered head to toe in lightweight armor that had the appearance of the camouflage fatigues the Army was famous for. The only visible part or their bodies were their faces. All of that extra equipment wasn't really necessary; it was worn more so as fanfare and to intimidate the general population.

The team now directed their attention to each other to formulate a plan. "This makes things complicated," Miles said.

"To be safe, we have to assume they're here for us," Ayla said looking at Miles.

"One of you three will have to go in and figure out if the contacts are still there," Miles said as he looked toward the others.

"Let me go, I'll do it," Raj volunteered himself enthusiastically.

"Absolutely not!" Ayla protested.

Miles, feeling a bit different said, "Now wait a minute. Think about it. They aren't going to be looking for a kid. He might be able to get in and get out without anyone giving him a second look."

"Miles, no, it's too dangerous," she said to him, concerned for Raj's safety.

"Okay, and how old were you when you first shot somebody?" he asked her rhetorically.

Knowing that she herself was only a little older than Raj when she first took a life, she reluctantly agreed to let him go. "Here, take this, it's not much but maybe somebody will recognize my brother." Ayla handed him the picture of her family that she excavated from behind her tenement house in Chicago. "That's him. It might help," she added shrugging her shoulders. She then removed the iodine from her pack and grabbed a small handful of moist dirt. She added the two together and began to smear it sparingly on Raj's face.

"What are you doing?" he asked her as he tried to dodge her

application.

"Stop moving, this will look like ash; like you've been digging through your burned down house," Ayla replied.

"Oh I got it," he said as he stood still to get the rest of the disguise applied.

"Now when you get in there, try to avoid the army, but don't look too suspicious. If they want to talk to you, you're going to have to improvise. Maybe tell them your parents were killed in the attack and you're looking for a relative or something. Ask around and see if anyone knows Evan Vural or Johnathan Morris and use the picture too. Just be careful, okay? Use common sense," she said.

"I can do this; you forget I'm from Chicago. I lie to enforcers all the time," Raj said confidently.

Ayla looked at him and said, "Okay, this is slightly more dangerous, so just be extra cautious. Once it gets dark, you can sneak in and find a place to sleep. When morning rolls around, you can start searching. Give it a day, if it's tomorrow night and you still haven't found anyone, come right back here to this spot and we'll figure something else out. Okay?"

"Got it," he said.

The five team members waited in hiding until it was dark enough to keep him out of site. They all wished Raj luck and he stealthily made his way toward the settlement. They watched as he found a small unattended break in the damaged city walls and in an instant, he disappeared through the crevasse. "Think he'll be all right?" Ayla asked Miles.

Hoping to ease her worries he said, "He's a smart kid, he'll get it done."

Chapter 13

Raj the Spy

Raj left the group at around nine p.m. and quickly made his way to the town walls of Pikesville. The walls themselves were made from the surrounding forest. Using trees they cut down, they stacked them vertically all around the outside of their town in the hopes of protecting the people. However, since the bandit attack, there were many spots that no longer functioned as designed. Raj found a spot just wide enough for him to slip through. With his pack on his back, he checked one last time that there were no soldiers around, and entered the town.

Once inside, he took in his surroundings. A few hundred yards away to his right stood a group of people consoling each other. Immediately to his left were the bodies of those who did not survive the bandit attack. He counted eight of them, each covered by a beige canvas with the blood from their wounds seeping through. One of the bodies was not nearly the same length as the others which indicated there was no prejudice in their attacks; killing whoever stood in their way, including children. Raj got chills up his spine looking at them.

He decided that his best option would be to join the group of survivors to his right. As he walked along the dirt pathway, he looked to his left and saw rows of small homes that were partially burnt to the ground. Most of them were no longer habitable, filled with the ashes and burnt logs of what used to be the walls and roofs. The structures were still smoldering from the attacks that ruined the lives of many town residents, some even still had glowing embers that could be seen in the dark of night.

As he approached the small group of survivors, he could see that they were huddling around a fire burning within an old metal drum. They must have lost their homes, he thought to himself. He counted eight of them; there appeared to be a small family of four, an older woman, probably in her seventies, two men that Raj guessed must be in their mid-twenties or so, and a young girl that looked to be around his age. Nearing closer, Raj could now feel butterflies in his stomach for fear of the people knowing he was an outsider. He knew if they asked him who he was he would need a backstory.

"Come over here, child, get warm by the fire," an older woman said to him.

"Thanks," he replied shyly.

"Don't think I've seen you around before, what's your name?" she asked him.

"No, ma'am, I'm Ra, Rodger," he quickly corrected himself.

"Where your folks?" she asked him.

"It's just me and my dad, but I haven't seen him since," He said as he paused and looked timidly at the destruction around him. "Since yesterday. We were just passing through," he improvised and hoped she believed him.

"Well, it's your lucky day. You can sleep there tonight," she said as she pointed to a small mattress that Raj was clearly too big for. Seeing the curiosity on his face she explained, "I used to be a baby sitter for some folks in town, so I had some lying around that we saved from the fires. Go ahead don't be shy," she said.

He approached the mattress on the ground and tested out his

new sleeping arrangement. "It's perfect, thanks," he said genuinely knowing that it would probably be the most comfortable sleep he's had since leaving Chicago. He sat up, pulled out his sketch pad, and continued drawing the picture of Ayla and Miles taking out the bandits that attacked them yesterday.

"What are you drawing?" Raj heard the voice from behind him and turned around and saw a young lady who was about his age. She had long blonde hair that was slightly curly, she was skinny and despite having ash and dirt on her face and clothes, Raj was sure he had fallen in love right then and there.

"Just a picture of my friends," he said trying to act cool.

"It's really good, she's pretty," the young lady said to him while she took it upon herself to sit down next to him. "I'm Laura," she said.

"I'm…Robert," he said almost blowing his cover once again.

"Okay, Robert. It's nice to meet you," she said. She then leaned in closer and almost in a whisper said, "If you're going to use a fake name, you should remember what it is."

As she spoke, he realized his dumb mistake and tried to cover, "Robert? No, I said Rodger, that's my name." He then tried to change the subject by asking about her family. "So, what's your story, are you alone?"

"I am now. You passed my family when you snuck in," she said to him, holding back tears as her lip quivered slightly.

He paused for a moment and realized she meant the people under the canvasses. "I'm sorry," he said and after another short pause he said to her, "I didn't think anyone saw me come in."

"Don't worry, I won't tell anyone," she said as she smiled at him and wiped away her tears, smearing some of the ash on her cheek. "So where did you come from anyways?" she asked.

Not knowing exactly what to say, he improvised once again trying to stick to his original story. "My dad and I we were passing through and heard the commotion, so we came running."

"Passing through, huh?" she asked him as Raj nodded. "You are really bad at this," she said laughing.

"No, really, that's the truth," he said unconvincingly while trying not to laugh. Internally, he couldn't believe that one pretty girl threw him off his game so bad, but at this point he was pretty sure he'd die for her.

"Okay, I'm going to get some sleep; maybe I'll see you tomorrow," she said.

"Yea, I'd like that," he said smiling.

"Maybe you can work on your cover story a little better," she teased him one last time as she walked away.

Raj, who had completely forgotten his mission, got comfortable and happily fell asleep.

The next morning, he was awoken to the sound of a nearby Pikesville resident shoveling the burnt remains of his home into a wheelbarrow. He didn't rise to his feet immediately. He instead took a look around from the small mattress to ensure it was safe to get up and begin his search for the revolutionary contacts who had been residing in Pikesville. Laura, the young girl he had met last night, was still sleeping. The two men in their twenties were standing near the barrel, attempting to reignite the fire. The family of four and the older woman were no longer around. He noticed that there were no soldiers around and determined it was safe to get up. Not knowing where to begin, he decided to approach Laura. He walked up to her, knelt down, and gently shook her awake.

"Robert?" she said to him in a surprised manner.

"No Rodger!" he corrected her and continued, "I need your help."

"Help with what?" she asked as she rubbed her eyes.

"Can you take me somewhere we can talk?" he asked. She looked at him, perplexed. "If you help me, I can get you out of here," he said to her not thinking clearly as he looked around to ensure no one was watching.

"What do you mean, get me out of here?" she continued to ask questions which made Raj even more nervous about drawing attention to them.

"There's nothing here for you any more," he said bluntly.

Laura looked around the town that surrounded her. She saw the burning homes, the dead bodies, and the people who were suffering. "Let's go," she said. As she climbed to her feet, she took Raj by the hand, and led him through the town.

As they casually walked to wherever Laura was leading him, Raj looked at the faces of the survivors in hopes of recognizing the adult version of the boy in Ayla's photograph. It was hard for him to pick anybody out because most were similarly looking to Laura; they had soot and ash covering their tattered clothes, hands, and faces. Some were rummaging through what remained of their belongings, others were still searching for family members, and some, for reasons unbeknown to Raj, were trying to rebuild already. "Why would anyone want to stay here?" he asked Laura as he imagined himself as a survivor.

"This is our home, most of us moved here from Wausau after the Sullivan Clan took control of the city," she explained.

"Say what now?" he asked.

"Wausau. It used to be a city not too far from here," she said.

"Who are the Sullivan Clan?" Distracted by Laura, he once again forgot that he had an important mission to accomplish.

"This guy named Bill Sullivan organized a bunch of bandits and formed an army. My parents said he was some crazy guy living out in the sticks before the war started. I was about ten when we left the city. My parents and some other people found this spot and helped build the town," she said.

"Why did they attack you?" he asked as they continued to navigate through the ruined settlement.

"We've always had problems with them but this time was different. Usually, there's like three or four of them that come looking for trouble. Normally, we can fight them off but it felt like there were fifty of them this time. It was terrible," she said.

"Yea, it's pretty terrible," he said as he looked around.

"In here," she said as she led him through the doorway of a half-incinerated home.

"This isn't very private," he said frankly as he noticed one of the walls had been burnt down entirely. She looked at him and motioned for him to follow her. They walked into another room where Laura reached down to the floor and pulled the charred rug away, revealing a door that led to a basement. She unlatched the lock, opened it, and the two newly acquainted friends walked down the short stairway into a small room that had been dug out of the Earth. It had dirt floors and walls, and the ceiling was made from the wooden planks of the floor above their heads. "What is this?" he asked her.

"This was my home, well upstairs was my home. My dad dug this out in case we needed a place to hide," she said. "So, Rodger or Robert, what's the secret?"

"I lied to you last night. I don't live north of here. I'm from Chicago," he said.

"Everyone here has heard of the Sullivans so I kind of knew you weren't from around here," she said.

"My name isn't Rodger or Robert either, it's Raj," he said.

"Okay, Raj from Chicago, what are we doing down here?" she asked.

"I'm looking for some men that are supposed to help me. Johnathan Morris and Evan Vural, have you ever heard those names before?" he asked.

"Actually, John Morris, he was good friends with my dad. He didn't make it though. He's one of the bodies you saw yesterday. I know an Evan Anderson, but he took off when the attack started. I saw him race away with some of my dad's horses. What a coward," she said.

"Do you think this might be him?" he asked as he showed her the picture of Ayla's family.

"It might be, yea I think it is," she said after looking at the picture briefly.

"So, he's definitely not here?" he asked.

"No, he definitely left; everyone was really pissed at him. Any other day he would be the guy who was helping keep them away. He just left us this time," she replied in an angry tone.

He looked at her and in a serious manner he said, "All right we need to leave tonight. If there's anything you want to take with you, better pack it now."

Chapter 14

Back at Camp

While Raj and Laura were organizing themselves to make an escape from the town, Ayla and the others were still in hiding on the outskirts of the Pikesville settlement. Zoe and Gabe had gone hunting in the early morning and the team again enjoyed some fire-roasted rabbit meat. After they ate their breakfast, Gabe made an off-handed comment, "It's too bad we couldn't steal one of those Humvees. That would make the trip a whole lot easier."

Ayla and Miles both looked at each other, then back at Gabe, "No, come on, I was just joking," he said.

"They have tracking devices," Miles said

"We could disable it," Ayla replied. "Do you really want to spend the next six months riding horses to Vegas? I sure don't. When Raj gets back, I'll go in and get one," she added.

"Oh yea, and just how do you plan on doing that, Rambo?" he asked sarcastically.

"Who's Rambo?" she asked.

"Never mind, what's your plan?" he asked again.

"Well, you'll obviously make a distraction; I know how you like to do that," she said jokingly.

"Oh I love it," he said.

"You distract, I go in, pop the tires on the other two Humvees and steal the third. Simple," she said.

"Hypothetically speaking, let's just say we pull this off and steal one of those Humvees, aren't you worried that you'll be spotted easily? And what about gas?" Zoe asked skeptically.

"It would be pretty rare to run into anyone. Plus, we'll disable the tracker and I bet they'll have guns in there. Do you see those panels on the top of that one, that's a solar panel so gas shouldn't be a problem," Ayla said, almost as if she was convincing herself.

"This sounds dangerous," Gabe added.

"What do you think we're doing here? Sometimes you have to take a few risks when you're fighting for freedom," Ayla said to him confidently. Miles and Ayla determined that the risk would definitely be worth the reward and Gabe and Zoe had no other choice but to go along with it.

The four of them sat together in a circle far enough away from the town to build small campfire, small enough not to give off a visible trail of smoke but large enough to keep them warm. "So let's talk distractions," Ayla said, prompting the group.

"We could start a big fire on the opposite side of town," Gabe suggested.

Ayla shut his idea down rather quickly. "No, it might work on a few of them but it's not enough to make all of them leave their posts."

Ayla got to her feet and began to pace back and forth as she methodically devised a plan in her head. The others watched her as it was obvious she was thinking deeply about something. Gabe was about to speak but Miles stopped him, "Wait, just watch," he said with a smile, keeping his eyes fixed on her.

Just as her path was becoming muddy from her repetitive footsteps, she spoke. "Bullets," she said matter-of-factly.

"Bullets?" Miles asked curiously.

"Yea, if they hear gunfire they're going to run toward the

sound. No one else is supposed to have a gun out here. We'll need everyone on this though. Three or four fires in the woods on the opposite side of town should be enough," she said to herself.

"Okay, I'm lost. Put it all together for me," Miles said as he looked up from his seated position on the forest floor.

Ayla looked at him like he should already know what she was talking about. She then crouched down next to him, and with a stick she found near the fire, she started to draw a map in the mud where she had been pacing. She began to explain the plan to the group, "This is the town here." She drew a circle in the mud. "We're on the eastern side of the town and so are the Humvees." After marking their place on the map with an X, she continued on, "You three are going to go through the woods to the western side of town and make three small fires, here, here, and here. Spread out by a few hundred feet and far enough away so they can't see the fires. At, I don't know, let's say eight p.m. you'll all throw a few bullets into your fires and hustle back here ASAP. When the bullets get hot enough, we'll have gunfire in three different spots. Hopefully they will hear it and scatter. While that's happening, Raj and I can steal the Humvee."

Miles smirked, looked toward Gabe and Zoe, and said, "This is why she was the youngest major."

"So you like it? Good plan?" Ayla asked Miles.

"Works for me. Sounds like a fine plan," he said.

"What about you two? Think you can handle it?" she asked Gabe and Zoe.

The couple looked at each other and Zoe then turned back toward Ayla and said, "We're in."

She reached into her pack and retrieved the box of ammo that once belonged to Ryan Gould. She handed each of them five or six 9mm bullets and said, "We need to keep these dry so put them somewhere safe. Our biggest obstacle will be actually making the fires hot enough to get the job done. Miles, I think you should all go to together. You can make sure each fire is where it needs to be before you light yours."

"I can do that," Miles said confidently.

With the plan in place, the team waited for nightfall and anxiously awaited the return of their youngest member. The fire had been extinguished and their eyes were locked on the gap in the city walls where Raj entered. After a short while, he emerged with Laura in tow.

"Okay, here he comes," Ayla said. "And he's not alone," she added.

"What do you mean?" Zoe asked.

"He's got some girl with him," she said as she pulled out her pistol.

"Do you really think you need that?" Miles asked her.

She gave him a look of displeasure but took his advice and put the pistol back in her pocket. Shortly after, Raj arrived at the camp and introduced Laura to the rest of the team, "Guys, this is Laura. She helped me and I told her she could come with us."

"Raj, that's real nice, but I think it's too dangerous," Ayla said to him rather sternly.

"She has nowhere else to go. I promised her," he said almost begging.

"What did you figure out?" Miles asked in an attempt to get back to what was important.

"Laura here says our guy Morris is dead and a man named Evan Anderson ran away with horses and a wagon. He was headed that way," Raj said as he pointed to the South.

Ayla then turned toward Laura and asked, "You saw all this?"

"Yes, everyone in town did," Laura answered timidly not knowing what she had gotten herself into.

Miles looked toward Ayla and said, "Looks like we're headed to Stevens Point."

"Who are you people?" Laura asked hesitantly as she noticed the guns.

"We're…" Raj attempted to explain the situation but was cut off by Ayla who was still not pleased he added another member to their team.

"Raj, you'll have to explain later. We're not done here," she said.

Chapter 15

The Heist

As Ayla watched Miles, Gabe, and Zoe disappear into the dark forest surrounding Pikesville, she explained the plan to Raj and Laura. "We're changing the plan, Raj. You see those Humvees over there?"

"Yes," he answered.

She continued. "We're going to steal one. Thirty minutes from now, our friends are going to create a distraction for us. Meanwhile, we'll camouflage ourselves and sneak over to the vehicles. When we get the signal, we'll make our move. Take this," she said as she pulled a short knife from a holster around her ankle and handed it to him. She continued, "When you hear gunfire, you're going to slash two tires on the first two Humvees while I disable the tracking device on the third and get it running. As soon as you slash them, get into my Humvee. Then we'll come back here and pick up everyone else and drive to Stevens Point."

"How are we going to camouflage ourselves?" he asked.

Ayla reached down and grabbed a handful of dirt and mud and smeared it generously this time on his arm and said, "That's how. Now, cover yourself completely, your skin and anything else that might stand out." Laura reached down and grabbed a handful of mud and raised it near her face. Ayla stopped her and said, "Laura, you can sit this one out. Just stay here and wait for the others to come back."

Looking a bit disappointed, she flung the mud out of her hand and reluctantly took a seat on the ground and said, "What if something happens?"

"You have the benefit of being able to go home. Just walk back into town and pretend you never met us," Ayla said to her. Laura accepted and sat quietly.

Ayla and Raj began to smear the mud on their exposed skin and checked each other's faces for any spots they may have missed. They then made their way toward the Humvees, taking care to stay hidden until they reached a portion of the city walls near their targets. While sitting with their backs leaning against the walls, they were within fifteen feet of the vehicles and one army patrol officer, who Ayla assumed was tasked with watching over the vehicles. They waited in hiding for their signal.

Meanwhile, Miles, Gabe, and Zoe had prepped the three fires and were waiting for the clock to strike eight p.m. Eventually, Miles checked his watch and gave them one last set of directions, "Ok, after we light this fire, Zoe you stay here and Gabe and I, we'll go to the next one. We'll light it and then I'll go on to the last fire. By the time I throw my bullets in, we should all have time to get back to camp before they start to pop. Now this is important, I'll throw mine in first when I'm sure it's hot enough, then when I get back to you, Gabe you'll throw yours in, and Zoe you'll wait until we both get back to you. That way we know the fires will be hot enough. Clear?"

Gabe and Zoe both nodded showing their understanding as Miles reached in his pocket to pull out his flint stick. Using the dull side of his knife, he dragged it across the stone rod and a wave of sparks crashed into the tinder pile igniting the first fire. Once they were satisfied that the fire was sustainable, Gabe and

Miles jogged toward the second location. Upon their arrival, Miles again used his fire striker to ignite the flame and then ran to his spot and repeated the process once more.

Once he deemed his bed of coals was hot, Miles strategically placed the five bullets into the fire and began to sprint back toward Gabe. Once there, he showed him a good spot to place his and they then ran to Zoe and did the same. The three then made their way back to camp where they were greeted by a wave from a somewhat confused Laura who was just sitting on a log looking out of place.

Ayla and Raj were still in position waiting to hear the gunshots from the campfires their fellow revolutionaries had prepared and ignited. A short while later, they heard the first shot. It echoed through the forest, followed by another, and then another and then thirteen more shots went off randomly causing chaos to erupt among both the townspeople and the soldiers who had assumed the bandits had returned for another attack. Residents screamed in fear as they fled to hide once again, and orders being commanded by the higher ranking officers could be heard through the pandemonium.

The soldiers convened and ran toward sounds of gunfire in the opposite direction of Ayla and Raj. "Stay here!" One of the officers yelled to his counterpart who was watching the vehicles.

"Give me that knife." Ayla whispered to Raj. He handed her the knife and without hesitation she snuck up to the left behind guard who was distracted by his fellow officers running toward the perceived danger. She flipped the knife around, and using the blunt end, she forcefully slammed it into the back of the young soldier's head. He let out a groan as he collapsed into the mud. She carefully tossed the knife back to Raj, who immediately and forcefully stabbed the large tires, which caused a high-pitched sound of air being released as they decompressed into the ground.

While Raj fulfilled his duty, Ayla positioned herself under the third Humvee and used the butt of her gun to dislodge the tracking device hooked into the undercarriage of the powerful vehicle. She then slid out from underneath and found the keys in the pocket of the unconscious soldier. She unlocked the doors and the pair entered the large SUV. Upon ignition, the Humvee roared to life and Ayla shifted it into reverse and slammed down on the gas while turning the wheel sharply. The vehicle turned so quickly in reverse that mud was flung wildly through the air while the front end of the vehicle slid to a stop. She shifted into drive and again threw mud toward the settlement as she hammered her food down on the gas pctal and they raced toward their team members.

As it made its way across the uneven terrain, the Humvee bounced violently in the air tossing Raj and Ayla about as they pressed on. Once she arrived near the camp, Ayla stomped on the brakes, and as the Humvee came to a sliding halt, the rest of the team, including Laura, emerged from the forest and hopped into the back seats of the Humvee. Ayla once again floored the gas pedal and the team sped away. It was a perfectly executed plan that couldn't have gone better.

The team of revolutionaries celebrated as the troubled settlement disappeared behind them with no signs of pursuit from the soldiers. They triumphantly high fived and hugged each other, retelling their favorite moments. Ayla watched them in the rearview mirror with a confident smile as she knew it is the first time the team had accomplished a real mission together, and the bonding taking place was fun to watch.

Ayla drove the vehicle through the darkness without ever turning on the headlights. Eventually, the bumpy, uneven, dirt road gave way to a smoother abandoned highway. With the team still enjoying the moment behind her she brought them back to reality. "Great job, everyone, but this is just the beginning. We've got work to do. Start taking an inventory of everything in here and keep a sharp eye out for anything outside."

Chapter 16

Evan Anderson

"So do I get to know what's going on yet?" Laura asked as Ayla drove the Humvee toward their next destination on Interstate 39, using only the moonlight to guide her.

Ayla answered her, "Just give us a few minutes. We don't have much time before we get to Stevens Point. Miles, did you check the back yet?"

Miles turned to investigate the rear portion of the Humvee and after a brief analysis he said, "We've got an m16, two more pistols, and a sniper rifle; not much, but better than nothing."

Frustrated that there were only a few weapons, she asked another question, "Has anyone found anything else useful back there?"

"There's nothing else here," Miles said.

"Raj, see if there's anything in the glove box," she said. He did as he was asked and upon opening it, a stack of papers, which had been folded into quarters, fell onto the floor. As he reached down to retrieve them, Ayla inquired, "What are those?" He whisked away the mud and slowly unfolded the papers. He showed the first one to Ayla. It was her picture and a description of what she looked like. "Give me that," she said. She began to read it out loud placing the pages on the steering wheel while doing her best to focus on driving as she read, "Wanted, Ayla Vural; brown hair, brown eyes, 5'8", athletic build, roughly 130 pounds. Read the rest of that Raj," she said as she handed him back the papers and continued to focus on the road.

"Ayla Vural is wanted by the United States government for conspiracy, treason, murder, and espionage." He flipped to the next page; it was a picture of Miles. He continued on, "Miles Lang, Zoe and Gabe Tyler, Raj Kassar, Ryan Gould; there's one for each of us," he said as he thumbed through them.

"They have Gould's real name? That can't be good for Jeffery," Ayla said.

"How do they have our pictures?" Zoe asked frantically.

"They don't," Ayla responded to her by slightly aiming her voice behind her while she drove. "They're sketches, but they kind of look like you."

"I knew that Jeffery would stab us in the back!" Gabe yelled out angrily.

Miles chimed in hoping to calm the others, "Everybody just calm down. Jeffery Gould is a revolutionary just like us. He did exactly what he said he was going to do. He made a search party. Hell, he might be dead for all we know now. We're going to continue on as planned, nothing has changed."

While the others kept quiet and occasionally shifted from side to side from the neglected highway, contemplating themselves as wanted criminals, Laura was looking quite shocked. She was coming to the realization that she had no idea who she was dealing with. Miles, having had the experience of dealing with a frightened teenaged girl before, did his best to explain to her the situation she unknowingly became a part of. "Laura, when you and Raj were little, Ayla and I were fighting in the war. We had lost and we both were hiding. I was in Los Angeles and she was in Chicago. Well, we're…"

Ayla, frustrated over his nurturing demeanor, interrupted him. While tightening her grip on the steering wheel and keeping her eyes locked on the desolate highway, she gave Laura an ultimatum. "Laura, we are the revolution, and we're going to take down the government. If you want in, we will teach you what you need to know. If you're out, then I'm sure you can find your way back to Pikesville." Miles looked at Laura sympathetically, and having not really been given a choice, she leaned back in her seat and didn't say anything; she only folded her arms and looked toward Raj who was staring at her amorously. "Well?" Ayla asked her again.

"I'll stay with you," she mumbled.

"Good, now we'll be coming up on Stevens Point soon. I'm going to park in the woods near the exit and I'll go in alone," Ayla said to the team.

"You sure that's a good idea?" Miles asked her.

"I'll be fine. He'll be expecting Ryan Gould, so seeing a familiar face will be the best," she said. In her head however, a different narrative played out, she asked herself if she even would be a familiar face for her brother. She imagined what it would be like to see him for the first time since thinking she had lost him so long ago. The last time she had seen him, he was barely a man in his late teens, now he was in his early thirties. She wondered how much he had changed, what happened to him after Atlanta, and how he even became a part of this second revolution.

Shortly after delegating herself the job of trying to find this Evan Anderson, the Humvee approached a sign that read, 'Exit 161', the exit for Stevens Point. Ayla merged onto the overgrown off-ramp and found an opening in the woods. She slowly drove the vehicle into the forest, far enough away from the road so it could not be seen by any potential army patrols or bandits. She shifted it into park and turned off the engine. "You guys try to get some rest." She said to the team as she unbuckled her seat belt and pulled out her pistol. She ejected the magazine, making sure there was a sufficient amount of bullets and reloaded her weapon. "Miles, if I'm not back by morning…"

He looked back at her and gave her a confident nod, and said, "I'll come and find you."

Without saying goodbye to the others she exited the vehicle, shut the door behind her, and made her way back to the spot where she drove the Humvee off the road. Doing her best to hide her friends, she grabbed armfuls of the wet leaves that covered the forest floor and threw them over the tire tracks that were imprinted into the soggy ground.

With her pistol in her hands at the ready, she walked toward the abandoned town of Stevens Point. The off-ramp seemed unusually long to Ayla and at one point, to her right, she could see tall stadium-type light posts protruding through the canopy of the forest; signs of life that used to exist here. She continued to walk cautiously on the narrow, one lane off-ramp, for about ten minutes until the road merged with one of the main streets of the town. Out of the corner of her eye, she could see something blue. She approached it curiously and moved the branches that covered the object. It was a sign that read, 'Welcome to Stevens Point'. She paused for a moment and examined the hand-carved wooden placard. She admired the forgotten trade through the misty cloud of her exhales from the falling temperatures.

A sound coming from the forest brought her back to reality. It was the clicking sound of someone pulling the hammer back on their weapon. Assuming that it was her brother, Ayla placed her hands in the air but still held her 9mm firmly. She slowly turned toward the sound and spoke, "Evan? Is that you?" She paused and waited for a response but heard nothing so she continued, "It's me…Ayla." She said hesitantly. A few moments later, she again heard the sound of the weapon's hammer accompanied by dragging footsteps walking toward her. As a precaution, she aimed her pistol toward the approaching sound.

"Ayla, is that really you?" a male voice asked as it emerged out of the darkness. As he stepped out onto the street, the moonlight hit his face and Ayla could see it was her long-lost brother. She immediately lowered her weapon and with a large smile, she wrapped her arms around her brother and squeezed tightly. "I can't believe it's you," he said in relief as he rested his head on her shoulders.

Ayla released him when she noticed the hug was not returned. As she wiped a sole tear from her eye, her focus shifted to his well-being.

"What's the matter? Are you hurt?" she asked him urgently.

Evan didn't respond, he simply collapsed in her arms and as she gently laid him down on the street, she noticed his blood-soaked pants. As she ripped open the left leg of his pants, he let out an agonizing moan. She inhaled sharply as she discovered a gruesome gunshot wound to his lower thigh, just above his knee cap. "Don't worry Evan, I got you," she said to him as she removed his belt and made a tourniquet just above his wound. She tightened it quickly, which prompted Evan to yell out in pain. "Come on, we've got to go." She said to him as she helped him to his feet. She placed his arm around her shoulder and the reunited siblings slowly made their way back to the Humvee.

"What about the horses?" Evan asked as he limped along in pain.

"Don't worry about them; we've changed things up a bit," She said in anguish as she supported the weight of her brother.

Chapter 17

Together Again

"That's when I met these three, Ayla's roommates..." Just as Miles was in the middle of explaining to Laura just how the group of revolutionaries had come together, the back hatch of the Humvee opened up. Startled from the noise, Miles started to draw his pistol. When he saw Ayla with her wounded brother, he put the gun back in the holster and sprang into action. He exited the vehicle and joined her near the rear hatch and began to diagnose the injury. "Check under the seats for a first aid kit, and give me something to clean this blood off." Zoe handed him a t-shirt from her pack and he cleaned the wound using the water from one of the canteens.

"Here, found one," Raj said as he handed the first aid kit back to Laura who in turn handed it to Miles. He opened the kit and found rubbing alcohol, gauze, and a small pair of tweezers. He rubbed his hands and the tweezers with the alcohol and then poured a generous amount over Evan's wound, which caused him again to groan in pain. With Evan's blood streaked across her forehead, Ayla looked on nervously. After disinfecting and cleaning his instruments, Miles began his attempt to extract the bullet from Evan's thigh. He probed the small hole with the tweezers, which caused Evan immense pain. "Ayla, hold him down!" Miles yelled to Ayla knowing she should have been doing so already.

After several seconds of digging around, Miles pulled the small bullet from Evan's wound and began to wrap his leg in gauze. "He should be all right; we just need to keep an eye on it; make sure it doesn't get infected." Miles said to Ayla as she approached her brother to comfort him. Miles, recognizing the situation, suggested they set up camp for the night. Confident they were far enough out of sight, he lit a small fire and the team started to turn in for the evening.

"Evan, I know this isn't the best time, but what did you do with my dad's horses?" Laura asked him.

Evan propped his head up in astonishment and in a raspy tone he asked, "Laura? What are you doing here?"

"I brought her with us," Raj spoke up from outside the Humvee in her defense.

"I put them in an old barn in the middle of town," Evan replied as he laid his head back down.

"I know you guys don't care but they need those horses back home," Laura said, hoping someone would sympathize with her.

"We aren't going back there," Ayla said sternly.

"If we let them go, they can find their way back home. They've lived in Pikesville their whole life," Laura said pleading with the team.

"Tomorrow morning, we will untie them and hopefully they'll go back," Miles said to her while looking at Ayla implying she needed to ease up on the young lady.

Ayla and Miles then helped Evan out of the Humvee and propped him up near the campfire. Knowing the two had a lot to talk about, Miles excused himself and returned to Laura and picked back up on the conversation he was having with her about the events that brought the team to Pikesville.

"Are you okay?" Ayla asked her brother.

"I'll live," he said. "What happened to you?" he asked her. Surprised that he asked the question, Ayla responded, "Me? What happened to you? They told us you were killed in Atlanta."

"I never even made it to Atlanta; we were ambushed on our way down there in Virginia. Most of us were killed but me and a few others escaped into the forest and made our way to Baltimore," he said.

"What was in Baltimore?" she asked curiously.

"Nothing much; I was hiding out with resistance survivors until they evacuated." He met his sister's eyes and she could tell the look he gave her meant he had something to say. "I'm sorry, Ayla."

"Sorry for what?" she asked hesitantly.

"They told me you were dead, that the resistance was dying," he said.

"What did you do?" she asked him nervously.

"I joined them," he said as Ayla looked at him with disgust. "I was only twenty, Ayla; I didn't know what to do."

"They killed our parents Evan! Did that slip your mind?" she asked him angrily as the rest of the team started to take notice of the altercation.

"They were going to kill me! I was just a kid. I didn't know what else to do," he pleaded with her hoping she'd understand his decision.

"So now what, you're back on our side?" she asked.

"A few years went by and I realized things weren't getting better, so I left again. I remember one of the guys I was hiding out with in Baltimore said he was going back toward Green Bay to find his family, so I headed that way too and found Pikesville. So, I just stayed there and made a life for myself," he said.

"How did you get involved again?" she asked him.

"This guy Ryan Davis would come through every six months

or so and meet with my friend John, so I eventually asked him about it. He was bringing correspondence back and forth from people involved and John was his contact. He would stay the night in Pikesville before going somewhere else. I kept pressing him and eventually they let me in," Evan said.

Ayla leaned back and tried getting comfortable near the fire and said casually, "His name was Gould."

"What?" Evan asked.

"Ryan Davis is actually Ryan Gould," she said.

"You know him?" he asked her in a surprised manner.

"I knew him. He's dead now; killed by the same bandits that attacked Pikesville," she replied.

Before they both fell asleep, Ayla explained her side of the story, where she had been the past several years, and just how she became part of the second revolution. "You should probably get some rest, let that leg heal," she said as she kissed him on the cheek. "It's good to have you back, bro," she said before she closed her eyes.

The next morning, Evan explained to Raj and Laura where he hid the horses and the two made their way toward the center of Stevens Point. When they finally found the spot, they set the horses free in the hopes that they would find their way back on their own accord. Meanwhile, Evan, Ayla, and Miles huddled around the small fire and waited for Gabe and Zoe to hopefully return with breakfast.

"So what's the plan now?" Evan asked Miles and Ayla.

"Ryan never filled you in?" she asked him surprisingly.

He replied, "I don't think he ever intended for me to continue on with you guys."

"Well either way, you're coming now," she said to him with a smile.

Miles interjected, "So the plan is that we're going to go to a town in Nebraska called Elsie."

"What's in Elsie?" Evan asked.

"An old gun store, we're to investigate and take whatever we can to help the cause. Then it's on to Los Angeles to meet with Dumont," Miles said as he wrapped up.

"Really? I get to meet Dumont?" Evan asked surprisingly.

"Actually, it's just Ayla that'll be meeting him. Dumont's a pretty paranoid guy," Miles said.

Just then, Gabe and Zoe returned from the woods but instead of wild game, they had plastic grocery bags. As the three newly reunited Western New Yorkers directed their attention toward the married hunting couple, they emptied their grocery bags onto the ground near the fire. "Baked beans, corn, and peaches? Where on Earth did you find canned food?" Miles asked them.

"We couldn't find anything to hunt and we wandered into town and found an old grocery store. It was mostly cleared out but we did find these little gems in a back room area. I'm pretty excited about it," Gabe said to the group with a positive attitude.

Using the same knife she used to knock the solider unconscious in Pikesville, Ayla opened the cans and set them near their small fire. Eventually, Raj and Laura returned after having successfully released her father's horses. The team enjoyed a hot meal reminiscent of the days before the first revolution. Following breakfast, they gathered their things and loaded up the mud speckled Humvee. With Ayla at the wheel, they drove off in the morning sun, headed toward the small, abandoned town of Elsie.

Chapter 18

Elsie

After a long day of driving and not seeing another soul along the way, the team arrived in Elsie, Nebraska. The sun had set and as Ayla navigated the small town roads without her headlights, Miles tried to locate the old gun store using the maps that were provided by Alexander Dumont. A lot of places like this were overrun with bandits or looters until there was nothing left, and then they'd move on, leaving the town to rot. Most of the buildings, although still intact, had crumbling foundations, peeling paint, and shattered windows. The streets were littered with abandoned cars and random reminders of the people who used to call the town home. It was quite clear that whoever forced the people out had their way with the quaint Midwestern city some time ago.

"Maybe I'm out of the loop a little but don't you think that this gun store may have suffered the same fate as the rest of this town?" Evan asked.

Before anyone had the chance to answer, Raj chimed in from the backseat he shared with Laura, "I don't know but this is stupid. This place is going to be the same tomorrow morning. I'm hungry, and ready to get out of this car."

"All right, I'll find a place to make camp for the night," Ayla said.

With no objections heard, she found a home on the outside

of town that was, for the most part, out of site from the main road. The long driveway led to an old rundown house that at one point was painted white but had lost some of its luster from the neglect it had suffered. She stopped the Humvee just in front of the old garage attached to the left side of the main house.

"Do you think this place has beds?" Laura asked optimistically.

Miles answered her, "I don't know but just wait and we'll all go in together, just in case."

Ayla and Miles approached the garage hoping to find space to keep the Humvee out of view. As they lifted the door, it let out a high-pitched squealing sound, reinforcing their thought that the house had long since been abandoned.

Inside they found the belongings of the family that once resided there. There were a few old cardboard boxes on the weathered shelves labeled with black marker. They read *Baby Clothes*, *Dad's Stuff,* and *Old Pictures*. In the corner was a dilapidated crib that most likely once held a newborn child to proud parents. Ayla took in the moment and walked around the garage. She felt the same sadness she felt when she first saw the picture of her and her family that she gave to Raj. She could only wonder the fate of this family and thousands of other families as they faced the oppression of the United States and the war that turned the country upside down.

Miles snapped her out of her daydream by clearing his throat and asked, "Do you want to give me a hand here?" He was standing near the driver side door ready to push. Ayla walked to the passenger side door, opened it, and the pair pushed the large military Humvee into the garage. They closed the door, which again made the same squealing and grinding noises as it closed.

Together the travelers approached the steps that lead to an

uneven and weathered porch. The wood creaked as it felt the pressure from the team of seven. Ayla reached for the doorknob and surprisingly it had been left unlocked. She and Miles entered first and instructed the rest of the team to stay on the porch while they investigated the house. Upon entering, Miles gave Ayla the signal for her to head to the right while he took the left. Both with their pistols drawn and at the ready they separated. Ayla began canvassing the kitchen where there were some broken plates and a few random utensils on the counter. She was tempted to open the fridge and the cupboards to check and see if there was any salvageable food but decided that it could wait. She continued cautiously to what appeared to be an old sitting room with a couch and an empty bookshelf. Unfortunately, it looked like some rodents had decided to call the couch home as random pieces of cushion lay strew across the amber colored hard wood floor. She also saw an old vertical piano made of dark maple. She was drawn to it and began to wonder about the last time she had actually heard someone playing the piano or any musical instrument for that matter. Just then, while she was distracted by the thought of music, a large rat ran out from the couch and nearly scampered over her feet. She jumped back and let out a quiet shriek.

Miles hopped out from the hallway that Ayla was approaching with his pistol drawn expecting her to be in danger. When he realized it was safe, he lowered his weapon and gave Ayla a look indicating he was curious to what startled her. "A rat." She said in a whisper. Miles gave her another look. "A big rat!" she said as she laughed quietly and held up her hands exaggerating the size of the small animal.

Following their brief exchange, the pair regained their seriousness and approached a set of stairs. They cautiously made the ascent with Ayla taking the lead. About halfway up, they were overtaken by a horrible stench. It was a smell they had both experienced before, and one they would never forget. They made eye contact with each other and no words were needed as they both knew what they were about to discover. They covered their faces with their shirts hoping to partially filter the sting of the pungent odor.

At the top of the stairs, to their immediate left there was a bedroom. Ayla opened the door and they both entered with their guns drawn. They found nothing but one twin mattress on the floor and some coat hangers in the closet. They now directed their attention to the long hallway to the right of the stairs where there were three more doors to check. The next door led to another bedroom. No mattress this time, only a dresser with one of the drawers missing. The door directly across from them was a full bath and if there was a shower curtain, it would actually look like it didn't belong in an abandoned house. It even had a cup with toothbrushes in it.

One bedroom left to check and the smell was stronger than ever. Miles slowly opened the door and even with all of their training and the things they had seen in the war, there was nothing that could have prepared them for the sight that was now in front of them. It appeared to be an entire family, dead on a large bed. Two small children, a man, and a woman, each of whom died from a gunshot wound to the head; at least as far as they could tell. The thing that left them unprepared was the fact that the man was still grasping a pistol indicating that it was him who took the lives of his family members. It wasn't unheard of in times of peril and distress, but seeing it in person was still hard to understand and just as hard to forget.

"What happened to these people?" Ayla asked aloud not

expecting an answer from Miles.

"Something bad, maybe it was bandits and the father didn't want them to suffer. That would explain why everything is missing," Miles said.

He then approached the man's body and knelt down, which prompted Ayla to ask, "What are you doing?"

"Getting the gun," he said casually as he pried open the dead man's hand and placed the gun in his pocket. Ayla gave him a look of disgust.

"What? We're here to get weapons, aren't we? Well, there's one," he said unemotionally to which Ayla just shook her head.

They made their way back downstairs and out to the porch where the rest of the team was still waiting. "Okay, the house is clear, just don't go upstairs," Miles said.

"Why, what's up there?" Evan asked as Laura and Raj looked on with curiosity.

"Dead bodies," Ayla said as she grabbed her pack from the porch.

"Are there any beds?" Laura asked.

"No, there's nothing of use up there," Miles said to her, purposely omitting the fact that there was one twin bed in the hopes of sparing her any trauma.

Ayla assigned her team members different jobs to prepare for the evening. Zoe and Gabe of course were responsible for finding some food and they took off into the woods that surrounded the house. Laura and Raj were told to find anything the team could use to cover the windows so they won't be seen by any possible bandits or any other dangerous vagrants. Evan, still recovering from his injuries propped himself up against the living room wall by the open fireplace and inspected it to ensure it was functional. Miles gathered firewood and Ayla took the first guard duty.

She walked down the driveway, toward the road that ran perpendicular to the house. With her hands on her hips, she scanned the surrounding area of abandoned homes and buildings. She was looking for certain signs and listening for any noises that would not seem natural to the area. Using only the light of the moon shining down on the abandoned town, all seemed quiet, and she returned to the porch for the remainder of her guard duties. Eventually, Miles came to relieve her and she retreated to the home's living room and joined the others who were resting comfortably

Chapter 19

Guns for Hire

The next morning, the team ate some breakfast, and packed up their belongings. They had one mission for the day and that was to find the small weapons store and see if there were any salvageable guns or ammunitions. As Ayla stepped out onto the old porch of the abandoned house, a cool fall breeze rolled through and rustled the brown leaves across the gravel driveway. She took a deep breath and stepped down the stairs toward the garage where Miles waited for her to open the aged door. Once again, it let out a loud screeching sound which caused the other team members to cringe and even prompted some nearby birds to flee from their hiding spots.

They piled in the Humvee and began to navigate the streets of Elsie. "The place should be right around the corner here, if I'm reading the map right." Miles said. As they made the turn, the weapons store came into view. "There it is!" he said as if he was surprised by his own navigational skills.

The weapons store had a large sign over the front entrance that was missing several pieces. The doors and the windows were secured by metal bars and a bulky chain was wrapped around the door handles with a large padlock. "How are we supposed to get in?" Evan asked Ayla who in turn looked to Miles.

"Stop the car Ayla," Miles said to her as he reached in his

pack and pulled out a set of keys.

"More secrets Miles?" Ayla asked, annoyed. He just looked at her and raised his eyebrows as if to say she should expect it by now. As Miles and Ayla exited, they instructed the others to stay put while they investigated. As they approached the door, Ayla cautiously placed her hand on her pistol but kept it tucked in the back of her pants. Miles first unlocked the pad lock and then the set of barred doors. Before opening, he made eye contact with her, prompting her to ready her weapon. He opened the door quickly as Ayla breeched looking for any potential threats. "It's clear," she said.

She holstered her sidearm and the two began to inspect the interior of the weapons store. This was the showroom area and much like her first meeting with Miles, the store had been abandoned for quite some time. Strewn about were empty display cases, old ammo advertisements, and empty bullet boxes. "Great, this keeps getting better and better," Ayla said.

"Patience my dear," Miles said as he pointed toward the ground. Under Ayla's feet was a large throw rug covered in dust and random pieces of trash. He motioned for her to back up. As she stepped off the rug, Miles pulled it up and tossed it aside, revealing a trap door which was secured by a keyhole lock. Miles located the correct key and knelt down to unlock the door as Ayla looked on wondering why he couldn't have told her about the store and the cache of weapons. She decided to keep quiet for the time being and ask him later once they accomplished their mission.

The lock clicked as he turned the key and Miles then motioned for her to come closer. Together they lifted the trap door open and it dropped heavily on the ground, causing a plume of dust to swirl around it. Ayla wafted the cloud out of her face as she coughed slightly. All that was visible in the opening of the gun store floor was a set of wooden stairs that disappeared into the darkness. Miles led the way down and Ayla followed him in. The steepness of the stairs caused her to use the ceiling for balance. Miles turned on his flashlight revealing a small stockpile of weapons. "Where did all this come from?" she asked him.

"A connection Dumont made in prison. For whatever reason they picked this as their stash house," Miles said as he rummaged through a case containing ammunition and hand grenades. "Okay, let's start loading these up and get out of here." He said as he handed her a cardboard box full of ammo. She set the box above her on the original floor of the weapons store. Two more identical boxes followed and she again set them on the floor. Next he began to hand her AR-15 rifles; one by one, she sets them on the floor near the boxes. In total there were twenty rifles, ten pistols, a box of hand grenades, C-4 explosives, and a bunch of ammo.

"That's all she wrote," he said and they climbed up the stairs and into the empty store. As Miles closed the trap door and locked it, Ayla examined the newly acquired weapons imagining where they came from and why they appeared to be brand new. Her thoughts were interrupted by Miles who asked her to help him cover the trap door with the old dusty rug. "Put some trash back on the carpet. If they're tracking us we don't want them to know we had a secret stash here." She did as he advised but remained silent, stewing over the fact that Miles was still keeping things from her.

Miles grabbed two boxes that were stacked upon one another and began to head for the exit when Ayla stopped him, "Wait," she said. Miles stopped before the door and slowly turned around as he already knew Ayla's curiosity would not let it go. "You said we were coming here to look for anything that was left behind but somehow you have a key to the building and access to a cache of weapons that look like they just came off the assembly line. I want to know what you know," she demanded answers from him.

"I have orders Ayla," he said to her in a stern voice.

"Last time you told me that I punched you in the nose. I deserve to be in the know here. I thought I was a General? Or am I just a pawn in Dumont's little game?" she asked.

"There are other people involved here that need to remain anonymous, people like Jeffery Gould who are high up in the power structure of the United States Government. The less people who know the better, that's all Ayla," he said to her while still holding the boxes full of ammo and other military supplies. Ayla still remained skeptical but accepted his answers for now. She grabbed two rifles and followed him toward the exit of the shop. She pushed the door open, which still had a small bell that rang as they walked out into cool fall air.

"Go get the rest of the stuff in there," she said to Raj and Laura in a displeasing tone due to Miles keeping secrets from her. She wondered how she could trust him now, knowing that there were probably other things he was hiding.

The team loaded the rest of the gear into the back of the Humvee, which was now considerably more cramped. "This should be a fun ride to Vegas," Evan said from the back in a sarcastic tone. Miles started the vehicle and the team began their journey to Las Vegas where, if all went according to plan, there should be a team of rebels ready to take their supplies and put them to good use.

Chapter 20

On the Road Again

"If I-70 hasn't been destroyed, it looks like we can take that straight to Vegas. Only nine hundred and seventy miles, if we drive straight through with a couple of rests, we should get there late tonight, depending on traffic of course," Miles said as he laughed knowing full well they would most likely be the only vehicle on the road.

After a few hours of driving, they pulled over for a break. Each team member got out of the Humvee and stretched their legs. Some ventured out into the forest to relieve themselves including Evan. Ayla paced outside the Humvee when Miles approached her. "When was the last time you saw your brother?" he asked her as he stared off into the woods.

"Twelve years ago I guess. Why?" she asked.

"I'm just confused by something. It's been bothering me. I don't ever remember mentioning that we were going to Vegas. All I told him was that we were going to Los Angeles after we got the guns. Earlier he said something about driving to Vegas. How did he know that?" Miles asked suspiciously.

"One of the others must have mentioned it to him," she said.

"Maybe, maybe not," Miles said curiously.

"What are you suggesting?" she asked in a disapproving manner.

"What if he's lying? What if he isn't even your brother?"

Miles said to her.

"Really? I think I would know if it was my brother or not," she said.

"Twelve years is a long time," he said as he leaned in closer to her. "Why would he give Gould his real name? Nobody would use their real name if they were hiding. They could have found somebody that looked like him knowing that you'd welcome him back with open arms," he added.

The rest of the team began to make their way back to the Humvee and they all piled in. Ayla chose to keep the conversation she had with Miles to herself for now, but she didn't totally dismiss what he said. Ayla, behind the wheel now, thought about any scars or identifying marks he had as she drove along the dilapidated highway. She recalled a time from their childhood when he had stiches in his wrist from a broken window. She continued to ponder about the possibility of him being an imposter or lying about what he had been up to over the last decade or so.

A few more hours passed and it was time for another break. The crew exited the vehicle and this time Gabe and Zoe disappeared into the surrounding forests to see if they could find a meal for the wary travelers. Meanwhile, Raj built a fire and Ayla took a seat next to her brother. She began to recount old stories and memories with him. As she talked, she managed to work in the story about him cutting his wrist, which prompted him to turn his hand over revealing the scar that he's had since he was a boy. Relieved that the scar was actually there, she and Miles could at least confirm that it was in fact Evan and not someone claiming to be him.

Zoe and Gabe returned with a small turkey. They cleaned, cooked and ate most of it before heading back to the Humvee to tackle the second half of their long car ride to Vegas. Ayla, feeling somewhat relieved that Miles's suspicion was incorrect, rested in the passenger seat while he drove.

A couple hours later, Ayla opened her eyes after taking a solid nap. The Humvee was pulled over and she found Miles, Gabe, and Zoe all around the fire. "Where are the others?" she asked through a yawn as she pulled her hair back.

"Laura and Raj went for a walk and your brother went to the bathroom. A while ago actually, now that I think about it," Gabe said.

Ayla made eye contact with Miles and he jumped to his feet. "You two stay here. If you hear anything, put that fire out and stay hidden," Ayla said to the hunters.

"What's going on?" Zoe asked hesitantly.

"Just being careful," Miles said as he looked in the direction that Evan walked off to.

"They should be easy to track," she said to him.

Shortly after they entered the woods, they picked up the young couple's trail and followed it for a few minutes until Miles noticed something had changed. "Look here," Miles said to her. "Third set of tracks, probably your brother's." They made eye contact and readied their pistols.

They continued to follow the now three sets of footprints for another ten minutes until suddenly they heard Evan's voice to their right. "Stop right there," he said as Ayla and Miles pointed their guns toward the sound only to see him using Raj and Laura as human shields.

"What are you doing Evan?" Ayla asked him sternly.

"My job," he said. "I'm a spy, Ayla! We had a perfect plan to ambush this little rebellion until you showed up."

"You liar," she said angrily still pointing the gun toward him.

Meanwhile, Raj and Laura trembled in fear.

"Come on sis," he said sarcastically, "I didn't lie. Well, leaving the U.S. was a lie but the rest was real. I've been undercover waiting for that idiot Gould to make a move. He and his brother thought they were so smart," he said with a sinister laugh.

"How did you know?" Raj asked while choking from Evan's arm around his neck.

We heard rumblings of a growing resistance and put agents in settlements all over the country. I volunteered," Evan said proudly while staring at his sister.

"Why do this now?" Miles asked.

"I figured you were going to find out sooner or later when you were asking about my scars. I knew you were suspicious, Miles, so I decided my best shot was when Ayla fell asleep."

"Listen Evan, it's not too late. You can let them go, and help us. We'll forget this ever happened," Ayla said to him hoping to change his mind even though she knew none of what she said would be possible.

"I'm a patriot, Ayla. I serve my country. You're a traitor. Don't get me wrong, it was great to see you guys but I've been working this way too long to get caught now," Evan said while still peering from behind Raj's head while pressing the gun into Laura's temple.

"You're an idiot," she said to him trembling from both anger and sadness.

"Maybe so, but these two are coming with me. And if you follow me, I'll kill one of them, Ayla. Do you want that on your conscience?" Evan asked.

"Where are you taking them?" she asked.

"Oh don't worry about them. They'll attend the finest universities to learn about the glory and honor of the United States," he said with a sarcastic smile.

Knowing full well he intended to place them in a reeducation camp to brainwash them, Ayla objected, "Just let them go, you can walk away right now. Just let them go." She urged him to change his mind.

"Sorry, Ayla," He said as he pointed his weapon at his new prisoners, "I want the Humvee, with the guns in it."

Miles and Ayla both continued to look at him without saying a word.

"Now!" he yelled in an agitated voice as he pulled the hammer back on his gun, keeping it pointed at his human shields. Again his request was answered with silence. "I'll kill them, Ayla," he said in a serious tone.

She finally responded as her pistol was still aimed at him and his hostages, "You're already dead, Evan; you just don't know it yet. If you kill one of them, I will put a bullet in your head. You know I can. So, no, you're not getting the Humvee or the guns, you can hide behind them like a coward and walk."

"I need those weapons, Ayla," he replied to her.

"So does the resistance. Make a choice, you can kill them, try your luck with me, and go for the Humvee or you can walk away with your hostages and your life. What's it going to be?" she said to him knowing he was bluffing.

Evan paused a moment and knowing his sister's marksmanship, he decided that walking away was his best chance to make it out alive. "This isn't over," he said as he began to walk backwards keeping his hostages between himself and Ayla's gun.

"You're damn right it's not over," she said to him as he slowly disappeared deeper into the forest.

After they ensured that Evan had continued on his path, Ayla and Miles turned and made their way back to the camp where Gabe and Zoe remained waiting by the fire. As they walked, they didn't say a word to each other as Miles wasn't sure what to say, and Ayla was filled with so many emotions trying to process what had just happened.

Upon arriving at camp, Gabe and Zoe immediately got to their feet. "What happened?" Gabe asked as Ayla walked past him and stomped out the campfire.

"Let's go, we're leaving," Ayla commanded as Gabe and Zoe both looked at each other. "Give me the keys, Miles." Miles, looking concerned, reached into his pocket and tossed her the keys. "Let's go," she said again loudly as she climbed into the Humvee and turned the ignition.

As Zoe got to her seat, she couldn't help but be curious about where the other three team members had disappeared to. "Where are the others? What happened to Raj, and Laura?" She caught Ayla's eyes glance at her in the rearview mirror as she sped down the empty highway. "Ayla!" she said urging her to give her an explanation.

"He took them," Ayla said quietly as she stared forward.

"What do you mean he took them, who?" Zoe asked frantically.

With Ayla choosing to remain silent due to her distress, Miles decided he better fill in the others. "Evan was a spy; he was working us the whole time."

"A spy?" Gabe asked.

"I think he was after the guns but he knew that wasn't going to happen so I think he cut his losses and took our friends as an insurance policy," Miles said remorsefully.

"What's going to happen to them?" Zoe asked frightened for their safety.

"They'll probably end up at a training camp as new recruits," he said.

"What does that mean, new recruits?" Gabe asked as Zoe leaned back covering her mouth with her hand in disbelief.

"It means they'll be brainwashed and made to serve in the army," Miles said.

"So you're just going to let him take them?" Zoe asked again as she clutched on to her husband's arm.

"We can't go after them," Ayla said as she glanced at the couple through the rearview mirror.

"Why not?" Zoe asked as tears began to slowly stream from her eyes. "Raj is family to us, Ayla. You can't just leave him behind."

"We are at war, and I'm a commanding officer, I can't sacrifice our mission. If we follow him, he'll know and he'll kill one of them. Evan isn't a compassionate person, at least not any more. We either continue on or risk their lives and our mission by going after them," Ayla declared. "He's not bluffing about killing; he has no problem with that," she concluded.

Zoe again leaned back in her seat in disbelief and placed her head on Gabe's shoulder for comfort. As Ayla saw this, she realized she must be coming off as cold hearted to her civilian friends. She stopped the Humvee, placed the vehicle in park, and turned to address them. "Raj is like a little brother to me, so believe me I'm disgusted by this. But we have to keep going. I promise if and when we have a chance to get him back, I'll do anything I can."

Not satisfied with her response, Zoe simply gazed out the passenger window as Ayla continued to drive to their destination.

"You know, if Evan already knew about Vegas, they could be waiting for us there," Miles said to Ayla.

She kept her eyes on the road and gripped the steering wheel until her knuckles turned white and said confidently, "We'll just have to kill them all."

Chapter 21

Sin City

The light from the moon once again illuminated the dark highway. The Humvee that contained the team of now four came to a slow stop along the side of the road. Ayla shifted the SUV into park and gently reached over to the passenger seat and nudged Miles to wake him. He was startled but quickly realized what was happening. "Where are we?" he asked as he attempted to become more alert.

"About five miles outside the city limits," she said calmly.

"What's the plan?" he asked her.

"I think we have to assume that Evan made it to his people or somehow contacted them," she said as Miles nodded in agreement. "We arm ourselves, approach with caution, and expect to come into contact with the army."

"What about them?" he asked as he motioned his head toward the back seat referencing the sleeping Gabe and Zoe.

"They're going to have to suit up. We'll have to see what they're most comfortable doing but if there are troops, we're going to need their help. If they want to survive, they don't really have a choice," she said to him.

"Well, I suppose we should get them up," he said.

Ayla nodded and reached back and shook Zoe's leg until she opened her eyes. "It's time," she said to her.

"Time for what?" she asked.

"We're about five miles from our rendezvous point. We need to get ready," she said to her calmly. "Get your husband up."

Ayla exited the Humvee and met Miles at the rear where he was loading guns with the proper ammo and filling his pack with grenades and explosives. "We won't be able to bring everything at first. We'll have to hide the Humvee and come back for the rest when it's all clear." He said as he stuffed a magazine into one of the 9mm handguns.

Zoe and Gabe both exited the Humvee and made their way to the rear. "So what's the plan?" Gabe asked.

Miles took the lead. "We're going to walk the rest of the way, stay out of sight until we know it's safe."

Gabe paused for a moment and asked another question, "And if it isn't safe?"

"That's what the guns are for, Gabe." Ayla said as she slung a rifle over her shoulder. "Now we're going to need you two if there's a problem. Are you ready?" She asked.

Gabe and Zoe both looked at one another. Zoe grabbed a pistol from the trunk of the Humvee, cocked it and said, "I guess we don't have a choice."

The team gathered what they could carry and Ayla found a good spot to hide the Humvee that held the remaining weapons and explosives. They left behind the Midwestern forests and now traveled through the dry cold deserts of the southwest. The resistance picked Las Vegas for a rendezvous point because it had long been abandoned. Even before the war, Las Vegas was running out of its water supply and now that most of the country's infrastructure had been abandoned, it had no hope of supporting any type of civilian settlement. The resistance, however, was able to transport water back and forth to the few soldiers stationed there by traveling from Los Angeles at night.

For the most part, Las Vegas had remained intact through the war. The United States government assumed it would neither be useful to the resistance or anyone else due to its lack of resources so they didn't feel it necessary to wipe it off the map like the other cities. Although it doesn't have the shiny lights and Elvis impersonators, it still resembled the Vegas of old except instead of majestic fountains there were now rolling sand dunes.

"Where exactly is this rendezvous point?" Gabe asked as they walked closer to the old neighborhoods of the city.

"At the airport, the soldiers should be in one of the private hangars on the western edge of the property. Once we get to the perimeter fence, we should be able to tell if the U.S. has been there or not, in theory," Miles said.

"In theory?" Gabe asked Zoe quietly, hoping Miles didn't hear his cynicism.

They hit the city's edge by traveling south from where they hid the Humvee until they reached a road marked Route 562, which eventually ran adjacent to the airport. They travelled along the dusty road where wind and Mother Nature had created swooping drifts of desert sand. Along the way, there were abandoned cars, empty lots, and endless rows of non-functioning street lights. Eventually, industrial complexes and department stores gave way to homes and residential neighborhoods. Many were in decline due to the harsh desert environment and neglect which occurred from the absence of their owners.

Once again, walking through the old residential neighborhood stirred up emotions within Ayla and the rest of the team. She, of course, remembered her once happy family living so far away in Orchard Park, a town much like the one they walked though. Gabe and Zoe wondered what type of life they could have made if they were able to grow old together like people did before the war. Miles, on the other hand, pondered what life could have been like if he never had joined the military. Would he have been able to settle down, find a woman he could love, maybe start a family of his own? No one spoke in this time of reflection and even though they each knew there was no point to wonder what could have been, they still couldn't help themselves.

After a few hours of walking, they passed what was once Sunset Park, having been abandoned by civilization, the once green grasses, where people played with their children and read in the shades of the trees, had now been taken back by the dry desert heat and sand. Just ahead of the park, the road continued on straight to their destination with empty plazas to the left and on the right was a long fence that once protected the sprawling airport property. The long flat runways were a relieving sight for the team as it marked another turning point in their journey.

"We still have a bit of a walk before we get to the hangar where our guys are. I think it's best if you and I split up," Miles said to Ayla.

"It's just the four of us now; you think that's the best idea?" she asked him.

"We can't risk it. If all four of us go and something happens, those weapons will be gone and the resistance needs them," he responded to her.

"So what are you suggesting?" she asked him.

"Give me those binoculars," he said as he pointed to her pack. "Ayla and I will get a closer look, you two stay here and we'll come back with a plan." As he spoke, Ayla removed the pack from her back and rummaged through until she found a pair of binoculars and handed them to Miles.

"You two cross the street and hide behind that truck until we get back." Ayla said as she pointed to an old pickup truck that had been turned on its side. "We'll be right back," she said before her and Miles stealthily followed the fence away from Gabe and Zoe with their weapons drawn.

Gabe and Zoe crossed the street and did as they were told. They took their position behind the beat-up, overturned truck. As they leaned against the metal, it was still warm from the hot day even though the colder evening air of the dessert had started to make its presence known. "It's pretty unbelievable how much our lives have changed in the past month or so, isn't it?" Gabe said to his wife.

"It's been pretty difficult sometimes," she said to him with a tear in her eye.

As it rolled down her face, Gabe placed his hand on her cheek and wiped the tear away and said to her, "I love you, Zoe. And I won't let anything bad happen to you." They looked at each other and then he kissed her; they remained behind the truck holding one another until Zoe spotted something out of the corner of her eye.

"What is that?" Zoe asked curiously as light shined into her eyes.

"Get down!" Gabe said as he grabbed his wife and pulled her out of sight of the oncoming lights. "It's them," he whispered to her.

"Them who?" she asks.

"The army, Evan must have found his people," he said as the bright lights got closer. "What are those?" he asked aloud.

Eventually, they both realized that the oncoming lights were army Humvees.

"We have to warn them, Gabe!" she said as she frantically searched through her pack before pulling out a hand grenade. Just then the Humvees all turned off their headlights to avoid detection.

"I've got a better idea," he said.

Meanwhile, Miles and Ayla had put some considerable distance between them and their partners. Peering through binoculars at their rendezvous point they could see the lights from the camp of their fellow revolutionaries. "I see five armed guards patrolling the perimeter, all wearing our colors," Miles said to Ayla. "No sign of the Army anywhere."

Ayla took the binoculars and looked for herself, "That doesn't mean they won't be coming though," she said.

"We need to get closer to these guys and tell them the Army could be on its way," he said.

"What about Gabe and Zoe?" she asked him as she placed her hand on his arm to remind him they weren't alone.

"They'll be fine," he said confidently as he took out a large knife and began to cut a hole in the fence that surrounded the airport. Just as the pair were about to enter into what once was a restricted area, a large explosion about a mile away made them both jump to their feet in shock.

"Gabe and Zoe!" Ayla said in a worried tone. She started to run toward the explosion but not before Miles grabbed her arm.

"Wait, we need a plan," he said.

"All hell is breaking loose, Miles; we don't have time for a plan," she said as another explosion in the distance lit up the abandoned desert city causing them both to shield their eyes. "You go to the hangar, I'll go to them," she said. Miles looked at her hesitantly but only for a moment until they took off in opposite directions.

Chapter 22

Battle at McCarran

"What do you mean you have a better idea?" Zoe asked Gabe as the small convoy of Humvees approached.

"What were you going to do?" he asked frantically.

"I don't know throw a grenade somewhere!" she yelled.

In a surprisingly calm way he began to explain his plan. "We've got a little bit of time before they get to us. We should try to rig up some sort of trap and try to and take them out." He reached in his bag and pulled out some of the C-4 explosives they brought from the Humvee.

"Like you know what to do with that?" Zoe yelled at him. He agreed with her and put it back in the bag and pulled out a few more grenades.

"Do we have any rope or string or anything?" she asked as they both started to rummage through their packs and the surrounding wreckage of the overturned truck.

"There!" Gabe exclaimed as he reached into the broken sunroof on the pickup truck and pulled out a spool of speaker wire.

"Okay, over there by the light pole, let's go," Zoe said. As the couple sprang into action, they tied the speaker wire to the light pole and suspended it across the road. Carefully, they tied the other end to the grenade's pin. From there, they held the grenade in place, weighing it down with a rock, creating a trip wire that would hopefully detonate as the Humvees passed through. They then rigged a similar type of trap a little further down the road.

The Humvees were now getting dangerously close to the couple as they sprinted to take cover behind another incapacitated vehicle. They both pulled out their pistols and prepared them to fire. As the roar of the Humvees grew louder Gabe turned to Zoe and with a smirk he said, "Just like hunting." Seeing that Zoe wasn't amused by his ill-timed humor, he immediately refocused on the incoming threat.

Moments later, the lead Humvee in the Army's convoy sped through the trap, detonating the first grenade. The delayed explosion allowed the first Humvee to escape; however, the timing was perfect for the second. The force of the blast caused it to be blown off the road, and in a ball of fire, it was sent tumbling through the airport perimeter fencing. When it finally rolled to a stop, it exploded and sent a massive fireball into the night sky.

Zoe and Gabe were shocked by both the heat and the noise. However, once they heard the squealing tires of the remaining four Humvees coming to a stop, they realized they may have to defend themselves. They quickly gained their composure and prepared for a shootout.

"Everybody out!" they heard one of the commanding officers yell over the noise of car doors being shut mixed with the crackling of flames from the dispatched Humvee. "Search the area!" he shouted.

"Do you think Evan is with them?" Zoe asked her husband as they hid behind an abandoned vehicle about fifty yards away from their enemies.

"I doubt it," Gabe whispered, "They probably took him to a

hospital or something."

"Got another trap here!" one of the men yelled to his commanding officers as he untied the speaker line from the second trap. "And footprints!" Several Armed men began to approach Zoe and Gabe's position.

"Are you ready?" Gabe asked his wife who nodded as she trembled in fear. As Gabe began to slowly raise his head to catch a glimpse of the men who were walking in their direction, several gun shots echoed through the desert and one by one the men began to fall.

"It's Ayla!" Zoe yelled in excitement as she could be seen in the distance walking quickly in their direction while firing toward the remaining men. This motivated Gabe and Zoe to join in and they both began shooting at the enemy. Before anyone had a chance to think, a firefight erupted in the desert.

Ayla eventually joined them behind the abandoned vehicle as bullets flew by them and ricocheted off the rusted metal. "Where's Miles?" Gabe asked as he ducked for cover.

"We split up when we saw the explosions, he went to the hangar," Ayla said as she loaded another clip into her pistol. "What happened?" she asked as she turned and fired a few shots hoping to slow their advances.

She again took cover and pressed her back against the old car as Gabe answered her, "We saw them coming and made a trip wire with a grenade but we only got one," Gabe said as he yelled over the sound of the army's gunshots.

"Nice!" Ayla yelled as she continued to return fire trying to hold them back. "Got any more of those grenades?" she asked. Gabe nodded, reached in his pack and handed her the last grenade he brought with them. Ayla peeked around the side of the car and spotted about fifteen more troops and quickly returned before a bullet pinged off the car near her head. "God, there's too many of them," she said disparagingly as she pulled the pin out of the grenade with her teeth and threw it toward the troops. It exploded taking out only a few and injuring a couple more.

"We're pinned down here. We need to get to the hangar," she said urgently as the three of them cowered behind the car. Bullets continued to fly by them making it impossible for them to escape. "Where are you Miles?" Ayla asked aloud. Just then a bullet ripped through the rusted vehicle and hit Zoe in the shoulder causing her to yell out in agony as she fell backwards onto the worn pavement.

"Zoe!" Gabe yelled as he rushed to help his injured wife while Ayla continued her attempt to hold back the encroaching threat.

"Keep pressure on it!" she yelled as she stood and fired off a few more rounds. As she aimed her weapon toward the enemy, she heard a faint whistling sound and before she could wonder what it was, an explosion sent her back through the air. She landed with a thud on the sand-covered road as chunks of earth and asphalt fell around her. She was disoriented and could see a blurry image of Gabe crouched over her. All she could hear was a high-pitched ringing sound and his muffled screams.

Another explosion shook the ground, this time closer to the enemy, followed by another and another. To Ayla, all she heard were muffled booms. She attempted to climb to her feet but the aftermath of the blasts had left her too rattled and she collapsed again. Another explosion rocked the nearby area followed by more muffled screams. Half-conscious, she lay there, looking at the stars with the occasional orange spark from the fires floating into her line of sight. Then, as if she were dreaming, she saw Miles leaning over her. He yelled something to her but she couldn't make out what he said. He picked her up and carried her away from the chaos. As she was carted away in his arms, she could see Gabe following close behind helping Zoe who clutched her shoulder. Behind them, all that remained were the burning chassis of the army Humvees and the bodies of their enemies. Soon, the smoke, fire, and night sky all became tunneled into one blurry image and she lost consciousness.

She was quickly brought back to reality by an excited question from Gabe, "What the hell was that?" he yelled as they further evacuated the scene.

"Artillery fire from our boys in the hangar," Miles yelled as he continued to run across the runways toward the resistance strong hold.

"You almost killed us!" Gabe yelled as Ayla tapped Miles on the shoulder letting him know she could walk now. "Miles!" he yelled again.

Miles stopped and while he lowered Ayla back to her feet he fired back at Gabe, "Yea and if we didn't fire you'd all be dead right now. Just be thankful. Ayla was with you because she's the reason we rescued you!" He was of course implying that Gabe and Zoe weren't worth wasting precious artillery rounds on; Gabe just stared at him not knowing exactly what to say. "Now just shut up and keep moving." He yelled as he helped Ayla limp along while they continued to make their way to their destination

When they finally arrived at the hangar, Miles helped Ayla get to one of the cots the soldiers stationed there slept on. Still reeling from the explosions and a bit disoriented she asked, "What happened?" She brought her hand to her forehead and groaned as she rubbed it.

"We blew you up with Artillery," he said as he chuckled and wiped away flecks of dirt that were stuck to her face. "You're all right though, all limbs accounted for." He laughed again hoping to make her feel better.

"Help me up." She said painstakingly as she extended her hand and grabbed hold of Miles'. He helped her to rise to a seated position. "Gabe and Zoe?" she asked hesitantly not quite knowing if the image she saw of them running behind Miles to safety actually happened.

"They're okay, just take it easy." He said to her as he helped her stand. "Zoe took one round to the shoulder but she should be fine."

"We don't have time to mess around here, who's the commanding officer," she asked as she began to start feeling like herself again.

"I am, ma'am," said a tall, fit officer named Lieutenant Hudson." Touching the revolutionary snake and shield on his hat as he saluted her.

"How many are you?" Miles asked him.

"There's about two hundred of us, sir," he responded.

Ayla took command of the situation and said, "We left a cache of weapons about six miles outside the city." Still breathing heavy she continued, "Hudson, take a team with you and get the Humvee. Miles, mark it on the map for them, would you? It's not safe here any more." She spoke louder so the rest of the men and women stationed there could hear her. "Your orders have changed. We're all going to Los Angeles now. We'll leave as soon as Hudson and his team return. I need a volunteer to go to Los Angeles ahead of the rest of us to bring Dumont up to speed, any volunteers?" she asked the rest of the revolutionaries.

This marked somewhat of a turning point for Ayla and Miles. He had done his part. He got her to Vegas but now things have changed and there were no more secrets that made her wary of taking charge. Maybe it was another near death experience or maybe it was because she was ready to do things her way, but from here on out she decided she'd be calling most of the shots.

"General, I volunteer." Ayla heard the voice of a young woman from behind a group of soldiers; she made her way to the front of the small gathering by weaving in and out of the platoon. She was medium height, very pretty, and wore her blonde hair in a ponytail which was covered by the same resistance hat Hudson had on.

Skeptical, Ayla approached her, "What's your name?"

"Ellie," she hesitated and continued "Ellie Dumont, ma'am," she said as she saluted Ayla.

"Dumont?" Ayla repeated her last name in somewhat disbelief.

"He is my grandfather, ma'am," the young soldier said to her while still standing attentive and staring straight ahead.

"How old are you, Dumont?" Ayla asked her.

"Twenty-five, ma'am," Ellie replied.

"Not enough experience, Dumont, any other volunteers?" Ayla asked but before she could continue her search, the young soldier interrupted her.

"Please, I can do this. Plus he knows me, he'll trust me," Ellie pleaded with Ayla.

Ayla, in reality, had no idea how much experience Ellie Dumont may have had. Her main concern was how Alexander Dumont would feel with his granddaughter's assignment. A young woman, traveling alone, usually garnered unwanted attention.

Ayla, however, admired her attitude and courage. In a way, Ellie reminded her of her younger self. She decided she'd give her a chance. "All right, Dumont, you want a shot, you got it. Just make sure you tell your grandfather it was your idea. Are you armed?"

Ellie pulled out her pistol and showed it to Ayla. "Miles give me your pack," Ayla said. She reached in and pulled out three more clips and handed them to Ellie. She also reached down and removed her knife that was holstered to her ankle and gave it to the young soldier.

Ayla glanced down at her shirt. Ellie was one of many wearing a black shirt with yellow and red stripes, a popular choice amongst the group.

"You'll need to change your clothes. Zoe, do you have any extra clothes with you?" she yelled over her shoulder.

Zoe looked up from her cot and while a field medic was addressing her gunshot wound, she said, "In my pack, there should be some stuff that fits her." Ayla grabbed Zoe's pack and began to rummage through her belongings and tossed Dumont a shirt, and a pair of pants.

"Go get dressed; we'll get one of the horses ready for you," Ayla said to her. The team stationed in Vegas arrived by horseback and it was their only means of transportation besides the Humvee that Ayla and Miles had brought with them.

Shortly thereafter, Ellie returned dressed in Zoe's clothing. "Are you sure you're up for this?" Ayla asked her again.

"I am, General," Ellie said with confidence.

"If you run into trouble, say you're on your way from El Paso to Los Angeles. You're looking for work and heard from travelers that Los Angeles had enough work for you to stop wandering and you hoped to settle down there," Ayla said to her as she bent down and fastened the ankle holster to Ellie's leg. "Keep your weapons out of sight and for God's sake don't give them your real name."

Another soldier walked through the hangar doors with a saddled horse which was brown and very healthy looking. Ellie mounted the steed and before she took off, Ayla wished her luck and looked her in the eye and said, "If you have to kill anyone, hide the bodies." Ellie nodded to affirm her understanding, tapped her heels against her horse, and began her journey to Los Angeles. As they watched the granddaughter of Alexander Dumont ride off into the early morning sunrise, Miles approached Ayla and said, "Are you sure you made the right call choosing her?"

Ayla turned and looked at Miles and said, "When I was her age you gave me a chance, I'm just paying it forward Miles. Plus she's got the right genes."

About an hour or so after Ellie Dumont made off on her solo mission, Lieutenant Hudson returned with his team of men and the Humvee full of weapons. He exited the vehicle and handed Ayla the keys. "Good work Hudson," she said.

"Thank you General," he said as he saluted her.

After that short exchange the team settled down for the night to get some sleep.

Chapter 23

Leaving Las Vegas

The next morning, while the soldiers all started their day, Ayla approached Hudson and gave him her first order. "I want to address your unit, have them fall in line," she said.

The men and women stationed at the hangar lined up in a standard military formation and Ayla began to address them regarding their new mission. "Good morning. For those of you who do not know me, my name is General Ayla Vural, and to my left is General Miles Lang," she said as she motioned toward Miles who nodded following his introduction. She continued on, "We've come a long way to get this far and we have a long ways to go. First, I want to thank you for your service here and to the revolution. It's dedicated and loyal soldiers like you who will win this war, and we are at war now, make no mistake about it," she said as she paced back and forth in front of the unit. "Last night's battle, albeit small, was the first step toward our victory. This location is no longer safe. Soon, when the United States realizes their men haven't reported back, they will send an even larger convoy here and we won't be able to defend it. So, now we're going to have to fast forward our plan. All of us will be riding to Los Angeles." She stopped pacing and looked at them all. "There will be no disguising our mission, we will be traveling as revolutionaries and we will kill anyone who tries to stop us. Many of us have lost friends and loved ones and were forced to

stand by while the United States killed the people closest to us."
She began to raise her voice, "It's time we put an end to the tyranny, an end to the oppression. This country belongs to the people! Let's take it back!" she yelled as she held her rifle above her head which prompted the soldiers to yell and cheer with enthusiasm. When the celebrating finally subsided, she concluded her speech, "General Lang will now provide you with the details of our mission."

She turned and walked back toward Miles who walked forward. As they passed, he whispered, "Not a bad speech, General." And he gave her a wink. Miles began to lay out the details for the traveling revolutionaries as Ayla watched on. "We'll need to take everything we can that will be of use to us. What we can't fit on the horses or carry ourselves we'll load into the Humvee. This includes all weapons, ammos, and rations. We'll burn any documents that are non-essential. When we travel, Lieutenant Hudson will lead by way of horseback, followed by General Vural and myself in the Humvee. Any other soldiers not on horseback will work security walking alongside and behind the convoy. We'll leave at sunset tonight. Are there any questions?" Miles paused and after no hands were raised, he continued. "Lieutenant Hudson, let's do it," he said. He looked toward Hudson who began barking out orders to the soldiers who in turn scrambled through the hangar preparing for their upcoming mission.

Miles joined Ayla who was talking to Zoe and Gabe. Zoe who was still resting her gunshot wound asked a question, "What about us Ayla, where do we fit in?"

"If there's room in the Humvee, you'll ride with us. If not, you'll have to walk," she said sympathetically.

Gabe, disapproving of her answer spoke up, "Absolutely not,

she's injured, she can't walk."

Miles, who was becoming increasingly annoyed with Gabe ever since the artillery bombing from the night before decided to address him. "You are no longer civilians; you said you wanted to be a part of this revolution, remember? So you'll follow orders just like the rest of the soldiers here. Got it?" They both nodded their understanding.

Miles walked away to assist the soldiers in preparing for departure. Ayla smiled as she said, "You guys are going to be great, I know it. Now, let's get ready. Okay?" The married couple nodded and they began to prepare themselves for the journey to Los Angeles.

The rest of Ayla's day consisted of checking in with the Lieutenant and getting to know the soldiers who would be serving under her command. She learned that many of them had similar stories of the struggles they had faced under the brutal leadership of the United States. Like John Hart, who sought out the underground movement in Los Angeles after his son was kidnapped and forced into a reeducation camp. Or Lisa Anderson, whose parents died from the flu after they were denied medical treatment because they couldn't afford hospital passes. Ayla's faith and determination grew stronger with each story she heard. It reaffirmed her commitment and belief that life should be and can be better for her fellow Americans. She was reminded that she wasn't just fighting for revenge or for hatred, but for a greater cause, one greater than herself.

Before they knew it, the Sun started to set and most of the preparations had been completed. Soldiers finished filling the Humvee with supplies, officers mounted their horses and everyone else tightened up their boots and prepared themselves for the long journey on foot. They'd travel along Interstate 15 which would eventually bring them directly to Los Angeles. The Humvees and horses would have to keep pace with those on foot in order to keep the convoy together, a journey that would take them up to five or six days. Traveling through the dry deserts that separate Las Vegas from Los Angeles would be no easy task. It would be hot and dry during the day and cold through the nights.

They began their voyage and left the hangar of the abandoned airport behind. As the group saw the airport slowly fade in the distance, the wind picked up and whipped grains of sand against the unlucky soldiers. They attempted to shield themselves using their coats and hats but it provided little relief. Inside the safety of the Humvee, Ayla slowly coasted along between five and ten miles per hour setting the stride of the unit. It suddenly hit her that she hadn't really given much thought to the well-being of Raj. She felt torn over her decision. On one hand, Raj was her friend. Should she have gone after him? But on the other hand, she knew that this was a war, and during a war you lost people that were close to you. It was just how it went. For a while she replayed this internal argument in her mind. She wondered if Raj held her responsible, or was angry at her for not going after them. After all, it was she that decided to bring her brother into the fold. She was blinded by her personal relationship with him and couldn't see the risk involved. Ayla and her other roommates were the only family Raj had left. If he couldn't trust her, who could he trust? She created many scenarios in her mind of what it could be like if they reunited and she couldn't help envisioning him hating her.

"It looks pretty rough out there," Miles said, breaking her train of thought. "You think we should get them out of this storm?" he asked her.

As they approached the outer limits of the city, Ayla honked

143

the horn on the Humvee in two quick bursts which prompted Lieutenant Hudson to turn his horse around and meet Ayla at the driver's side window. She covered her face with her jacket and rolled down the window. "We need to get out of this storm Lieutenant... Over there!" She yelled over the whipping sandstorm as she pointed to a white structure on the right-hand side of the highway. The convoy veered right and approached the building which still had some of its green porcelain letters attached to the side facing the road. Even with the darkness of night and the raging storm, you could still make out the words, *Heenan's Irish Pub*.

Hudson and another soldier forced open the doors and the small military convoy entered, hoping to wait out the storm. Ayla instructed Hudson to assign watch duties and to conceal the horses. She also encouraged the others to take advantage of the situation; getting as much rest as they could, and reminded them that they will leave as soon as the storm passed. As she found an old booth to lie in, she propped her back up against the wall and examined the room around her. The old pub was mostly wood paneled with a dark maple stain. The aged beer taps had cob webs and all of the liquor shelves were emptied, probably robbed before the city was abandoned. There were still old pictures hanging on the wall of regular patrons and celebrities from before the war. She could also see empty silhouettes where memorabilia and advertisements once hung on the walls. As she took in her surroundings, she imagined what it was like in the old pub before the war. Was it filled with locals who gathered for a good time, or was it where people spent their last few bucks after emptying their bank accounts? Her eyes slowly closed and eventually she got some much needed rest.

A few hours later she was awoken by Lieutenant Hudson.

"General, wake up," he said to her as he gently shook her shoulder.

"What is it?" she said as she took in a deep breath, "Has the storm quit?"

"No ma'am, one of my men reported lights in the distance headed this way."

Alerted by the report, she immediately gathered herself. "How much time do we have?" she asked him as she sat upright and rubbed her eyes.

"Thirty minutes, maybe less. It's hard to tell with the storm," Hudson said to her as Miles listened close by.

"Okay, get everyone inside, tell them to be ready for anything," she ordered the Lieutenant. "And make sure those horses are out of sight!" she yelled as he headed off.

"What's our play Ayla?" Miles asked her.

"We do nothing."

"Nothing?" he asked her skeptically.

"Chances are they can't track us in this storm, we keep quiet and hide and hope they pass us by," she said to him as she readied her pistol.

"And if that doesn't work?" he asked.

"Then we'll have to use these guns sooner than we thought," she said confidently.

As the lights came closer, all of Ayla's soldiers eventually made their way inside the pub. Most of the soldiers crouched beneath windows and readied themselves for a firefight. "Here they come, nobody move, don't make a sound," she whispered to her team. Not long after that, eight Humvees filled with United States soldiers steadily drove by without slowing down or giving any indication that they knew their whereabouts. Ayla and the rest of her team let out a sigh of relief but before they got too

145

comfortable, she reminded them that they weren't in the clear just yet. "Don't get too excited, this changes things," she said.

The team continued to lie low until they were sure the convoy was long gone. A short while later, Miles spoke up. "Hudson, get your men back to their positions until we figure out our next move."

Miles and Ayla got together at one of the tables that sat in the middle of the pub. "Taking the road is out; we're going to have to cut across the desert," he said to her.

"Yep, I just hope our girl is close, or she has the brains to get out of sight if she sees those Humvees coming," she said referencing Ellie Dumont who rode ahead to warn her grandfather of the changed plans.

Chapter 24

The Mojave Desert

With winter approaching, the desert was cold and the wind made conditions worse for the team of rebels. They managed to find one of the numerous trails that sprawled throughout the landscape. These were once frequented by adventurers and tourists seeking to experience the Mojave Desert in its natural splendor. For Ayla and the others, however, it was anything but splendor. Much like the rest of the terrain, most of the trails had been taken back by Mother Nature with small shrubs and dunes. Although the trails were uncomfortable, the mountains surrounding the desert would have been much worse to travel on.

Leading her band of revolutionaries from within the confines of their stolen army Humvee, Ayla and Miles had some time to discuss the team's next series of moves as they prepared to rendezvous with Alexander Dumont. "Did Dumont tell you anything about what we're supposed to do when we get there?" she asked Miles as their bodies swayed back and forth from the slow bumpy ride.

"Originally it was supposed to be just us, but now we have a small army. I think our best bet is to send you in with a small team. You have your meeting, and we go from there," he said.

"What did he tell you?" she asked him.

"You're my mission, Ayla. I was supposed to find you and convince you to meet him. This whole weapons thing was just supposed to be a quick and easy delivery but here we are driving through the desert," he said.

"So you don't know what his plan is?" Ayla asked him as she was getting annoyed by the mystery of it all.

"He's not a very trusting person. I think he tells you what he wants you to know and nothing else," he said and seeing she wasn't quite satisfied, he elaborated further, "Look, all I know is that he has a plan. He told me that he had everything in place but he needed you."

Despite still being annoyed by the secrets, she decided not to waste any more of her energy on why. She had already come this far and she wasn't going to change her mind now, so she figured she might as well meet Dumont and hear what he had to say. "We should get a few hours rest." She said after a few seconds of silence between the two.

As the team made camp for the evening, Ayla closed her eyes and reclined her car seat. When she was almost asleep, the sound of laughter from outside of the Humvee caused her to open her eyes. She noticed a young couple, both sporting their revolutionary symbol proudly on an arm band, much like Ayla's. They were holding each other near one of the fires and she was suddenly reminded of her lonely life she had chosen to live.

Growing up through her teenage years and through her twenties, there was no time for love in her life. She was a young military commander who never saw the point of falling for someone. She watched too many friends die next to her in battle. She always thought, what was the point of loving someone when you can lose them so easily? Living in Chicago, hiding as a clothing vendor, her best chance at anonymity was to distance herself from others. She always felt love would be impossible for her if she had to lie about who she was. The fear of letting someone get too close forced her to put up walls and alienate herself from others.

The happy military couple, who kept themselves warm in the cool desert air, made her ponder what her life would have been like, or what it could be like, if she had someone special to share it with. As she reflected, she realized that there were really only a few people who truly knew her: Miles, Gabe and Zoe, and Raj. Even including her roommates in that list was a stretch. As her thoughts drifted, she remembered how close she and Raj were. She shed a lone tear over the fact that he was taken, and that he was out there somewhere, scared. She blamed herself for allowing Evan to manipulate her and her sadness quickly turned into frustration and anger over the entire situation. Before she drifted off to sleep, she made a promise to herself that if the opportunity presented itself, she would do whatever she could to find and rescue him. After all, Raj was her family and she owed him that at least.

The next morning, the team left their resting spot just as the rising sun breeched the desert horizon. Ayla and Miles decided that they would rotate out of the Humvee and walk alongside the troops they were commanding. They gave Hudson a chance to drive a little and even allowed some soldiers to ride on the top of the Humvee, resting their legs. They continued on their journey through the American Southwest drawing closer and closer to their final destination of Los Angeles.

"According to the map, we're going to run into some problems when we get out of the desert. Looks like Angeles National forest will be too rugged to drive through unless we take the roads." Miles said aloud to Ayla as he examined the map while he walked.

"Got any suggestions?" she asked him as she squinted from

the bright sun.

"It looks like Route 138 through Palmdale is straight ahead. If we can make our way there we could hop on Route 14. That would take us to some northern suburbs of Los Angeles through the forest," he said as he folded up the map and continued, "The only problem though is we have no Intel on either of those locations or Route 14. We'd be going in blind."

Ayla knew that whatever they chose to do would be difficult. They either would have to take all the ammo and weapons they retrieved on foot through the mountains, or take a risk and drive through the forest on Route 14. She kept to herself for a moment while she thought about the choices Miles set forth. After a few minutes she made her decision. "I think we should take Route 14, we've travelled on the roads before and we were able to hide when we needed to. Worst case scenario, we fight our way through. I think we have enough people and weapons to do it if we had to."

Miles nodded in agreement and said, "Okay, Route 14 it is." As he looked at his compass, he walked toward the convoy leaders and informed them of the change in plans and pointed them in the right direction.

Several hours later, the team reached the outskirts of Palmdale where Ayla stopped the convoy. As the winds picked up and the sand began to whip across the flat desert, she informed the entire squad of the new plan to again travel by road. She made them aware of the unknown nature of the travel conditions and how they would not know who they might encounter. "When we get through Palmdale we're going to split into two teams. I'm going to lead a smaller group on foot up ahead to scout out any threats. The rest of you will act as security for the Humvee and travel behind the first group but we'll figure that out once we get there."

After several hours, the convoy passed through Palmdale. The desert city had looked to be abandoned with most of the surviving structures being consumed by sand. Large dunes covered the roads and some of the houses were almost completely swallowed by the giant mounds. As they reached the southwest border of the city, the team watched as the landscape slowly changed from endless sand to small shrubs, and then, eventually, the trees that made up the rugged mountainous terrain that separated them from their final destination.

They finally reached the access point to Route 14 just west of a spot on the map titled *Lake Palmdale*. As the convoy rested and prepared itself for its last leg of their journey, Miles approached Ayla who was behind the Humvee readying herself to lead the scout team. "What if you run into trouble?" he asked her as he leaned his body against the side of the vehicle.

"If you hear gunshots, then come quick," she said with a smirk as she put her bag on her back and put her arms through the loops.

"Before you go, you might want to check on your old roommates," Miles suggested to her.

Ayla, who had completely forgotten about Gabe and Zoe, put her hand on her head and sighed knowing that they probably felt abandoned by her. She approached her old friends for a quick reconnect and checked on Zoe's gunshot wound. They exchanged pleasantries but, for Ayla, the relationship had changed. She felt awful for this, but at least for the time being, she really struggled to care about how they were doing. They fought alongside her up until this point, which Ayla was grateful for, but they really didn't have a choice. Now, with Zoe's brush with death, she suspected their commitment to the cause wasn't as resolute as it had once been. She told herself she'll know how they really feel once they arrive in Los Angeles. It was at this point that Ayla offered them another opportunity to opt out and told them there would be no hard feelings if they changed their minds and decided to stay in Los Angeles to live out their lives.

"We'll think about it," Gabe said with his arm around his wife. Knowing that he could have lost her, made him second guess getting involved in the conflict. Zoe, after getting shot had already been secretly regretting the path they chose.

After Ayla walked away from them, Gabe turned to his wife and said, "I know you wanted to help but..."

Zoe interrupted him and said, "I just want to go home."

He kissed her on the forehead and there were no words that needed to be spoken between them, as they both agreed that living a life of oppression was better than living a life without each other. They decided that when the time was right, they would tell Ayla that their involvement would end once they were able to safely escape into the city.

Chapter 25

Route 14

As Miles looked on and the majority of the convoy continued to rest, Ayla began to corral her four volunteers who would round out the scout team for Route 14. The team consisted of four men, all with a history of seeing some sort of combat experience. As they began their journey, Miles marked the time. He and the rest of the team would leave in about an hour and follow behind the scout team. Eventually, Ayla and her team disappeared in the distance and Miles gave the okay for the rest of the crew to start their traveling preparations.

After the scout team reached the city limits of Palmdale, it was clear that Route 14 was a terrible choice. The road turned into a giant abandoned multilane highway with no cover whatsoever on either side. Ayla decided that she and her team would wait for Miles and the rest of the convoy to reevaluate their choice.

"All right, this clearly was not a good idea," she said to her small group. "You, what's your name again?" she asked the man directly in front of her.

"Private Tidwell," he replied.

She rolled her eyes slightly and asked, "What's your first name?"

"Frank," he replied.

"Okay, Frank, I need you to go up there and see if there's

anything out there. Make sure we're good to wait here," she said as she pointed to the large embankment that enclosed the highway.

"On it," he said plainly.

"Wait!" she yelled and as he came back to the group, she handed him a pair of binoculars. "Be subtle," she added.

While Frank headed to the lookout, Ayla attempted to get to know the others who were traveling with her. "So let's see if I remember." She pointed to the solider to her left. "Your name wasssss," she drew out the *s* trying to remember. "Couchman, Tim!" she exclaimed.

"That's me," said the soldier to her right. "That's Ruiz, and that's Jake." He finished up pointing to the solider resting close by who waved back to Ayla.

Feeling slightly embarrassed, she welcomed the return of Frank, who reported that there was no danger on the horizon. "Okay, let's hang here until they catch up," she said as she pulled out one of the maps and sat against a guardrail to plot out any possible alternative routes.

Miles and the rest of the team met up with Ayla after almost an hour. "What do ya got?" he asked her.

"We're too exposed out here, I don't like it. They could roll up on us anytime, and we'd be sitting ducks," Ayla said as her brown hair swirled around from the dry winds that seemed to be picking up as they spoke.

"Have you scouted any other routes?" he asked her.

"It's not going to be easy but I think we need to take this road here." She pointed to a small road that led into a national park just outside of Los Angeles. "It'll take us to this canyon, right outside of the city. I think it would be a good spot to have the team wait when I go meet Dumont. Once we get there, we can

154

set up defensive positions just in case. It's the best I got," she said reluctantly as she looked toward Miles to judge his reaction.

"I think it'll work but there's no way we're going to make it there tonight. Let's find a place to make camp, rest up and go for it tomorrow. It's been a long day today anyways."

Chapter 26

All My bags are Packed

Ayla was excited about leading her small platoon to Los Angeles. She could remember the news reports back when Dumont had started causing chaos for the country. It wasn't as though she was in awe of Dumont; after all, it was his violence that ultimately led to the deaths of her family. It was more so just the culmination of so many events and stories that were linked to him that she had heard and had witnessed over the years that made her so eager to meet him.

In terms of her parents and their deaths, she didn't blame him; she knew that it was the overreaction of the government that killed them, not Dumont. She did however want to meet the man face to face; the man that jumpstarted a revolution and the man that was now trying to start another. She admired the fact that even after all these years, after being in prison, and going through who knows what, that he still wanted to see his vision come to fruition.

Ayla came to realize that the members of her scout team seemed pretty reliable. Once she got to know them and what their talents were, she decided that for the sake of continuity, they would also accompany her to meet Dumont. The small group consisted of four former resistance fighters and they each brought unique skills to the team. Couchman was skilled and experienced in combat, both hand to hand and weaponry. He was tall and skinny and had a rugged five o' clock shadow. Under his revolutionary hat he had thinning, light brown hair. Rafael Ruiz was an expert in explosives during his resistance days. Having to learn how to use what was available to him; he now could make a bomb out of almost anything and got pretty good at disarming them too. He was short with thick dark hair but his small stature never held him back. In terms of personality, Frank Tidwell was probably the least impressive. He seemed to stay pretty unemotional, but he was brave and knew the area pretty well. Frank was built solid; he was average height but was strong with a square jaw line, broad shoulders, and big hands. The last member of the group was Jacob Brown, but everyone called him Jake. He was a computer whiz and was pretty handy with technology. Jake didn't have the stereotypical computer nerd appearance though; he was definitely the tall dark and handsome type and Ayla certainly took notice of that.

Once they found a good place to camp for the evening, Ayla informed her new team about the next leg of their journey. Each member was equipped with weapons that could be hidden away. Things like hand guns, knives, small explosives, and anything else that may prove to be useful if they encountered any government resistance along the way. They were also forced to give up any identifying pieces of personal property. For Ayla, she gave Miles the picture of her family and her resistance arm band. As she turned them over, she remembered how it wasn't so long ago that she was in the weather-beaten backyard of her tenement home in Chicago, clawing through the mud to retrieve the very same items she was turning over to him.

She looked at Miles and said, "I didn't think I'd be giving these up again so soon."

He looked her in the eye and said, "Don't worry, it won't be for long. I'll keep them safe. You worry about yourself and your team. They'll be counting on you."

"I got this," she replied with confidence.

"Don't get cocky," Miles said jokingly. "Here's Dumont's address, his operation is based under a fish market. I'm assuming he's still there but, you never know."

"A hundred and twenty South Main Street. That sounds easy enough," she said.

"Well, it won't be. It's in the middle of the city with lots of enforcers around. But you'll be able to blend in, it's a busy place," he said

"Yea, but they have my picture still," she said with concern.

Miles grinned and held up a pair of scissors and a bottle of hydrogen peroxide he found in the Humvee's first aid case. "How about a makeover?" he asked her.

By this point, Hudson had already got the camp's perimeter security set up and many of the traveling soldiers began to relax in their newly formed social circles within the platoon. Among the small campfires, laughter and conversations could be heard while they managed to eat what little food they were able to bring with them. Meanwhile, Ayla and Miles were discussing ways that she could alter her appearance.

"Are you ready for a haircut?" Miles asked her as he clipped the scissors in his hands.

She looked at him with a face that suggested he was out of his mind. "If you think I'm going to let you cut my hair, you're crazy!" she said as she laughed. "There's got to be someone here that can cut hair," she said as she looked out at the group of rebels.

After asking around, they found a woman named Lana, who once upon time gave her family haircuts during the days following the war. She was around the same age as Ayla but the similarities between the two ended there.

In preparation for her haircut, Ayla found a small boulder to sit on. She took off her coat and then to the surprise of the onlookers, which included Miles, she removed her t-shirt wearing only a black sports bra. Ayla, who was still very beautiful despite the years of conflict and a postwar Chicago lifestyle, drew some commentary from the crowd. Miles quickly reprimanded them. "Hey now, this is still your commanding officer."

Ayla let down her long hair and gave it one more caress with her fingers as if she was saying goodbye. For some reason, she looked out to the crowd of soldiers and out of all of them she caught eyes with Jake Brown, one of her traveling companions for tomorrow. It only lasted a couple seconds and she then gave the go-ahead to Lana. She chopped away and the locks of brown hair began to fall onto the sandy ground around Ayla's feet. Throughout the haircut, Miles, Lana, and Ayla traded small talk back and forth about their lives before, during, and after the war. For the first time in a long time, the focus was not on the mission at hand. The night served as an impromptu get-to-know-each-other session in the desert as similar conversations were taking place throughout the makeshift camp.

After a short while, Lana transitioned the conversation back to Ayla's hair and said, "Okay, I think you're all set. You look like a badass," she said as she swept some hair from the back of her neck.

Ayla was astonished at how much hair was on the ground around her and as she ran her fingers through her now pixielike haircut, she exclaimed, "Oh my god, there's nothing there!" At first she was in shock, but it didn't last long. "It feels great!" she said while laughing.

She grabbed her army green t-shirt to put back on, but before she could manage it, Miles said to her, "Hold on now, you're not done yet." As he held up the bottle of peroxide that they found in the Humvees' first aid kit. "You're going blonde."

Not knowing exactly how to feel about the idea, Ayla hesitantly put her shirt back down and in an unsure voice she said, "But I've always been a brunette." She eventually agreed though and while still in just her black sports bra, she allowed Miles and Lana to begin dying her hair with the hydrogen peroxide.

"I've technically never done this before so I have no idea what's going to happen." Lana said as she began to slowly pour peroxide onto Ayla's hair.

"That's not good," Ayla said as she shuttered from feeling the cold liquid touch the top of her head. "Well, if it only changes a little I guess that will be okay still, just don't make me bald or I'll kill you." To which Lana laughed but Ayla just stared up at her as her head dripped with peroxide, which made Lana's laugh turn more into a nervous chuckle.

After it was thoroughly wet with peroxide, Lana wrapped Ayla's damp hair in her t-shirt that she had removed earlier and said to her, "I'll go find you another shirt."

"How do I look?" Ayla asked Miles, winking at him. He just laughed because he was slightly uncomfortable; having known her since she was just a teenager, it was a bit awkward for him seeing her as a grown woman. Lana returned with a new t-shirt and Ayla gracefully pulled it over her wrapped head ending Miles's discomfort. "How long do I have to wear this thing?" she asked Lana.

"I have no idea?" Lana responded as she shrugged her

shoulders "This was his idea," she said pointing to Miles.

While the rest of the team continued to enjoy their respite, Ayla and Miles discussed how they would continue on separated and where the best location would be for the second group to wait for Ayla to return from seeing Dumont. "I don't like the idea of splitting up this early, for one we still have a long ways to go and two, we'd have to come all the way back up here to get you," Ayla said to him.

As he spread the map out on the hood of the Humvee, he pointed to the road she picked that meandered through the mountains and said, "Well, this is the road you picked, I don't see many choices."

They stood in silence for a moment as she examined the map biting her lower lip as she concentrated on their options. "What's this little road here?" She asked as she pointed to a spot on the map near the border of Los Angeles County.

Miles leaned in closer and said, "It looks like some sort of hiking trail or something, oh wait here *Mount Lukens Truck Trail.*" She looked at him waiting for his response as she implied it could be an option. "Okay," he said without much objection.

He didn't ask her to provide a good explanation, but she went ahead and did it anyways because she got the sense he was not totally sold on the idea. "It's much closer to the city, there's probably plenty of places to hide if need be, and I bet there might be some sort of shelter at the trail entrance."

"All right, I guess getting this close to Los Angeles is going be risky no matter where we split up at. Let's gather up the troops and let them know." They called over Hudson and Ayla's team and let them know the new plan and told them to spread the word around the camp.

"Plan to leave at sun up, let's get some rest; we'll switch out

161

guard duty and put out the fires," Ayla said as she finally took the t-shirt wrap off her head. "Well?" she asked Miles.

He shrugged his shoulders and said, "Well, I mean it might be a little lighter, but I wouldn't call you blonde."

"Oh well, it'll be good enough," she said as they all started to make their sleeping arrangements for the night.

The next morning, Ayla was slowly waking up to the warmth of the sun and the birds chirping until she heard a loud voice yell, "Holy Hell!" It was Miles.

Ayla jolted out of her sleeping position and as she grabbed her gun she was looking around for the threat "What is it?" she asked loudly, still half asleep. She soon realized that Miles was looking right at her and then he burst out laughing. "What?" she asked again this time more perplexed.

"That peroxide must've needed a little more time," he said to her while still laughing.

"Oh no," she said as she ran to the Humvee to check her hair. "Oh my gosh," she said as she examined her new pixie cut hairdo. "It's white!" she exclaimed.

"Well, on the plus side, they definitely won't recognize you now. They aren't looking for any senior citizens." He said as he doubled over in laughter. Not enjoying his humor at her expense, she gave him the finger and walked away as he continued to have a good laugh.

"You," she pointed to a skinny young recruit. He pointed at himself in a nervous manner as she stomped toward him. "Give me your hat."

"My hat?" he asked in timid voice.

"Yes, your hat, give it to me." She took the plain black hat off his head and placed it on her own and shooed him away. She gave one more look to Miles who was still trying to contain himself. She made a childish face at him and decided to go eat breakfast with her old friends Gabe and Zoe.

She sat down next to them and they both stared at her white hair sneaking out from under the hat. "What?" she said pointedly.

Picking up on her sensitivity they both replied, "Nothing." and gave each other a look.

"Good," she replied. "Have you guys decided where you're going to go once we reach the city?"

"Not really, just find somewhere to earn a living and hope for the best, kind of like we did in Chicago," Gabe said to her as he grabbed Zoe's hand.

Zoe chimed in, "Maybe start a family."

Ayla looked at her and paused for a moment thinking about how strange that idea sounded to her at times like these but she quickly snapped out of it and smiled, "You guys are going to be great parents. I'll do what I can to help."

She finished her breakfast and returned to Miles who had finally stopped laughing at her. "Are you ready?" he asked her.

She looked around and briefly examined the team of revolutionaries who were all still enjoying their breakfast. Knowing that this might be their last stress-free morning she replied while still gazing at her troops, "Let's give them ten more minutes."

"Once you get to the trail, I think you should wait for us. It might be good to regroup one more time before you head into the city," he suggested.

"Okay, good idea," she said as she adjusted her new hat and tucked in a few escaping locks of her now almost white hair. "I'm going to get my guys together and start moving. Give us a two hour head start."

"Ok, see ya soon," he said as she started packing up her things.

Chapter 27

The Angeles Forest Highway

Although the new road Ayla chose to take was likely less traveled than their original path, it was still dangerous. The winding road was cut into the mountains with high walls of rock on both sides. The small team of five had to keep their wits about them as they had no idea what to expect. Any knowledge they had was all theoretical. "Frank." Ayla motioned for Tidwell to come and walk next to her. "You're my lookout man, right?"

"I suppose so, ma'am," he said compliantly.

"You see how we're closed in here by the rocks?" she said as she pointed to the walls surrounding the highway.

"Yea, I see it, sure," he said.

She continued, "Next time there's a break in the wall, I'm going to need you to go up top, and walk up there. If there's something out there that we can't see you can give us a heads up. Think you can do that for me?"

"I think I can definitely do that," he said.

Feeling much better about the situation, they continued on their journey. While looking up to her man on the rocks every so often, Ayla took this time to reflect on the upcoming challenges of making her way through Los Angeles, finding Dumont, and what she'd say to him. She hoped he at least had a plan that made all of this worth the effort.

They had been walking for some time now and Ayla was

feeling both tired and hungry. She figured the others must be feeling that way as well. "Let's take fifteen, shall we?" She asked them and without hesitation, they all started taking off their packs and found a shaded spot on the side of the road. Frank Tidwell began to make his way down and Ayla stopped him. "Sorry, Frank, you got to stay up there and keep an eye out, buddy."

"Yes, ma'am," he said again without showing any preference to her decision one way or the other. He turned around and made his way back up to the top of the rock wall and took a seat still keeping an eye out for danger.

"Think we'll run into any resistance when we get near the city?" Jake asked her attempting to make small talk.

"Hopefully not," she said as she chewed on a snack she took out of her pack. "I mean we're dressed like civilians, we have a back story. If we run into any enforcers or the army, we don't engage. Just play the part and they should let us go."

"What if they recognize you?" Ruiz asked.

"Well," she paused. "I guess that's why we brought the guns. But it shouldn't ever get to that point. We've got Frank up there who can tip us off; we're small enough that we can hide. Los Angeles is pretty busy, shouldn't have any trouble blending in there."

After several minutes of chatting strategy, Ayla decided it was time to start moving again. A few more hours of uneventful travel passed and she and the team rounded a large bend. In the distance, they could see the entrance to the truck trail her and Miles found on the map. This was the meeting point they had arranged to come together one last time before entering into the city. Just then, Frank got Ayla's attention by throwing a small rock near her feet. She looked up at him and he held up the number two with his fingers and pointed toward the truck trail.

165

She took out her binoculars and aimed them toward the entrance and parking lot of the trail. Through the lenses she saw two soldiers that appeared to be standing guard. "What do you see?" Ruiz asked her.

"Two guards," she said as she handed him the binoculars. "Not sure why they're there, I don't see any Humvees." Ruiz handed her back the binoculars and she again looked through them. "They must be here for something," she said thinking out loud as she scanned the rest of what she could see. Through the trees she made out what appeared to be a roof. "There's some kind of structure down there. They must be guarding that."

She waved Frank down from his elevated lookout position and addressed the other four members of her team. "All right, so we need to take care of this problem. We can't have our entire unit hide here if the army's here too. We either need to find a new spot or go in and investigate and see if we can take them out. I tell you what; I'm not running away from these dicks any more," she said as the other four nodded in agreement and smiled. "Frank, I want you to walk back the direction we came from and find the rest of the group and tell General Lang what we're doing."

"Right," he said and turned to start walking.

"Wait," she said to him in a hushed voice. "You don't know what we're doing yet."

He stopped and again in a more drawn-out voice he said, "Right."

Ayla shook her head which drew a few chuckles from the other members of the team. She continued on, "Jake and I are going to go through the woods and make our way down to that building and try to figure out what's inside." She then addressed Couchman and Ruiz, "You two sneak down to the front side of the building. Just lie low there until you hear from us. You're going to be my insurance policy. If we get into trouble, flank them and take them out." They nodded showing their understanding. "Now, if there's a bunch of them down there, we'll come to you guys and we'll all back out of there nice and quiet. But if we can take them without any trouble, wait until we make our move, do what you have to, and meet us around the front side."

"We good?" After a brief pause where they all looked confident, she continued, "Okay good, Frank, go ahead and go, we'll see you soon." Frank gave them all a nod and headed back toward the rest of the platoon. Ayla and the other three climbed over the old rusty guardrail and began to trek through the wilderness toward the guarded structure. The downhill terrain was a mixture of desert-like shrubs and trees. Halfway down their hike, Ayla made the call for them to split up and head toward their respective destinations. It was at this point she took out her pistol and Jake followed suit.

After a thirty minute walk through the forest, they finally arrived at the building. It appeared that it once was some sort of utility garage. It was pretty long, Ayla guessed it was around forty feet in length and probably at one point was used to house equipment used to maintain the trail. It had a green metal roof and the walls were a beige color also made of metal. Like many other buildings left unchecked, Mother Nature had left her marks as there were many rusted out holes along the bottom edges of the building's exterior.

Ayla leaned up against the back carefully, trying not to make the metal crimp and bend. She motioned for Jake to join her. As they leaned against the building, she carefully peered around the side to see what, if anything, was there. She saw a gravel road that led further down the trail with nothing else to see as it weaved through the woods. She also noticed a window on the side of the building. She held her hand out telling Jake to stay put and she cautiously turned the corner. Crouching, she quietly walked toward the window. She slowly rose to a standing position and peered through it.

Inside, she saw what appeared to be a medium-sized room. There was a desk which, to Ayla's surprise, had a closed laptop resting on its surface. There was also three sets of bunk beds; two sets were along the wall opposite of the desk. She quickly realized that the third set was along the same wall with the window that she was currently looking through. She stood up a little further and looked directly below her and saw a soldier sleeping in his bed. She immediately ducked back down and in doing so kicked up some dust from the dirt road the building resided on. She held her breath until she knew all was quiet on the other side of the wall.

She continued her reconnaissance and stealthily made her way to the next corner. Here she slowly peered around the edge which gave her a glimpse of the front of the building. There was a green door that matched the roof color which led into the room she saw from the window. Just past that, she could see a green garage door, definitely wide enough to fit all sorts of vehicles, she thought to herself. Beyond the building she could see the entrance to the truck trail and the backs of the two guards Frank pointed out to her earlier. She returned to the wall with the window and counted in her head. "Two on duty, probably two sleeping and two more beds. There must be two more somewhere."

Around the same time, she deduced that there were two more soldiers somewhere, she heard voices approaching her from the trail that led into the wilderness. "You're dreaming, man, I totally had you." She heard as she scrambled to get to the back side of the building to regroup with Jake. Once there, she placed her finger over her lips and the two waited in silence.

"That's not what the score card said, bro," the other soldier said. Their voices grew louder as they walked toward the building, continuing to banter back and forth until they reached the green door and entered.

Ayla motioned to Jake to follow her lead as they began to head back into the woods away from the structure. Once they were at a safe distance, Jake asked her a question. "So what are you thinking?"

"This is a big chance to get some info from these guards and there was a computer in there. We need a plan," she said.

Upon hearing this, Jake's eyes lit up and he excitedly began asking her questions. "What kind? Was it a desktop or a laptop? Was it an Apple or a PC?" Jake loving technology as he did couldn't believe they had a computer; he hadn't even seen one since the end of the last war.

"Let's just focus on getting a plan together, need to take care of these guards first," she said to him trying to ease his excitement.

"Are you crazy?" he asked her sarcastically, which prompted her to shoot him a look, reminding him of who he was talking to. He tried again. "What I mean is the computer needs to be top priority. If I can get my hands on it, I can probably access information that those guards don't even know about. If there's some sort of network they're connected to, who knows what I'll find."

After his sales pitch she decided that he probably had the right idea. She asked him some more questions. "What kind of information?"

"If I can get online and get into their system, I might be able to find things like troop movements, supply lines, maybe communications they've sent," he said excitedly.

"What about reeducation camps?" she asked him as thoughts of her friend Raj filled her head.

"Maybe," he said.

"Okay, we'll make the computer a priority to save," she said.

As they wrapped up their conversation, she sent him away to fetch Couchman and Ruiz. Once they all returned, the small group made their way back to the highway where they first spotted the guarded structure. Ayla began formulating different attack scenarios in her head, trying to determine the best course of action to save the computer and take out the guards.

When they arrived back on the highway, Miles was there waiting for her. Already partially filled in on the situation from Frank, he was ready to hear more. "What do ya got?" he asked her.

"Looks like there are only six of them, I mean I saw six bunks and counted six soldiers. Not sure what's in the garage part, we had to get out of there pretty fast." He nodded to show that he was following along and eagerly waited to hear more. "I was thinking, just go in and overtake them, but Jake, that guy over there," she said as she pointed in his direction. "There's a laptop and he thinks that it could be useful, so maybe the plan should be a little more finessed to try and get our hands on it."

"I'm assuming you have a plan already?" Miles asked her.

"I'm guessing that when night rolls around, the two soldiers who were sleeping will go on duty. We wait until they make the shift change, and the other four go to sleep. We take out the two guards first, and then take the other four by surprise. All while

170

getting our hands on that computer before they do."

"And what happens after all that?" he asked her.

"We carry on with our original plan. You stay here, pose as U.S. soldiers and wait it out until we get back to you," she said as if he should have already known. "After we find out what's on the computer though," she added in.

"What else do you think is here? I mean these guys aren't here guarding a laptop, are they?" he asked.

"Jake!" Ayla motioned for him to join her and Miles. He left his conversation behind and jogged over to join his commanding officers. "Got any guesses as to why these guys are here?"

"If I had to guess, I'd bet the laptop is connected to something nearby. This place could be something like a power station or some sort of communication hub and they're using the computer to monitor or control it. Or it has nothing to do with that and it's just used for communication. Either way, I think its import—"

"So you don't know?" Miles asked disappointedly.

"That's it for now, thanks, Jake," Ayla said to him.

"That wasn't much help," Miles said unenthusiastically. Ayla shrugged her shoulders as if she knew it was a long shot for him to know why they had the computer. "The sun's already going down." He said as he squinted toward the horizon. "Let's get the troops together and pick who's doing what."

They gathered the older veterans of the group including Ayla's handpicked team of travelers and started to delegate responsibilities. Surrounding Ayla were Miles, Jake, Ayla's yes man Frank Tidwell, Ruiz the explosive expert, Couchman the battle-tested soldier, and of course Lieutenant Hudson, the group's leader prior to Ayla and Miles arriving. "Okay, each of you is going to lead a small team on this. Couchman, your team will be taking out the two guards on duty. This needs to be done quietly and take them alive if you can."

"Understood. How many should I bring with me?" he asked her.

"I'd take four or five, we want to outnumber them but be small enough so they can't see us coming. When you get to your spot, look for my signal near the corner of the building." He nodded and she continued on, "Frank, you'll continue to be my lookout guy. Take ten or fifteen troops and spread out around the perimeter of the property and make sure we're alone and keep it that way."

"Got it," he said while doing his patented salute.

"Ruiz and Jake, you'll be with Miles and me. We're going to get a few more soldiers and we'll breach the sleeping quarters. Once Couchman's team takes the guards out, we'll make our move. Ruiz, do you think you can bring something to get us inside if need be?" she asked him.

"I have the perfect piece," he said excitedly.

"Hopefully, we won't need it, but better to be prepared. Jake, your job is to get that computer before they do. You're the expert so we'll be counting on you to get it out," she instructed him.

"Yes, ma'am," he said enthusiastically with a smile on his face.

"After we breach the door, we'll take out the sleeping guards. If we can take them alive great, if not, oh well." She then focused her attention to the most senior officer besides her and Miles. "Hudson?"

"Yes ma'am," he said ready for orders.

"You're going to be on standby with the rest of the platoon. If anything goes wrong down there, like if you hear a bunch of gunshots, we'll need you to come save the day."

"Understood," he replied.

"Okay, everyone on the same page?" she asked as she looked around the huddled group of soldiers including Miles. With no questions or comments, she instructed them further, "Okay, get your teams together. We'll reconvene here in six hours and make our move around two a.m. Until then, get some rest." She gave her final order before their moonlight operation.

The team had pulled their Humvee off the side of the road and had all found a place to rest, out of sight for a few hours. There was a mixed bag of emotions throughout the fireless campsite. For some, they were excited to get back into action, ready to take on their enemies once again. Others, who besides their lone rescue op at the Las Vegas Airport, had never seen combat and were quite nervous. Ayla and Miles, who had a bigger goal in mind, saw this as one small step on their journey to Alexander Dumont. To them, the real war hadn't even started yet.

Chapter 28

Truck Trail Conflict

The hour had arrived. It was almost two a.m. and Ayla and the separate teams were ready. They had all changed their clothes to all-black attire and some even used mud and dirt to darken their faces. They all started the downhill trek together through the wooded mountainside as Hudson and the rest of the soldiers waited quietly at the campsite. Halfway through their journey, Ayla silently gestured to Couchman to take his team, split off, and head toward the front of the building. Frank Tidwell designated two members of his lookout team to follow suit to keep their eyes on the road.

The rest of the team continued on through the woods toward the back of building. After a few minutes, they finally arrived. Ayla signaled to Frank and the remaining members of his squad to spread out around the property and take their positions to ensure there was no one else out there.

Now, with everyone in place, Ayla carefully took the same route she did earlier on their reconnaissance mission. She slowly and silently stood up slightly to peek into the window and saw exactly what she was hoping for. Four occupied bunk beds with sleeping soldiers, the laptop closed on the desk, and it appeared that no one ever suspected any late night visitors.

She crouched back down and approached the corner of the building. As she peered around the edge looking toward the driveway, she spotted the two guards on watch duty. One was standing on the left side of the entranceway staring off toward Los Angeles, admiring the glow against the dark countryside. Despite it only being a fraction of what it once was, the cityscape at night was still a spectacle. The other guard was in a white plastic lawn chair either sleeping or gazing up at the night sky.

She waited a few minutes to ensure Couchman's team was in place and gave the signal. She quickly turned a flashlight on and off. She waited, but nothing happened. She signaled again, on and then off. Seconds later, she saw a dark figure emerge from the woods and then another. They grabbed the guards from behind and put them both in a choke hold. After ten seconds or so of struggling, the guards stopped fighting, their legs stopped kicking, and the two revolutionaries pulled their victims into the woods and just like that they were gone. Ayla remained at the corner of the building and waited until Couchman and another member of his team returned from the woods, wearing the uniforms of the dispatched guards. He looked in Ayla's direction and nodded his head to confirm the first phase of their plan was completed.

Now it was Ayla's turn. She signaled to Miles who was with Jake and Ruiz behind the building. They carefully joined her at the corner and then they all made their way to the green front door of the structure. Ayla placed her hand on the round golden door knob and slowly tried to turn. She continued to turn and when she felt that there was no resistance, she nodded to the others implying it was indeed unlocked and they could enter quietly. With their weapons drawn, she opened the door and the four of them entered the dark room. Before anyone did anything, Jake unplugged the laptop and quietly stepped out of the room to secure the device.

Realizing she had the upper hand as she stared down at the four sleeping soldiers, she looked toward Ruiz and motioned for him to flick the light switch on. As the room illuminated, the bewildered men didn't even have a chance to figure out what was happening to them. When they heard Ayla's voice order them to stay where they were, they were all shocked to see the guns that were pointed in their direction. They started to scramble but again Ayla spoke up, "Nope, don't move another muscle." The four of them all accepted defeat at this point and did as they were told. With her gun still pointed at them, she pulled a small cluster of black zip ties out of her pocket and tossed them at the soldier in the bunk facing her. "Put those on," she said. The man did not comply at first; he just sat there staring at them. "Now!" she said as she pressed her gun against his head.

"Okay, okay," he said nervously as he started to slip his hands through the loop.

"No, tie them up first," she said as she pointed her gun in the direction of his bunk mates. The half-dressed soldier did as he was told beginning with the man who was on the top bunk. He then moved to the other set of bunk beds where he tied the next set of hands. As he stood to restrain the last man, the young soldier on the top bunk shoved him out of the way while drawing a pistol from under his pillow. Before he even had the gun pointed in their direction, Ayla took the shot. The young man was dead and slumped against the wall in his bunk.

Splattered in blood, the shocked soldier who was still unbound stared at his friend. Ayla, swearing under her breath, grabbed the ties and restrained him. "Why did he do that?" she asked herself out loud. "Stupid kid," she muttered to herself again. "You three, sit against the wall," she said pointing to the ground in front of the bunk beds. "Ruiz, watch them," she said as her and Miles turned and left the room.

"What the hell was that?" Jake asked frantically from just outside the building.

Miles held his hand up at him telling him not to ask and he then directed his attention to Ayla. "You okay?" he asked her as they stepped out into the darkness.

"I didn't really want to shoot some kid but other than that I'm fine," she said dramatically.

"He didn't give you a choice," he said, to which she didn't respond. "It was him or us and I'm glad you picked us," she nodded and appreciated his efforts to make her feel less guilty about taking his life.

She waved to Couchman who ran over to their location. "Good job," she said to him. "There should be four more uniforms in here, go ahead and give them to your team, and you can stay in charge of guard duty." He nodded and went to search for the other uniforms. "Jake, where are we with the computer?" she yelled out not knowing exactly where he was.

"Working on it," he yelled back from around the corner.

Just then, Lieutenant Hudson emerged from the woods. "I heard a gunshot, but looks like we're good?" Ayla pushed open the green door and Hudson looked in and took note of the casualty. He nodded and continued, "Should I go get everyone else?"

"Let's take a look inside first, make sure we know what we're getting into," she said to him. They grabbed a key ring full of keys from a hook inside the door and approached the garage. The door was secured with an old rusted, silver padlock. Ayla flipped through the collection of keys and tried a few duds before finding the right one. The padlock clicked open and they proceeded to lift the green door. Unlike the garage in Elsie,

177

Nebraska, this door opened with ease. They found a light switch and as they flipped it on, the few lights that hadn't been burnt out slowly flickered on. Inside the concrete floored garage, they saw a few things that could be useful but nothing that would require the protection of six soldiers. Along the right side was an old workbench with several tools lying about in an unorganized manner. There was an ATV that was plugged in charging, an old army Humvee much like the one the team had stolen earlier in their journey, but this one was almost completely dismantled, and a locked metal cabinet that held a few rifles in it.

"That was uneventful," Miles said.

Ayla and Miles entered to take a closer look around. The ATV appeared to be something they used often, it had fresh dirt on its wheels and there were tracks leading in and out of the garage. There were tools and car parts lying around that suggested someone was attempting to repair the Humvee but wasn't having much luck. They also found a pantry with canned food and other non-perishable items that looked well stocked. She found the key for the gun cabinet and unlocked it. She motioned for a random soldier to come over. "Go ahead and give these guns out to anybody that doesn't have one."

"Yes ma' am," she said, as she began to pull the guns out one by one and hand them to another fellow soldier.

Ayla turned to look at Miles who put his hands up suggesting he was not sure what to do next. "Let's go chat with our new friends," she said.

They returned to the sleeping quarters, finding that the body of the young soldier had since been removed. Couchman had ordered a few of his soldiers to dig a grave for him and the other two casualties. The remaining three prisoners were all still tied up and sitting on the floor of what used to be their bedroom. She crouched down in front of the same soldier she had instructed to tie up his friends. His face was speckled in the dried blood of his former roommate. At first, she didn't say anything. She just looked into his eyes, holding her gun. She wasn't pointing it at him, but she made sure he could see it.

After a few uncomfortable moments of this silence, the guard began to look around to see if anyone else knew why she was staring at him. He tried to speak up, "What—"

As he tried to ask his question, Ayla interrupted him. "What are you doing here?" he began to open his mouth and she interrupted him again, this time more intensely, "Why are there six guards here watching over a broken Humvee and a dirt road?

The prisoner started to talk, "There, there's a—" He was elbowed by the prisoner next to him. "Do you want to die, Tim?" the prisoner shot back at his friend. "I don't. Not for a damn radio tower." He turned back to Ayla and continued. "Like I was saying, there's a small power substation, a distribution station down the trail road about a mile. There's also a radio tower that we use to contact our bosses in Los Angeles."

Ayla waited a moment and then said, "Go ahead, keep talking."

"We're just here to make sure nobody trespasses, and to keep it working," he said.

"What about the computer?" she asked him.

"Oh, that's nothing." he said. "We use that to run diagnostics on the power station. That's it."

Not completely sold on what he said about the computer she stood up and left the room and Miles followed her. She instructed Ruiz to find a partner to help him watch their new prisoners. She also told Hudson to return to the rest of the team and have them come down to their newest place they would call home. "What

179

are you thinking?" Miles asked her.

"I'm thinking it's late. We accomplished our mission today. We bring everyone back here and we can sleep in the garage. We'll keep the same guard rotation going to keep up appearances just in case. We can figure out our next move in the morning," she said even though they had both already started thinking ahead. Eventually, the rest of the revolutionaries arrived at the structure and they tried to get some sleep. "The sun is going to be coming up soon, try to get some shuteye," Ayla gave out one last order before she found a spot to lie down.

Jake, who didn't want to sleep at all, was tapping on the keys of the laptop in the corner of the garage continuously. After almost an hour, he suddenly stopped and raised his eyebrows. Talking quietly to himself he said, "I did it. I'm in." After a couple seconds he yelled it louder. "I did it!" This startled some awake and even drew some groans.

"Shut up, Jake!" One soldier yelled from across the room.

Ignoring the moans and groans from his fellow comrades, he closed up the laptop and ran over to Ayla. His excitement was halted, however, because when he arrived at her side, Ayla seemed to be in distress. Her eyes were closed but he could see them moving wildly beneath her lids. She was clutching her arms tightly around her body and moaning quietly. He placed his hand on her shoulder and tried to gently wake her. "General?" he said as he nudged her lightly. She began to moan louder so he shook her a little harder. "General, wake up." Ayla then violently sat up letting out a loud sound as if she had been frightened.

"What?" she asked loudly. "What's going on?"

Jake, forgetting about his progress with the laptop was more concerned about her. "Are you okay?" he asked her sincerely.

"Yea, I'm fine. It's nothing," she said wiping the sweat off

180

her forehead.

"Are you sure? Doesn't seem like nothing," he said.

"Sometimes I get nightmares, you know, every once in a while," she said and immediately realized she was being uncharacteristically vulnerable. She tried to brush it off again. "It's nothing really. What do you got?" she said casually as she looked at the laptop trying to gain her composure.

Jake was unconvinced of her answer but knew his place and decided not to push the issue. He began to describe what he found. "So this computer is used to monitor both the substation and the radio tower. They have programs loaded on here that allow them to run diagnostics and make changes to internal processes for both, but, if you dig a little deeper... See this here?" He asked her while using the mouse to show her a small desktop icon that looked like the flag of the United States but in the shape of a large capital *I*. She nodded and allowed him to continue. "If you click that," he said while double clicking the icon, which prompted a screen to pop up asking for a user name and password.

"What's that?" she asked him.

He began to vigorously tap on the keyboard again. "I'll show you. So if you bypass the encryption and use a standard algorithm to hack into this..." he paused while still typing away. "Voila!" he said and turned the laptop back to face Ayla.

She read the top of the page aloud. "U.S. Security Intranet." Stunned she looked at Jake and asked a question, "They have internet?"

"Well sort of. It's an intranet. It's basically a private network that's using the same technology as the internet. It's just limited to those who have access to it," he replied.

"What can it tell us?" she asked him.

He continued on, "Depending on what you want to gain access to, there are more and more levels of security, but assuming I can gain access to most of it, we could see everything from troop movement and who knows? Maybe even communications between the President and his cabinet."

The cabinet wasn't like what it used to be. Before, in the old days, they were educated people that helped the president make decisions on different issues for the betterment of society. Now, it had become basically a group of wealthy individuals trying to keep themselves in power.

"That's really great work, Jake," she said to him. "How about reeducation camps?" she asked him.

"Let me see," he said as he typed away. "Looks like there are only a couple left in operation, but they don't really come out and say where they are. Why do you want to know about that?" he asked her curiously.

"Just some personal stuff," she said while realizing she shouldn't allow her own agenda to get in the way of their mission. "We can come back to those later, I guess. See what you can dig up on troops in and around L.A," she said to him.

"You got it," he said as he rose to his feet. He started to walk away but then said one more thing to her, "Hey General."

"Yes?" she said to him.

"I'm a good listener, you know, if you need to talk to somebody," he said to her charismatically.

"Thanks, Jake, I'll be all right," she said with a smile as she turned and rolled back over.

She struggled to fall back asleep as she thought about her conversation with Jake, so she decided to go find Miles. She headed toward the open garage door and slowly walked past her soldiers who were still resting on the concrete floor. As she stepped out of the structure, the sun was just beginning to rise on the camp. She looked to her left and saw two of Couchman's soldiers masquerading as security guards at the entrance.

She looked to her right and peered through the trees and saw one of Frank Tidwell's team members keeping an eye on the perimeter of the property. She approached the door of the sleeping chambers and entered. The smell of fresh brewed coffee filled her nose. After she took a deep breath in, enjoying the aroma, she looked around and saw Ruiz and his partner both asleep on the bunks as Miles was crouched down talking to the other remaining captive guards. As she entered, Miles looked over his shoulder. "Ah, good morning, General," he said. "How about some coffee?"

"Yes, please. I don't remember the last time I had a cup," she said smiling as he poured her some from the pot on the desk where the computer had once lived.

"Sorry, no creamer," he said with a smile.

She took a slow sip, taking care not to burn her mouth, and swallowed. "So good, man, I missed that," she said.

Miles allowed her to enjoy a few more moments of caffeine-induced euphoria before he asked if there was anything new she had learned. He motioned toward the door, "Let's take a walk," he said as he nudged Ruiz awake to take over guard duty. The two walked down the dirt road away from the building. "So where are we with the computer?" he asked her.

She moved the cup of black coffee away from her lips and answered, "Jake did confirm that these guys were using the computer to maintain a radio tower and substation. He also gained access to what he called the intranet for the U.S. I guess it's like the internet but not really." Miles nodded to show his understanding despite her poor description. "Anyways, he said he needed more time with it but should be able to get us some intel about a lot of stuff, maybe even troop movements."

"That will definitely help," Miles said.

"What about you? Did you find anything out from the guards?" she asked as she took another sip of her coffee.

"Our friend who's doing all the talking, his name is Bill Ingram. He's been enlisted for two years and he's been posted here for just a couple of months. Doesn't seem to have any loyalties to anyone. He told me he joined up because he didn't know what else to do," he said.

"Did he have anything worthwhile to say?" she asked him.

"Not really, nothing much more than Jake found out. Although he did say that their replacements would be here in another three weeks. So I guess we have a timetable now of when you need to get to Dumont and back," he said. "Oh, and about the guy you shot, Bill said he was a real loyalist, and I'm quoting him here 'a really big douche', " he concluded with a smile.

"Thanks, Miles," she said. It didn't really make her feel any better, but if she had to shoot someone, she was glad it was someone like him rather than a guy like Bill, who was just enlisted because he didn't want to go hungry. That was the real appeal for people joining up with Army or becoming a city enforcer. Sometimes in this post war America, you had to make the hard choice of going hungry or joining up with what was causing the people to go hungry in the first place.

After her conversation with Miles, Ayla decided that it may be time to start organizing her team that will journey into Los Angeles to find Dumont. The sun was now bleeding through the tree line as it rose up above the horizon. The warmth on her face coupled with the cool mountain air made her feel refreshed. She took a minute to finish her cup of coffee and took off her hat to feel the breeze in her hair. The bright sun made her newly dyed hair appear even whiter as the light bounced off her head.

"Good Morning, General," a soldier said as she passed by.

Ayla stopped her, "Hey, can you do something for me?" She asked her.

"Yes ma'am. What do you need?" she asked.

"I need you to get Jake, Ruiz, Couchman, and Frank Tidwell. Tell them to meet me in the garage in an hour," she said to the obedient soldier who quickly did as she was told and headed out to complete her mission. In the meantime, Ayla found Zoe and Gabe to catch up and see how they were doing.

Chapter 29

Prep Time

Jake was the first to arrive in the garage. He had the laptop in tow, ready to share some more knowledge with his General. He opened the computer and set it on the hood of the broken down Humvee and told Ayla about his newest discoveries. "So this software is nothing like what we had before the war. It's very basic. But there's an online database about troop movement I was able to access. The most recent entry is a large relocation of troops from the capital to the Las Vegas Airport."

"I guess we know why they were headed there." She said referencing their encounter a week ago.

Jake continued on, "Now in terms of us getting there, the road we are on now is Route 2 which takes us nearly into Los Angeles There's only one checkpoint along that route and it's well into the city, so we should be fine getting there with minimal risk of running into any trouble; at least according to this info," he said just as the other members of the team arrived.

"Great job, Jake," she said to him as she placed her hand on his and gave it a quick squeeze. She hated the idea of being close to someone but she kept finding herself opening up to him. Ever since she saw him in the hangar at the Las Vegas airport, she often found herself seeking him out in the groups hoping to catch a glimpse of him. She couldn't help being attracted to him, even when he was being a computer nerd. For a moment, their eyes met, but only briefly as the others joined them near the old Humvee. She forced herself to refocus on the mission, "Miles!" She yelled. He was across the large open room chatting with some soldiers. She waved him over to join the group to discuss their next move.

"Okay, so this is the team that will make contact with Dumont, excluding Miles. He'll be running point here until we complete our mission." She began to lay out a map on the hood of the Humvee. "Thanks to Jake, we're fairly certain we can continue on this road until right about here," she said as she pointed to a section on the map where the road merged onto a highway. She then laid out the rest of the journey the team would make on foot and included the details about where the checkpoint was and how they could avoid it. "Any questions about the route?" she asked.

"What's our back story?" Couchman asked as he raised his hand.

"Let's keep that simple. We're all friends from a settlement that decided to come to Los Angeles for work." She paused and thought for a moment and continued on, "Miles, where are some settlements north of here that would make sense?"

He looked at her and while shrugging his shoulders he gave a suggestion, "I think there are some small ones around Salt Lake City."

"That'll work; we can hash out some finer details as we go." Couchman nodded showing he understood. "Any other questions?" she asked. After waiting a moment she continued on, "Okay, once we get past the checkpoint, we'll head directly to Dumont." She looked to Miles to see if he wanted to add anything.

He stepped forward to address the team, "Los Angeles is not

your average city or settlement. These days, most people are all clustered in and around the downtown area. It's going to be busy and bustling. There will be a lot of city enforcers, some soldiers, street merchants yelling and shouting, women and men selling their bodies, not to mention crooks; if they aren't trying to pick your pocket, one of their buddies probably already did. You'll need to keep your wits about you and stay focused. There are lots of distractions."

Ayla started in again, "It should take us about a day's walk to get to Dumont from here. It's too late to leave today so get yourselves together and pack supplies you think you'll need. Rest up. Tomorrow will be a long day. We'll leave at first light. Remember, pistols only," she added in as the group dispersed.

"I have some more information for you," Miles said to Ayla as it was just the two of them now at the Humvee. "When you get to the fish market, you'll want to find a guy named Juan, he'll probably be chopping up fish somewhere. When you see him, ask him 'what was the catch of the day this time last year?' His answer should only be 'tuna, just like this year.' If it's anything else, then you get your men and get the hell out of there."

"Really, we have code words now?" she asked sarcastically.

"Yea, I know, but Dumont grew up watching those old spy movies and has a lot of trust issues," he said as Ayla nodded. "Now you keep that to yourself, don't tell any of your team."

"What if something happens to me?" she asked him.

"You tell your guys that if you get killed out there, they're to report directly back here, no matter how close they are to Dumont. If they show up without you then they're as good as dead anyways."

"Dead?" she asked confusingly.

"Trust issues. Remember?" he said raising his eyebrows.

"Right," she replied. "I wonder if Ellie ever made it," she asked out loud.

"Hudson thinks she's very capable. I'm sure she made it," he said confidently.

The sun glared down into the garage through the open door. Ayla could see beads of sweat forming on Miles' forehead. She motioned to the back of the garage, and the two found a shaded spot to sit and continue their chat.

Ayla had a lot on her mind and Miles could tell. "Do you think we should have gone after Evan?" she asked him.

"There was nothing we could do, Ayla, we couldn't risk going after them. Plus, you could see it in his eyes, he wasn't going to let us get them back. He would have killed them before we even got close," he said to her, trying to ease her guilt.

"I just hope Raj is okay," she said as she hung her head between her knees.

"He's a strong kid; you saw what he did in Pikesville. He'll do what he needs to survive and when we get him back, he'll be even stronger," Miles said reassuringly.

"I hope you're right," she said.

"I'm always right!" he said jokingly, "Now, go find Jake; I'm sure he'd love to talk to you more about his computer," he said sarcastically, which prompted Ayla to open her mouth in shock. "I see everything," he added.

Ayla found an old greasy rag lying next to her and threw it at him playfully as he walked away. She sat alone in the garage thinking about what Miles said as he left her. Why she was attracted to him was obvious. Jake was a tall, good-looking man, but there was something else about him that Ayla was drawn to. However, being as stubborn as she was, she decided to ignore Miles' suggestion. Instead of finding Jake, she found her old friends Zoe and Gabe. After visiting with them, she spent the rest of the day socializing and getting to know her troops better.

The light of day eventually started to fade and outside the garage, a small ways up the dirt trail, there was a campfire that had been started in preparation for the coming night. Those who weren't on guard duty or watching the prisoners had gathered there for a relaxing evening of fun and laughter. Here, she again found Gabe and Zoe. The couple was sitting by the fire eating some stew that some of the soldiers threw together from the cabinet of assorted canned foods and spices. Ayla grabbed herself a small bowl and found a seat next to them. "Mind if I join you?" she asked.

Zoe, still nursing her bullet wound, responded first with a smile. "Not at all, how's everything going?" she asked.

"Oh you know, just enjoying this brief moment of normalcy," she said. "How are you guys?"

Gabe answered, "Us too, it's nice here, enjoying it while it lasts." They all smiled and gazed at the fire which had become bigger and brighter as the night got darker. Gabe broke the silence after a few moments, "We heard you're heading into the city tomorrow."

Keeping her eyes on the fire Ayla replied, "Yep, going to see the man tomorrow. Hopefully problem free, but that's usually not the case."

"Take us with you," he said to both Zoe and Ayla's surprise. Although she was taken aback by her husband's request, Zoe decided to wait and see how she would react.

His words broke her focus on the dancing flames. She didn't exactly know what to say. She hesitated for a moment before speaking. "I don't know guys, it's dangerous. It's just going to be the five of us and we're all trained to handle anything we run

190

into…"

Gabe interrupted her. "We won't get in the way. Remember the airport? We handled ourselves there, didn't we? Once we get close to the city, we'll just disappear and start over." He reached for Zoe's hand and she grabbed it to show her support.

Ayla really did want to help them. They were her roommates and the closest thing she had to a family for a long time; but she knew the right thing to do was to keep her focus on the mission and having these two accompany her team would jeopardize everything. She decided to stand her ground but play it off like it was for their benefit. "Listen, I want that for you guys, I really do, but if something happened to you out there, any chance you have at a new life is over. Zoe, you've already been shot once. Just stay here with Miles; he'll keep you safe until we figure out what's next. I promise I'll get you into the city to start over, just not tomorrow," she said as she stood up. "I'll talk to you guys soon." She bade them goodnight, hoping she had put their adventurous ideas to rest.

As she turned to walk away, she took one last look at the fire and through the flames her eyes met with Jake's who had been watching her talk with her friends. For a brief moment they stayed locked in on each other until Ayla turned and headed back toward the garage. He watched her walk away and decided to make his move. He had been debating whether it was a good idea or not, she's his superior officer after all. But he went with his gut and scrambled to his feet. He casually walked after her trying not to draw too much attention.

Ayla looked over her shoulder and saw him following her. She quickened her pace and after she rounded the bend in the trail she hopped off into the woods. Watching through the trees, she saw Jake round the same bend. He stood there confused not

191

knowing where she went. Ayla took a few moments appreciating his good looks. She then purposefully snapped a branch she had been standing on. He turned and saw her leaning up against a tree looking both vulnerable and as beautiful as ever. He smiled at her and she seductively bit her lower lip. He walked toward her, ducking beneath a branch and the two came together. He waited just a second to be sure she consented and then he kissed her passionately and she kissed him back. He ran his hand through her short, white hair while the other hand, gripping her hip, slowly made its way up her side. Ayla, caught up in the moment, allowed him to keep going but only for a second as she realized she wasn't quite ready for anything further. She grabbed his hand and held in place as she pulled her lips away from his.

While breathing heavily and still holding each other, they both started laughing realizing how ridiculous it was they just had a make-out session in the woods, as if they were teenagers at a party. "Does this mean I'm getting promoted?" he asked with a smile.

"Maybe," she said teasingly while looking in his eyes. But before he got any ideas, she stopped him in his tracks. "But not tonight, big day tomorrow." She patted him on the shoulder, stepped around him, and walked out of the woods as if nothing had happened, leaving him dumbfounded. Playing it cool, she never even turned around to see his reaction, but she couldn't help herself from smiling ear to ear as she walked down the trail. Eventually, she found her way back to the garage, climbed inside the old broken down Humvee, and fell asleep.

Chapter 30

The Road to Dumont

Ayla was awakened the next day by the sound of her wristwatch beeping. It read eight a.m. but it was actually much earlier because she had not yet made any adjustments for the time zone changes. It was still dark, and all she could think about was getting more of that coffee. She quietly made her way to the soldiers' office and sleeping area. She knocked softly on the door and a soldier who was on duty watching the prisoners opened it seconds later. With her arms folded across her body trying to stay warm in the cool morning she asked him, "Got any of that coffee brewing?"

"I can get some going," he said.

She said thanks and turned back to start waking up her team who had all at some point made their way back to the garage from the fire last night. Ruiz and Couchman were both sleeping on the opposite end of the garage, and Frank slept outside under the stars. Meanwhile, Jake, who she hadn't noticed before, was leaning up against the side of the Humvee using a backpack as a pillow. She slowly walked up to him and watched him while he slept, listening to his small snores and thinking about her late night encounter with him. Eventually, she snapped out of it and gave him a soft kick to his foot.

He was startled but once he realized who kicked him, he smiled. "Good morning," she said to him.

"It's still dark out," he mumbled and closed his eyes again.

She then took a more drastic measure and pulled his makeshift pillow out from under his head which caused it to bounce off the Humvee tire. "Ow," he said while slowly opening his eyes back up and looking up at her.

"Go wake everybody up and meet me by the door." She ordered him and then left him lying there to go get her hands on some of the coffee that was brewing. He slowly got himself to his feet and really wanted to chase after her, but he followed her cues and figured now was not the best time to talk about their intimate moment from the night before. He did as he was told and left to find his fellow soldiers.

Ayla headed back toward the office area and found Miles, who was already pouring her a cup. "Ready to go?" he asked her as he handed her the steaming coffee.

"I will be as soon as I get this," she said smiling as she reached for the cup. "I don't know how I have survived so long without you," she said to the coffee as she took a slow sip taking care not to burn her mouth.

"Where's your team?" he asked her.

"Jake is rounding them up; they'll be here in a few," she said as she took another sip while Miles gave her another look, "Oh, be quiet, Miles. I'm almost forty years old. I know what I'm doing."

"I didn't say anything," he said.

"I know that look," she said back to him.

Just then, the rest of the team arrived and Ayla ran through a last minute checklist. "All right, everyone, today is the day we go see Alexander Dumont. We all have our pistols and a couple clips in our bags?" she asked as the four soldiers nodded. "Jake, please don't tell me that you have that laptop in your bag."

"You mean this laptop?" he said as he pulled it out of his pack.

"Are you crazy?" she asked him. "If they catch us with that, we'll probably be shot on site and then they'll know to come here."

"Well, they won't catch us if we're tracking their troops," he said in his own defense.

Ayla thought about his response for a moment but stuck to her original decision. "No, check it out one more time before we go and then give it to Miles. It's too risky." Jake looked a little deflated but complied and opened the computer to take one last look. It didn't take him more than a minute before he closed it up and handed it over to Miles. "Well?" she asked him.

"Nothing's changed since their last login," he said.

"All right, let's do this," she said as she took her black hat and placed it over her short, almost white hair. She looked at Miles. "We'll see you soon," she said confidently.

The team of five began their daylong trek down Route 2 toward Los Angeles. Frank Tidwell again took point, traveling the higher ground, keeping an eye out on the horizon for any oncoming dangers. The journey was much easier than the one that took them to the truck trail; the terrain had shifted to a downhill descent with spectacular views of the valley on the winding mountainous road.

After a couple of hours of walking and small talk, the team took a break. Ayla picked one of the many scenic lookouts that motorists used to use to take in the views of the Angeles National Forest. "At least, we didn't destroy this," Jake said poetically as they all stared out toward the untouched beauty of Mother Nature.

After taking in the sights, they all sat and shared a small

snack, had some laughs, and hashed out some more details of their cover story just in case they encountered any resistance.

Ayla checked her watch "Okay, time to get moving, team." She said as she stood and dusted the loose dirt off her pants. The team gathered their belongings and resumed their trek toward Dumont.

Eventually, they left the wilderness behind and began to enter more residential areas. With the new infrastructure of the city not being able to support these outlying communities, the large suburban neighborhoods were all but abandoned. Boarded up homes with overgrown lawns served as a reminder of what life used to be like here. As they continued on, houses became more condensed, and the landscape became more and more urban. As they inched closer to their destination, they began to see people who dared to live on the fringe of society, in what was now considered the outskirts of the city.

"All right, this is a good spot to get off the main road," Ayla said. "Let's turn here, it should lead us right to downtown and we'll miss the checkpoint," she said as she pointed toward a road while still looking at the map.

The team followed her lead and they headed down the street hoping to avoid any confrontations with enforcers or the Army. The journey from here consisted of more turns and small streets and alleyways. They also began to see more and more signs of life as they passed buildings that were used for housing. Much like Ayla's old tenement house, these buildings were over populated and were in rough shape.

The team also got a somber reminder of why they were once again pushing toward war with the government. As in Chicago, humanity suffered greatly on the streets of Los Angeles Besides tenement houses, there were scores of tents and makeshift homes lining the streets; more than Ayla had ever seen in Chicago. People were covered in filth and the sick lay dying on the street because of the lack of medical care. The team didn't say much to each other as they passed through this area. It was hard to summarize how they felt but they each experienced different moments of anger, pain, and sympathy as they observed the downtrodden of society. Ayla turned back and her eyes met Jake's; there were no words spoken, just a shared moment of disbelief at what they were seeing.

The hustle and bustle of the city intensified as they inched closer to their destination. As they walked through the section of tents and apartment buildings, the atmosphere was quiet and still, now it was full of action and even exciting. Street peddlers were shouting prices and the names of their goods. "Hot food!" shouted one gentleman. "Fresh Water!" shouted another.

Pretty soon, the team found themselves walking through crowded streets surrounded by both merchants and their customers. There must have been a couple thousand people crammed into the small area. Ayla wondered how there could be such a contrast between the squalor of the tent city they had passed and this, but it was short lived as she was soon engulfed in all the action.

This is what Miles was talking about. The downtown area of Los Angeles was full of life. Ayla found herself becoming distracted just as he had warned against. She was gazing at local artwork, clothes with vibrant colors, and taking in all the smells. The aromas that filled the air came in waves; first, it was roasted meat, then fresh smelling fruits, coffee, sweets, and then an aroma that reminded her of the mission, fish.

Ayla honed in on the smell and looked around the market. Soon, she heard chopping sounds like that of a butcher knife on a block, wack, wack, wack. She walked toward the sounds with her team in tow and as the sounds grew louder, the smell became stronger. Trying to block out all the noise around her, she heard the sound again, WACK, WACK, WACK. She jumped up trying to see over the heads of the people and then she saw it, a fish getting flung through the air, and then again WACK, WACK, WACK. She could now see the green sign with hand painted white letters that read "Los Angeles Fresh Fish." She meandered through the crowd and eventually made her way to the source of the chopping sounds. Just as Miles described, there was a large man wearing a white apron covered in fish debris. As she approached the butcher block he slammed down a giant cleaver chopping a fish head clean off, causing her to flinch slightly. This has to be Juan; Ayla thought to herself as he carried on with his business and continued to chop the dead fish, WACK, WACK. She got closer but soon regretted it as his next chop caused the soaked butcher block to spray a mist of fish guts and water in her direction.

"Hey!" she yelled at him as she wiped the fishy water from her mouth.

"Back away if you don't like the spray!" he yelled routinely as if it was something he said often.

He caught another fish and, WACK, off goes the head and more fish mist at Ayla. "Hey, would you stop for a second!" she yelled, irritated by his persistence.

Juan, rolled his eyes, stopped what he was doing, and looked at her annoyed. "What do you want? I don't take orders, that's inside," he said as he raised his hand up for another chop.

"Wait, what was the catch of the day this time last year?" she yelled quickly, trying to interject before he swung again.

Juan stopped mid chop and stared at her and after a brief

moment he laid his cleaver down on the fish scaled covered block. "Tuna, just like last year," he said with a straight face. He looked over his shoulder and yelled, "Hey, Ramon, I'm taking a break!" His eyes again met Ayla's and he said, "Follow me." Ayla and her team began to follow Juan through the crowd toward the front entrance of the shop. Once near the door, Juan again spoke to her. "Your friends will have to wait here."

"Oh no, where she goes we go," Jake said.

Ayla secretly appreciated that Jake was worried about her, but she didn't show it. "I'll be fine, Jake," she said to him. "I'll be back soon, blend in," she said again as her team watched as the two weaved their way closer to the door and eventually disappeared inside.

Following Juan made it easy for Ayla to navigate through the customers inside the shop; his wide body cleared the way. After a couple minutes, he brought her to a brown, wooden door. He knocked on the door in a specific rhythm. Three quick knocks followed by three slow knocks. Despite the loud murmuring from the customers in the store, she could hear the old door creak open as a very serious-looking man appeared from the other side. Ayla looked at Juan who motioned for her to continue on as he held the door open for her. "He's been waiting for you," he said as Ayla walked through the door leaving him behind.

She placed her hand on the smooth railing and began to walk down the creaking wooden stairs. The dimly lit decent had a turn halfway down so she still could not see what was waiting for her at the bottom. The cool air from the basement began to pass through her clothing. The stench of the fish market slowly faded and was replaced with the smell of a musty basement combined with cigarette smoke. As she turned the corner of the stairs, she could hear two men speaking softly. "I'll get this to my superiors right away," she heard one of them say in a Spanish accent. The man exited the room and passed Ayla on the stairs. The two made eye contact as he stuffed an envelope into his jacket pocket and continued on his way.

She finally reached the bottom and found a very modest looking set up. The concrete floor was stained and there were several bulletin boards hanging on the dark walls with bits and pieces of information haphazardly pinned to them, and an old filing cabinet pressed in one of the corners. There was also a large bookcase filled with literature, which reminded her of Dumont's reading habits as Miles had told it. There was a very large man with a pistol sitting in the corner; Ayla correctly assumed it was Dumont's body guard. Under the only hanging light bulb in the basement was an old metal desk, where a tired-looking Alexander Dumont was sitting. He was an elderly looking man with wavy gray hair down to the back of his neck. He was wearing modest clothes in an attempt to not stand out in the crowds. Upon seeing Ayla, his eyes widened. "Ah," he said in a happy tone as he took one last drag of his cigarette and put it out in the ash tray. "You must be Ms. Vural, pardon me, General Vural," he said as he reached out toward her with his wrinkled and weathered hands.

"I am," she said cautiously as she shook his hand.

"I'm Alexander Dumont. It's a pleasure to meet you. I've heard so much about you from our mutual friend General Lang. Speaking of which, where is he?"

"He's about a day's walk north of here," she said, not wanting to give away any more details.

"Please, take a seat, we have much to discuss. Do you mind?" he asked as he held up a pack of cigarettes. Ayla motioned to him that it was fine, and he lit up another one. Pulling on the lit cigarette, he paused before exhaling. "You changed your hair," he said curiously. Ayla had forgotten about her white hair and gave him a grimace as she touched the back of her neck. He tapped the ash off his smoke and continued. "Tell me, Ayla, can I call you Ayla?" She nodded and he continued, "Why are you here?"

"Miles told me that you were leading the charge on another revolution, so here I am," she said bluntly.

Dumont took another drag of his smoke and exhaled. "Why come at all? Why not stay in hiding and live out your life?"

"You already know the answer to that," she said.

"Indulge me," he pressed on.

"Well, before Miles came to see me, I guess I was just trying to stay alive. But after we had our little chat, and two of my roommates were murdered, I decided to come and see what you had to say."

"Go on," he said as he leaned back in his chair still smoking his cigarette.

"You haven't said anything yet, so I'm not sure what you're expecting," she said, unimpressed by his routine.

"You came all this way just to talk to an old man?" he asked rhetorically and continued, "We both know you've already made up your mind regardless of what I have to say."

"All right fine, yea I plan on seeing this through whether I like what you had to say or not," she said annoyed at his insight. Prior to Miles showing up in Chicago, Ayla had never thought she'd get a second chance to save the country. Now that the door had opened back up, she was determined to walk through it, no matter what.

"That's what I wanted to hear," Dumont said with a smile as he continued to puff on his second smoke. "I need someone like you, someone who wants to take this country back just as much as I do."

"How do you plan on doing that?" she asked him, trying to get to the point.

"I have a few tricks up my sleeve, but for now, the plan is to take down this pathetic excuse of a government and return it to the way it was. Bring this country out of the damn dark ages." At this point he stood and started to pace around on the cold concrete floor. "Those people in Seattle, they did this to us! First with the martial law, then they skipped straight to full on genocide." He stopped, put cigarette number two out, and placed his hands on his desk and looked at her. "I have dozens of groups of soldiers just like yours, ready to come together and fight."

"What do you need me for?" she asked.

"To lead them!" he said pleading with her. "I need someone they can believe in. Everyone in the resistance has heard tales of Major Vural, the liberator of Albany, fighting in the name of justice. You're my hero in all this; rallying the people to fight back!"

"What about Miles?" she asked.

"Miles is too old. Like me. It has to be you," he said.

"Before we get into this, I have some men with me today, they're all still outside." She said.

"I'll have Juan bring them inside," he said to her as he looked back toward his bodyguard who then left to see the task through.

"Okay, so Miles told me I needed to hear your plan, let's hear it," she said to him.

"Now, we're not going to go marching into the capital, that would be suicidal, we need to get them to come to us. All I need from you is to take control of Los Angeles," he said as if it would be a simple task.

"Oh is that it?" she said with a scoff.

"You'll have the manpower, I assure you," he said.

"Okay, what happens next?" she asked him.

"When they come, and they will come, you and Miles will defend our new city," he said.

She looked at him perplexed, "I know I'm new to the whole military strategy game, but how is taking over Los Angeles going to 'take the government down' as you put it?"

"Like I said, I have a few tricks up my sleeve," he said with a smirk.

"I'm supposed to just trust you on this? I mean you want me to take all of our soldiers that you claim to have lying around waiting for me, bring them here and take over an entire city without knowing the rest of the plan?"

"Well, yes," he said bluntly. "This whole movement will never be successful if I just lay everything out for everyone. There are spies everywhere. There are people in our ranks right now that will do anything to get a taste of the good life, like running to their local governor's office looking for that reward, the easy way out," he said as he lit his third cigarette. "I've already been betrayed too many times to risk telling you things, that, for now, you don't need to know. You've traveled this far, trust the process and know that in the end you and I want the same thing."

After hearing his plea, Ayla paced around in the damp basement, thinking to herself about Dumont's strategy. After a few moments she looked at him and said, "Okay, but if you screw me over I'm going to shoot you."

He let out a raspy laugh followed up by a tar-filled cough. "I'd expect nothing less," he said with a smile on his face.

They continued their conversation about what to do next and

the upcoming conflict. Dumont sprawled out a large map of Los Angeles onto his desk and pulled out a red marker. He pointed out and circled locations such as security checkpoints, the barracks for the city enforcers, the governors' office, and other locations that could help Ayla take control of the city.

After spending most of their meeting discussing strategy and mobilization, they eventually moved on to more personal matters. Ayla brought up the reeducation camps, the place she feared Raj had been taken. She and Dumont both agreed that if they weren't brainwashed already, those people who were forced into the programs shouldn't be punished. She also brought up her brother, which was a sore subject for both of them. Ayla still harbored a lot of hatred for him but he was still family, which made her a little uncomfortable when Dumont said that he should be shot for betraying him. She brought up Ellie, his granddaughter, and asked if she made it safe. Although she arrived without any problems, Dumont wasn't pleased Ayla sent her as the messenger. No one doubted Ellie's abilities, but even the most experienced soldier would be no match against a large crew of outlaws.

After what seemed like hours, they finally started to wrap up their meeting. "You and your men can stay here for now; there's plenty of space upstairs above the shop," he said to her. She nodded and turned to go back up the old stairs. "Oh I almost forgot to mention, there's a tavern around the corner, the food is decent and the drinks are cold. Treat them on me tonight," he handed her some money along with a key.

"What's the key for?" she asked.

"That's for the door outback and up the stairs. There's a few extra beds up there. It's not much, but should be better than what you've been sleeping on," he said to her.

"Thanks, the guys will appreciate it. When will I see you next?" she asked him.

"I'm too old to fight, or else I'd be by your side. I'll have to leave town before you start your mission or it will be too dangerous for me to travel." He continued on, "You know what you need to do now and now I've got to do my part. We all have our role in this war."

"You mean the role you won't tell me about?" she asked him sarcastically.

"That's the one," he said chuckling. "If all goes well, I'll see you once you take over and secure the city, and then we'll discuss our next move. I'll be sending one of my associates over to you in the morning to help you with your next mission. Just do me a favor and don't die."

"I'll do my best," she said as they both climbed up the stairs out of the old basement and into the now-closed fish market.

He placed his old cabbie hat on his head and said, "This is where we part ways for now. Good luck, Ayla; hopefully next time we meet we'll be one step closer to getting our country back."

She shook his hand one last time and he walked out the door, disappearing into the dwindling market crowd.

Chapter 31

Los Angeles Nights

As Ayla reemerged from her basement rendezvous, she realized how long she had been talking to Dumont. It had been several hours, and the lively market had died down and the crowds had dispersed. She no longer had to fight her way through hordes of locals or struggle to hear herself think over the commotion. As she stood in the middle of the empty fish store, the reality of what Dumont told her was starting to sink in. With Miles at her side, she was going to be leading the entirety of what would eventually be the second coming of the revolutionary army. At first, it seemed like a daunting task, however she was confident in both her abilities to lead and her knowledge of fighting on the ground. Still grasping the key to the backdoor of the market, her thoughts were interrupted by Juan.

"Your friends are up these stairs," he said, pointing to another set of stairs across the room from the basement door.

She thanked him and walked up the stairs and found her team anxiously waiting for her return. As she opened the door the first one to greet her was Jake. "Hey, how'd it go?" he asked impatiently.

"Um, it was interesting," she said trying not to give anything away.

"What's he like?" Jake asked as the rest of the team surrounded her.

She paused for a moment, thinking of the best way to describe him. "Cocky," she said bluntly, questioning her own description.

"Cocky? That's all you got?" Jake said wanting to know more.

"Cocky and old," she said smiling as she walked toward one of the bunks. "Smells like smoke," she added. She scanned the room and noticed two green duffels lying on the ground. Knowing full well her team only brought the clothes on their backs and small packs; she asked suspiciously, "whose bags are those?"

"Yeah about that," a familiar voice said from behind a wall as two people peered around the corner. It was Gabe and Zoe. Besides looking exhausted and Zoe's arm still bandaged from her Las Vegas gunshot wound, they appeared to be unharmed.

"What the hell!" Ayla said loudly as she turned to her team looking for an explanation.

"They followed us. They showed up a little after you left, Juan brought them upstairs," Jake said.

Ayla turned to Private Tidwell. "Frank! You're supposed to be my lookout guy. What happened, man?"

"I was looking forwards, not behind me," he said unapologetically.

Ayla placed her hand on her forehead in disbelief. "We're sorry, Ayla," Zoe said. "We saw this as chance to get out and we took it."

"You could have been caught, tortured, forced to give information, or even killed. I told you to stay put!" she said, worried about their safety.

"We're hunters, remember? We're good at not being seen," Gabe said.

207

Ayla stood with her hands on her hips and tilted her head toward the ceiling with her eyes closed. She took a deep breath and began to speak, "Okay, well, the important thing is that you're here and you made it. Come here," she said as she opened her arms and hugged them both simultaneously.

After their embrace, Zoe spoke up again, "We're hoping that maybe you could talk to Dumont, see if he could get us a job and a place to stay?"

"I'm not so sure you are going to want to stay here in the city," she said without any other context. Zoe and Gabe just looked at each other not knowing exactly what she meant. "Just stick with us for now until I can decide what to do."

"So what do we do now?" Ruiz asked her

"We're going to stay here for a couple nights at least. Tomorrow, Dumont's sending someone over to talk about some details and we'll go from there," she said. They all looked discouraged that she didn't have more for them. "Good news is that Dumont's buying us dinner and drinks tonight at a bar around the corner," she said hoping to cheer them up.

"All right, you heard the lady, let's go get some grub courtesy of one of the most notorious men in the country," Jake said, trying to support her efforts as he led the group outside and down the stairs.

As they made their way back onto the much quieter street, Ayla decided to make a quick detour and was soon back at the basement door of the shop. She remembered the secret knock that she watched Juan do earlier in the day and repeated it. Three quick knocks followed by three slow knocks. She waited. No answer. She tried again. Three quick knocks and then three slow knocks, again no one came to answer. She tried the handle and to no surprise the door was locked. She curiously pulled out the key that Dumont gave her for the back door of the upstairs apartment. She slid it in the keyhole, and it easily clicked all the way in. As she turned it, the lock clunked open. She turned the handle and slowly pushed the door. It let out an audible squeak. She looked around and decided to once again enter the basement.

As she stepped in the doorway, a voice startled her, "What are you doing?" It was Jake who came back for her.

"Go to the tavern, Jake," she said to him as she continued down the stairs.

"Not without you, what if Dumont finds you?" he asked as he followed her down the stairs, periodically looking back toward the door that was left slightly ajar.

As they made their way into the now-empty basement, they were met with the same cool, damp air from before, only this time the light was off and the smell of smoke was replaced by the more pungent smell of ashes and smothered cigarette butts. "Dumont went home; pretty sure he doesn't sleep here." She said as she felt her way through the dark until her legs bumped into his desk. She reached up blindly and found the hanging chain for the lone light bulb. She pulled it and the room illuminated. She contemplated leaving but couldn't help herself. She was soon on Dumont's side of the desk opening the middle drawer. Besides some cluttered papers, there were a few empty cigarette boxes, and a small loaded pistol. Finding nothing of interest she closed it.

"What are you doing?" Jake asked her again impatiently as he looked toward the stairs.

"I didn't exactly get the full picture. He's not very trusting," she said as she opened the bottom drawer and rummaged through the junk. She found nothing and let out a disparaging sigh.

"He trusted you enough to give you a key for down here,"

Jake said to her.

"Yea, I can't really explain that one," she replied.

"Well, he's old, maybe one key is easier to remember," he said jokingly.

Ayla laughed but then quickly moved on as she remembered the old filing cabinet that was tucked away in the corner. She grabbed the cool metal handle on the top drawer and yanked. It was locked, as were the other two drawers, and it was clear that her key would not work this time.

"Stand aside General," Jake said proudly.

"Oh my hero," she said to him sarcastically.

"Watch and learn," he said slyly as he pulled out a Swiss Army knife from his pocket. He extended the file part of the device and using the butt of his gun, he swiftly, and with a decent amount of force, jammed it into the keyhole. As he turned the red handle of the pocketknife, each lock gave an audible pop as it released. He put his knife away and looked to Ayla for approval.

"Okay, not bad Jake, not bad," she said to him impressed.

"A little trick I learned during my hacker days," he said proudly.

She rolled her eyes and then started pulling on the top drawer. As she opened it up, she again gave Jake a look of approval. This drawer contained all of the personnel files on her and her many acquaintances she had made since leaving Chicago. There was a folder for both Malik and Juliette with the word "Deceased" written in a red marker across both of them. There was also one for Raj, Miles, the Gould brothers, one for her brother and several other names she did not recognize. Resisting temptation, she closed the drawer and moved onto the second one. This one was mostly empty but it did contain one folder that was labeled "GHT", she opened it and found a very vague letter.

She read it aloud.

Dear AD,

As we discussed, MP agrees to assist you and your movement contingent with RGHT. Please advise, failure to follow through will result in severe repercussions. Reminder, this must be kept classified due to current affairs. Once your plan is in motion, please rendezvous at our predetermined location to begin phase one.

Regards,

H.

"That's weird and cool," Jake said wide-eyed, "Let me see." She handed him the letter and continued on to the third drawer. As he read it to himself, Ayla dug around and found nothing of value.

Just as Jake was about to point something out on the letter, the heavy footsteps and creaking floorboards above their heads caused them both to freeze.

"Give me that," she whispered to Jake as she swiped the letter from him and placed both documents back into the cabinet. She slowly closed both drawers and clicked them shut as quietly as possible. They heard more creaking above them and both looked up nervously as dust from the floorboards fell after each heavy footstep. Jake reached up and pulled the light cord slowly to minimize noise. It clicked and the room went dark.

The creaking continued above, but it moved away from the door of the basement. Ayla grabbed Jake, prompting him to follow her as she crept toward the bottom of the stairs. Taking care to step softly as they made their ascent, they reached the top without making much noise. She peered through a crack in the open door to see big Juan behind the counter of the fish shop with his back toward them. He bent over and pulled out a bucket from under the counter and began cleaning off the tools used to cut and clean the day's catch. He reached into his pocket and pulled out a small rectangular yellow object that had a matching colored cord wrapped around it. He uncoiled it, placed the two ends in his ears and pushed a button on its side. They then could hear faint music playing.

Jake gasped excitedly as Ayla turned to shush him. "I think that's an MP3 player!" he whispered to her excitedly.

"A what?" she asked but quickly changed her mind, "Never mind, just go." As she motioned him out the door, he left ahead of Ayla, snuck past Juan, and left out a side entrance. Ayla quietly closed the basement door, locked it behind her, and followed Jake out of the fish shop while Juan carried on with no knowledge of their trespassing.

As they emerged out into the street, the sun had all but set. The busy daytime market had now become a tranquil evening setting. They headed toward the sound of music and people chattering. It was the tavern that Dumont had suggested they visit. Before they entered, she looked up at the hanging circular sign. Along its top it read *The Wandering Cricket*: Just below the name was a hand-painted cricket wearing a suit with a top hat carrying his luggage. They opened the door and to their surprise, they found a packed house. The open floor plan was filled with wooden tables and chairs, there was a bar with rustic stools, and the wall décor was comprised of a wide variety of miscellaneous items from taxidermy to old sports memorabilia. The people were having a great time eating, smoking, and listening to the man playing the piano. They looked around the cloudy room and eventually Jake spotted the team in the back corner where two seats were saved for them. Zoe saw the pair first and waved them over.

It was very odd for Ayla in particular. She had never seen anything like this in Chicago. The tavern was proof that there really was a class system that had developed in Los Angeles. You had the homeless people living in tent city with no way of providing themselves with food or shelter. Most of the tavern's patrons either worked for the city or made their living in the market. Ranking above them were those that worked for the governor or the United States government like city enforcers.

She didn't dwell on the demographics of Los Angeles for very long though, as the allure of the tavern was hard to resist. They made their way toward the group who were laughing and carrying on while they enjoyed a cold beer from the bar. It was so surreal for Ayla. For a moment it was like there was never a civil war or a coming conflict. She could have been meeting her friends at their favorite bar for happy hour. Jake, who must have been more excited than Ayla, was somehow already several feet ahead of her racing to the group. To his credit though, he remembered his manners before getting too far ahead and turned back to her. "I'll get us a drink, beer okay?" he asked her.

"Yea," she said with a smile. "A beer sounds great."

Before heading to the bar he returned the smile and said, "All right, be right back."

"So, what did I miss?" she asked the rest of the team as she sat down.

"Oh just sharing some stories. Like, Frank here wanted to be an actor when he was a kid," Couchman revealed.

"Really?" Ayla said astounded as Frank nodded his head. "But you're so... Frank," she said as they all shared a laugh at his expense.

Jake returned with a beer for them both, she thanked him and he then addressed the group. "So I guess they don't really have a menu but if you look over by the register there's a chalk board with what food they have. You order at the bar and they'll bring it out to you when it's done."

"Great, I'm starving. I don't remember the last time I ate at a restaurant like this, this is awesome," Ayla said excitedly.

She gave him her order first and Gabe and Zoe followed suit. While the others placed their orders, Gabe leaned over to Ayla and quietly asked, "So did you ask about us?"

"We've got a lot to talk about, but best not to do it here," she whispered back. "Let's just have fun tonight," she said.

Gabe nodded but then gave Zoe a look of uncertainty. Ayla pretended not to notice but she knew they would be disappointed to hear that what they thought was going to be their chance to get away from the war, was actually throwing them right into what will become ground zero.

The rest of the time spent at the tavern was filled with laughter, as the team enjoyed a night to themselves. They told stories of their old lives while trying not to give away any clues about their current mission to any would-be eavesdroppers. Once the food arrived, the chattering mostly stopped as the group enjoyed the first homecooked meal since well before their journey began.

They stayed in the tavern for almost two hours longer enjoying each other's company and the cold beverages on tap. "We ought to wrap this up," Ayla said looking up at the clock near the bar. "We've got a lot to talk about in the morning." She stood up and took the last sip of her beer and threw some money down on the table. They all groaned and unenthusiastically stood from the table. Couchman and Ruiz finished their drinks as Frank thanked the bartender. They exited the tavern and made their way back down the street to the fish shop that they would call home for an undetermined amount of time.

The door to the upstairs apartment was at the stop of an outdoor staircase. They all trudged up to the top and after Ayla unlocked the door, they all started to look for a comfortable place to sleep. The upstairs apartment was mostly unfurnished. There were tarnished hard wood floors and the walls had pealing white paint. In the kitchen was an old wooden table with a few chairs. There were two bedrooms: each had two cots in them. Couchman and Ruiz helped themselves to one of the rooms, claiming the two cots. Gabe and Zoe chose the other bedroom and they pushed their cots together to be a little closer for the night, just as they used to do in Chicago. That left Frank, Ayla, and Jake standing alone in what would have been the dining room just off of the kitchen. There were two twin mattresses lying on the floor, on opposite sides of the room. Frank, with his keen eye and blunt attitude spoke up first, "I think I'll take my chances on the kitchen floor." Knowing full well that Ayla and Jake had eyes for each other, he did his best to give them some privacy.

Jake was visibly excited but trying to play it cool. After his few drinks at the tavern he had gained a little liquid courage and made the first move. "So should I just slide these together?" he said in a suave tone motioning to the mattresses. Ayla who was deep in thought just stared out the window. "Hmm?" Jake said again after an awkward silence breaking Ayla's concentration.

She looked at him and after a brief moment she realized what he was purposing. "First of all, gross, look at those mattresses. Secondly, everyone would hear us, and most importantly," she said as she walked toward him, "I would need at least three dates before I would consider it." He opened his mouth to respond but she cut him off, "And no, the tavern does not count as a date." She leaned in and kissed him on the lips softly but only for a

215

moment. Jake was caught by surprise by Ayla once again and before he could say anything she started in on him again. "Plus we aren't done yet tonight."

"What are…" Jake began to speak but with snoring sounds already emanating from the bedrooms Ayla pushed her finger on her lips and shushed him for being too loud. He tried again but this time a little softer, "What do you mean we aren't done tonight?"

"Just follow me, and keep an eye out," she whispered as she reached in her pocket and pulled out the key. Although the night was fun and filled with laughter and camaraderie, in the back of her mind she kept thinking about the papers in the filing cabinet. She needed to know more. They quietly walked down the stairs to the wooden door that led to the basement headquarters of the unofficial leader of the resistance.

"What are we doing?" Jake asked in a worried manner as he drunkenly bumped into the wall making a loud banging sound.

"Shhhh, it will be fine, he's not even here," she said as the lock popped open.

"What about Juan?" he asked her.

"Don't worry, stay here and if somebody comes, give me a signal," she said calmly.

"What? What signal, what are you talking about?" Jake asked as he held in a burp.

"I don't know, whistle or something," she said as she left him at the top of the stairs. She entered the dark basement and this time instead of reaching for the light cord, she pulled out a small black flashlight that she brought with her from the mountain hideout where the rest of the team was waiting. Before she got started, she returned to the bottom of the stairs and spoke once more to Jake. "Throw me that knife," she said to him, which prompted him to turn and toss her the small blade.

She opened the drawer using Jake's method from earlier, and once again rifled through the folders until she got to her name. While holding the flashlight in her mouth she analyzed the pages. The first page she came across was basic information listing her hometown and her biometrics. Also included were some brief snippets of information on her family. The next page was her war record from the first civil war, or at least what Dumont could get his hands on as Ayla noticed there were some large gaps. The last page was her information about her residency and activities in Chicago. She closed the file and stuffed it back in the drawer. She was almost disappointed in how boring it was. She continued on and perused several more folders including Miles's and her brother's, but found nothing that stuck out.

She opened the second drawer where the cryptic letter was stored. She found a pencil and a scrap piece of paper from the desk and wrote down the clues, "MP, RGHT, H." She circled them and read the letter one more time to herself.

She moved on to the next drawer but before she could continue she heard Jake's whistle from the top of the stairs followed by another beer burp. She decided it wasn't worth the risk to continue digging. She stuffed the file back where she found it and carefully returned the pencil to the desk, trying not to leave behind any clues that she had returned. She used her flashlight to find the base of the stairs and then using the handrail for guidance, left the basement once more.

"Hey," she whispered to Jake. "What's going on?" she asked him.

"Nothing, it's just too dangerous. Plus I'm shot; I can't keep my eyes open," he whispered back to her. "And I have to pee," he continued on, slurring his speech.

She rolled her eyes at him, which she found herself doing

more as she got to know him better. She poked fun at him. "Light weight," she whispered as Jake gave her a look of disbelief. But she too thought she had spent enough time snooping; after all, she didn't know what tomorrow would bring. "All right, let's go," she said.

"What else did you find?" he asked her as they climbed the stairs to the apartment.

"Nothing new really," she said, "just wanted to be sure."

As they returned to the apartment, the rhythmic snores and heavy breathing made it clear that the others had slept through all of their sneaking around. Jake had already started making himself comfortable on his small twin mattress. Before he could say goodnight, Ayla had slid her mattress over to his. She could see the look on his face and before he was able to make any assumptions, Ayla set him straight, "Don't get any ideas there, drunky." She lay down with her back against his chest and snuggled up next to him. She grabbed his arm and placed it around her stomach and placed her hand on his. She closed her eyes and felt comforted being in his arms.

"Goodnight, Ayla," Jake whispered in her ear and held her closer.

"I'm glad you're here, Jake," she said in a soft voice.

"Me too," he replied as they both eventually drifted off to sleep.

Chapter 32

The City of Angels

"Ahem." Ayla was awakened by the clearing of Frank's throat while still wrapped in Jake's arms. Slightly embarrassed, she slowly rose to her feet as Jake gradually came to.

"What's going on Frank?" she asked him as she rubbed her face.

"Nothing, I just figured you'd want to be up before the others," he said.

"Yeah, good call, thanks," she said as she patted him on the shoulder as she walked by.

The sun was starting to creep through the dirty windows and was gradually warming up the cool apartment. As the sun rays crept in, you could see the dust particles floating through the air of the seldom used living space.

There was one amenity the team had been without for some time and that was a bathroom. As Ayla made her way toward it, the floor boards creaked beneath her feet. She closed the door behind her and turned the faucet on. To her surprise, the water was somewhat warm unlike her old bathroom back in Chicago. She cupped her hands under the water and rinsed her face off in the sink and as she patted herself dry, she caught a glimpse of herself in the aged mirror. How different she looked she thought to herself. She examined her very short very light-colored hair and chuckled. "Hopefully that doesn't last too long," she said aloud as she turned her head, investigating the sides of her haircut. She placed the towel back on the rack and opened the door where Jake was waiting for his turn.

"Morning," he said to her with a smile.

"Hi," she said as she smiled back. The two crossed paths without saying anything more.

Ayla returned to the living room where Frank was patiently waiting for his next set of directions. "Why don't you go wake everybody up, I'll go see if I can find us some breakfast." Frank nodded and the two headed in opposite directions.

Ayla made her way back down to the first floor where the employees of the fish shop were just starting to get ready for another day of activity. She stood aimlessly for a moment in the middle of the room, looking for any familiar faces. Just then, she noticed Juan walking toward a row of aprons hanging from hooks on the wall. "Hey, Juan," she said to him.

Juan played it cool. He was used to dealing with Dumont's secret visitors. "We don't open for another fifteen minutes, ma'am, but I'll be glad to help you out when that happens." He said to her in the same booming voice that yelled at her while she stood too close to his chopping block.

Ayla quickly picked up on his act and joined in, "Oh, well do you know where I can get some food, other than fish?"

"There's a bakery across the street," he said as he tied his apron around his waist.

Ayla thanked him and made her way across the street and found a cozy little shop selling freshly made baked goods. It was so surprising to Ayla at how much more Los Angeles had going for it than Chicago. She ordered some food for her team and waited on the cashier bagging up her items. As she looked around, the people began to fill up the small marketplace. She thought it odd that there weren't really any city enforcers out or any Government patrols even though Miles had warned them that they would be lurking. She assumed that's why Dumont picked this place as his headquarters. They must just think everyone here is only interested in buying and selling, she thought.

"Miss." Her thoughts were interrupted as the small old woman behind the counter handed her a brown bag full of assorted pastries. Ayla handed her the rest of the money Dumont left for her and returned back to the fish shop apartment.

She headed back upstairs and placed the bag of miscellaneous breakfast staples on the table and the team slowly gathered around to see their choices. As they picked through the freshly made items, they begin to poke and prod Ayla for information. "So what's the plan?" Jake asked as he ripped apart a croissant and began chewing on it as the others looked on anxiously while getting their food.

Not really sure how to begin, Ayla nervously looked toward Gabe and Zoe as she chewed her bagel. "Why don't you two go for a walk. It's actually really nice out there; not like Chicago at all." Ayla said to them. They took the hint and gathered some of their stuff and headed down to the streets. Ayla waited for the door to close and then turned to address her fellow rebels. "The less they know the better," she said.

"So what did Dumont say?" Ruiz asked.

"He didn't let me in on his grand plan but he did tell us our role and he asked me to trust him," she said.

Jake could see the uncertainty on her face. "So, do you trust him?" he asked.

"No, but in this case we don't have a choice," she said. "We're staying put and we're bringing Miles and everyone else here to fight and hope that draws them in. Dumont showed me some places that'll be of value, but ultimately he left it up to me to figure out how to get their attention." She looked around the room and could see the excitement on their faces to not have to walk back through the Angeles County forest. She paused and waited to see if anyone had any questions or comments but besides a Ruiz and Couchman high five, they were ready to hear more. "Dumont wants us to bring the fighting here and that's really all I was told." Since she had no idea what it meant, she decided not to bring up the letter they had found.

Couchman spoke up first, "So our mission is to take over Los Angeles?"

"Pretty much it, yea," she said.

"Now, stupid question," Ruiz spoke up this time, "How are we going to do that?"

Ayla unfolded the map on the table revealing the circled locations she and Dumont discussed. "Like I said before, he's leaving it up to us to come up with a plan. I haven't really thought out the details yet, but I think if we took down the enforcer barracks first, that would definitely get their attention." She said boldly as the rest of the team was taken aback by her suggestion. She could sense their apprehension and decided to sugarcoat it a little, "Look when the rest of us get here, I'm guessing it will be a cakewalk all right."

"Yea, about that?" Jake asked, "How's the rest of the gang getting here?"

"I'm not quite sure about that yet either. Dumont told me he's going to send one of his people here to help us get started; I'm hoping they have a plan for that. So for now we're going to have to wait it out until we hear from them. I don't want to make any moves with just the five of us here," Ayla explained to them.

"You mean seven of us?" Frank added referencing Gabe and

Zoe.

Ayla corrected herself, "Yes, seven of us, thank you Frank." She said as she was really starting to appreciate Frank's no-nonsense attitude.

Just then, there was a knock at the door. The team looked at each other and then scrambled. Ayla quickly grabbed the map on the table, folded it back up, and placed it away in her pack which she hid in a cabinet under the sink. The boys all hid behind corners with their guns drawn as Ayla reached for the door handle. She gave her team one last look and placed her hand in the air to remind them to stay calm. Ayla placed one hand on the knob, while the other clutched her pistol. "Who is it?" she asked in a cordial tone as she looked back at Jake who showed his disapproval of her greeting. She shrugged her shoulders and mouthed, "I don't know," admitting that it was a poor choice of words.

A woman's voice answered, "A friend."

She opened the door just a crack and peered out ready to draw her weapon if necessary. Much like when she answered Miles's knock on her apartment door back in Chicago she was surprised to see the face of young Ellie Dumont whom she sent off from the Vegas Airport to find her grandfather.

"Can I come in?" Ellie asked.

Ayla opened the door all the way and motioned to her friends that the coast was clear. They all breathed a collective sigh of relief.

"When Dumont said he would be sending one of his people over to coordinate with us I wasn't expecting you," Ayla said as Ellie entered and looked around the room. She certainly looked different than the last time Ayla had seen her. One major difference, and for obvious reasons, was she was wearing street clothes as opposed to her combat gear she was wearing before. Her blonde hair, which was surprisingly long, was braided down her back. Ayla wondered how she had managed to stuff it all under her hat back in Vegas. As she closed the door, Ayla peered outside quickly to ensure there was nothing out of the ordinary. "You look different," Ayla said to her as she spotted a brown paper bag she was carrying by her side.

"I could say the same about you, General." She said as Ayla gave her a perplexing look. Ellie looked toward Ayla's hair and pointed to her own head.

"Oh right, the hair," Ayla replied as she combed her fingers through her short, white hair.

"So what's in the bag, Private Dumont?" Jake asked.

"Oh, actually it's Colonel now Jake," Ellie said with confidence as she sat down and placed her bag on the table. "Thanks to you sending me on my little adventure, my grandpa thought I deserved a little promotion. Oh, and this is lunch," she said as she motioned toward the bag. "Sandwiches."

"Hey, that's not fair. I want to rank up," Couchman said in a whiney voice.

Ayla rolled her eyes. "Fine, you can all be captains now," she said.

"Don't forget about Hudson," Frank added.

"Yes, he can be a captain too," she said, satisfying Frank's team first attitude.

Ellie sensed Ayla's frustration and decided to change the subject. "So, fill me in, what's going on?"

Ayla knelt down to the cupboard where she left her pack, retrieved it, and pulled out the map that they hastily hid away when Ellie knocked on the door. She then rolled it back out onto the table. "I was just explaining what Dumont had planned for us," she said as she sat down next to her.

"So what is the plan?" Ellie asked as she opened the brown bag and pulled out a sandwich wrapped in tan parchment paper. She motioned toward the other team members, urging them to eat but as they all just had breakfast they declined the offer. As she looked back to Ayla, she continued to unfold her food and took a big bite of her sandwich.

"You don't know?" Ayla asked her. Ellie shook her head as she chewed.

She quickly swallowed most of it and said, "I was told to come to here and find you and a small team. They weren't kidding when they said small," she said as she looked around the room. "Where's everyone else?"

"Outside the city, north of here, about a day's walk," she replied. "So the first part of the plan is getting them all here. I was hoping you had some ideas for that."

Ellie leaned back in her chair and put her hand up to her face as she took a couple moments to think to herself. The rest of the crew began to wonder what she was doing before she spoke up. "North of here?" She asked.

"Yea, we came down through the Angeles County Road," Ayla said, which drew a confusing look from Ellie.

That was when Frank chimed in. "Angeles Forest Highway," he said correcting her.

"Yea, that one," Ayla said as she pointed to Frank, to which he nodded back to her.

Ellie too nodded her head and paused for a moment. "There's a supply convoy that comes in every couple weeks, a few army trucks with minimal security and usually a semi. They come from the capital, down 210 and they use the Pasadena checkpoint," she said aloud as she traced the route on the map with her finger.

"Where exactly is everybody else?" she asked.

Ayla looked to her man Frank again. "Mount Lukens Truck Trail." Ellie gave him a confused look. "Right here," Frank said as he pointed to the location on the map that was sprawled out in front of her.

"210 is right here." Ellie pointed to the highway on the map. Ayla stood up and saw just how close Highway 210 actually came to Miles and the rest of the team.

"This has got to be the play," Ayla said as they all huddled around the map. "We'd have more than enough man power to take them down. It would be the best way to get them in the city without being seen. What do you know about this area here?" Ayla asked as she pointed toward a section of Highway 210.

Ellie tilted her head to see the area Ayla was referring to. "It's hard to say, Los Angeles is so big and there's pockets of people living all over the place. If I had to guess based on what I know, I'd say it's probably pretty desolate over there." They all stared at the map for a few minutes until Ayla spoke up. "Right here."

"*Devil's Gate Reservoir*," Couchman said as the name seemed to spark a little fear in him. "Why do you have to pick that place?"

"It's a perfect place for an ambush. Look, this is JPL, the Jet Propulsion Laboratory. That has to be empty, right?" she asked Ellie.

"They barely have enough people to patrol the streets," Ellie said.

Jake with his tech background was a bit more of an expert. "Most people in the scientific community sided with us. A lot of them didn't make it. I highly doubt they have that many working for them up in Seattle."

"All right, then that's that. We'll get everybody together at

JPL. We'll have to send word to Miles so he can meet us there; we grab the trucks, and…" she paused and looked to Ellie. "How often do these trucks come again?"

"Once a week and I think they already came this week so we've got some time," Ellie said.

"Frank, I'm going to need you to be the one that goes and gets the rest of the team to JPL. You know the route the best," Ayla said to him. "You'll leave tonight as long as we can figure out a plan to make this work," she concluded and he nodded confirming his understanding.

After studying the map and talking with Ellie about the area, Ayla addressed the small team once again. "I want all hands on deck for this. We need to come up with a plan to get this convoy to stop on the highway while salvaging the vehicles. Everyone take a look at the map and brainstorm some ideas. We'll eat lunch and then come back together to see what we've got." With no further questions, Ellie began passing out the sandwiches she brought and the team sat in silence as they ate and thought about the plan.

After several minutes of thinking and listening to the sounds of each other eating, Couchman spoke up first. "What about playing dead?" he asked and seeing the confused looks he was getting, he decided to elaborate. "You know, one of us lies in the highway, they see a dead body, they stop and investigate, and then we attack."

Ayla thought for a moment, then answered, "There's no guarantee they would stop. They could drive right by or run you over for all we know. We can come back to that one." They all kept eating and thinking.

Out of nowhere, Jake gasped loudly, but by doing so he inadvertently began to choke on his sandwich. What ensued was a coughing fit that lasted almost a minute with Jake holding his finger in the air asking the team to wait while he choked on his bread. The coughing finally subsided and they all had a laugh at his eating mishap.

"You okay there, Jake?" Ayla asked him with a smile on her face.

"Yes," he said while clearing his throat one last time. "I've got an idea."

"Okay, let's hear it," she said to him.

"We've still got an army Humvee," he said with no follow up.

"And?" Ayla asked him.

"Okay, so we get the Humvee on the same road as the supply convoy, and pop the hood. We get some people in the uniforms from the guys at the truck trail place. Now we've got a broken down Humvee and soldiers in need of assistance." He waited for approval with a proud smile on his face.

The rest of the team waited to take their cue from their General. Ayla paused for a moment and leaned back in her chair and took another bite of her sandwich. She finally spoke up after she swallowed her food. "I like it. It's as good a plan as any. My only issue is we have to make sure the entire convoy stops but I think we can make it work."

Ellie chimed in, "Maybe we can combine Couchman's idea. Broken down Humvee, maybe there's an injury to someone. You said you have a few uniforms, right?" Jake nodded and she continued. "You could have the Humvee taking up one lane and the two uniformed soldiers in the other lane, so they can't just pass through. Oh, I got it!" she exclaimed with excitement. "Someone has a heart attack; they stop in the middle of the road, pull the victim out and do CPR!"

"Okay, let's stick with that, I like it. Nice work," Ayla said.

"Do you have any connections within the city enforcers? If we're going to do this, that has to be our first target," Ayla asked as she pointed to the map where the barracks were marked.

"Let me do some digging around and see what I can find out," Ellie said.

"Wait a minute," Ayla said interrupting Ellie's thoughts. "We're getting ahead of ourselves. When exactly do these convoys come into town?" she asked her.

"It can vary but usually Monday morning. They typically are bringing supplies in for the week," she said.

Ayla getting excited said, "Okay, this is perfect. Those buildings for JPL are probably all empty. They'll be big enough for us to house everybody in one spot. Frank, when you bring the team back, that's where we'll be, inside one of those warehouses. Ellie, you said the trucks bring supplies. Do they bring them to the enforcer barracks?"

"Every week," Ellie said.

"So that's our way in. We set up our ambush here," she said as she pointed to the section of highway near *Devil's Gate Reservoir*. We'll take the supply trucks using the fake heart attack play, we then load up the entire team, go straight to the barracks under the guise of delivering the supplies and take it by force." She sat down somewhat out of breath from the excitement and took a bite of her sandwich. "Man, I love it when a plan comes together," she said with a mouth full.

"You also avoid the checkpoint that way too," Ellie added in.

Just then the door burst open which caused the entire team to draw their guns and point them toward the action. It was Zoe and Gabe who had been gone all morning. They entered the

229

house laughing but it quickly turned to fear as they were staring down the barrels of five pistols. "I totally forgot you guys were here," Ayla said as she put her gun down on the table. The rest of the team followed suit while shaking their heads at the near catastrophe.

"What are they doing here?" Ellie asked.

"They aren't supposed to be," Ayla said.

"So any news on what we're going to be doing?" Gabe asked as he walked past the table eyeing the map and all the notes the team had scribbled on it.

During the excitement of planning the next phase of the revolution, Ayla had totally forgotten that Gabe and Zoe followed them here looking for an escape and that she still hadn't told them that Los Angeles was about to become a bit more dangerous. "Why don't you guys relax a bit, I need to have a chat with Gabe and Zoe." Ayla said as she rolled up the map, trying to hide as much information as possible from her two former roommates. This was done for two reasons, one Ayla knew from experience that you can't be too trusting of anyone no matter how close you were to them, but also if either of them was to be captured and questioned, they wouldn't be able to tell the army their plans. "Let's go over here," she said as she pointed toward one of the bedrooms.

"What's going on, Ayla? You're making me nervous," Zoe asked in a suspicious tone.

They sat down on the small cot. It was an old army cot that someone had painted white. Most of the paint was chipping and the springs made an annoying sound as they sat down on the green cushion that covered them. Ayla sat down against the wall across from them and they were now looking face to face.

Ayla looked toward the ground before she started speaking,

"I know you guys had hoped to find somewhere you could call a home here in Los Angeles." As she finished her sentence, her eyes rose and met theirs and by the look she gave, Zoe and Gabe already knew they were in for bad news.

"Oh no," Zoe said.

"It's not going to happen here. In fact, as your friend, I would advise you to get as far away from here as you can," Ayla said.

"What are we going to do now?" Zoe asked in a panic. "This is not how I want to bring my baby into the world," she said as she started sobbing into Gabe's shoulder.

"Oh my god, you guys are going to have a baby?" she asked excitedly. Zoe just nodded with tears flowing down her cheek. Ayla got up and moved closer to them and gave them another group hug. "I'm so happy for you guys."

Zoe started laughing, "This is not the way I wanted to tell you," she said as she wiped the tears away from her cheeks and with one of her arms wrapped around her small baby bump, she continued, "What are we going to do?"

Gabe, realizing he needed to be strong for his expecting wife, placed his arm around her and spoke with confidence, "We'll go somewhere else." He looked to Ayla for confirmation to which she nodded in agreement. "We'll get out of this city, and find somewhere we can raise our baby away from all this craziness," he said as he rubbed her shoulder.

"I'll speak with the Ellie and Juan, maybe they can get you out of the city," Ayla said trying to reassure her friends as Zoe nodded rubbing away another tear before it rolled down her cheek. "I'll give you guys a minute. I'm going to go back into the kitchen," Ayla said as she rose to her feet. "I'm sorry I don't have better news for you," she said as she walked out of the bedroom.

As Ayla walked back into the room, Jake called to her from

his seat at the table, "Hey, Ay— I mean General." Catching himself from calling her by her first name as he did in private. He stuttered and continued, "We have another idea about the plan." She placed her fingers over her mouth signaling him to be quiet. She motioned with her head toward the bedroom making the rest of the group aware she didn't want Gabe and Zoe to know more than what they needed to.

She approached Ellie. "So, can you get them out of town?" she asked, again nodding her head toward the bedroom.

"General, I've been planning on how to get people into L.A, not necessarily how to get them out," she said.

"Ask around, you must know people who are smuggling things in and out of here right?" Ayla asked.

"I'll see what I can do," Ellie said hesitantly.

"Good, because I love those two but I can't have any distractions, and that's what they're becoming. So see what you can find out," she said, keeping the real reason there was more urgency to herself.

As Ayla finished her request, Ellie nodded her head. Ayla continued to stand and stare at her. After a moment of awkward nothingness, Ellie asked, "Now?"

"Yes, now. Go. The sooner the better, this is happening fast, Frank is leaving tonight and we only have less than a week to get our stuff together," Ayla said.

"Oh okay. I'll come back tonight hopefully with some news," Ellie said as she grabbed her things and began walking out the door.

"Wait. Take Couchman and Ruiz with you. We need to start getting our bearings here." As the two soldiers walked toward the door they concealed their pistols. "Start getting a lay of the land," she said as they walked past her and out the door. "And bring back dinner," she yelled one last order as they headed out.

Now, all that remained in the house were Frank, Jake, Ayla, Gabe and Zoe. The moment of serenity was interrupted by a growing commotion outside. The regular sounds of the outdoor market grew louder and louder until it sounded more like a mob with screams and yelling. The five remaining in the upstairs apartment all looked toward one another with confusion. They sat up and made their way toward the windows but before they got close enough to see, the sound of gunfire popped loudly and was followed by screams from the crowd. Ayla assumed the worst; she expected to see Ellie, Couchman, and Ruiz dead in the street. She ran the rest of the way to the window with her hand on her pistol that was tucked in the back of her pants.

They all peered outside and saw a small group of Los Angeles city enforcers. Ayla counted nine. She was relieved to see her soldiers looking on from the crowd from just below the stairs. Her attention now focused back on the enforcers. They were dressed similarly to the Chicago enforcers but they had a cleaner look to them, as if their standard blue pants and black bulletproof vests and shirts were brand new. Some of them looked like they were straight out of combat, while others looked like they had never fired a weapon before. They were obviously a mix of people who loved the job and others who were just going through the motions.

Her focus was interrupted as one of the more experienced looking enforcers fired his rifle in the air three times, sending the crowd into a panic and dispersing into the nearby streets. The other enforcers were dragging reluctant citizens and forcing them into the back of a camouflaged truck with a covered bed. Since there were no bodies in the street, the team all assumed that the first gunshots they heard must have been from the same enforcer shooting more warning shots. It appeared as if they were wrapping up whatever they were doing. Ellie looked up to the apartment and caught Ayla's eyes to which Ayla motioned with her head implying that they needed to get out of there as soon as possible. Ellie nodded and the three soldiers took off in the opposite direction of the enforcers. Again, the moment was interrupted, this time by a single gunshot which caused Zoe to gasp in fear and sulk to the floor. Ayla looked back to the enforcer and saw that he had killed one of the detainees right in the street. The man looked around, put his pistol away, and returned to the vehicle. The plume of black exhaust that spewed from the tailpipe upon ignition seemed to hover over the woman's body as the truck drove away from the scene.

Ayla ducked down in the kitchen and sat on the floor. She pulled Jake down with her who had been peering out the same window. Frank slid down the wall and joined the rest of the team on the kitchen floor. "I guess Los Angeles isn't that much different than Chicago after all," she said in a deflating tone. The event was a stark reminder to them all that, although the last couple of days in Los Angeles seemed like a small vacation, they were indeed in the middle of a dangerous conflict where the slightest mistake could get them all captured or killed.

Ayla looked around the room at the other three and they all were reflecting on the moment. Frank and Jake sat silently staring straight ahead. Meanwhile, Gabe was consoling Zoe, who before this event, desperately wanted to find peace, and now was just overwhelmed. Gabe had his arm around her shoulders and pressed a kiss against her head as she shook in fear.

Ayla didn't exactly know what the others were thinking in this moment but for her it reignited the fire within. Watching an innocent life be taken was a cruel reminder of why they were in

Los Angeles. She decided she would capitalize on this moment and from here on out, the vacation was over. No more enjoying the town, no more croissants from the bakery, and no more drinking at the tavern.

A few hours later, Ellie, Couchman and Ruiz all returned from their outing into the city. As they entered the upstairs apartment, Ellie came in first followed by the other two, who set a couple of paper bags full of food down on the table. "So what did we find out there?" Ayla asked, regarding Gabe and Zoe.

"Well, not much," she said tiredly. "No one is willing to risk it. I did find somewhere they might be able to wait everything out in town and get out of your hair for a bit."

"Is it safe?" Ayla asked her.

"Is anywhere going to be safe after next week?" Ellie asked her in return.

Just then, Gabe entered the kitchen. "What's going on?" he asked.

Ellie and Ayla exchanged looks and Ayla decided to let him in on the discussion. "We're just trying to find somewhere you and Zoe will be safe," she said.

"And?" he asked her.

"We don't really have a plan, yet. We can't smuggle you out, and pretty soon it will be too dangerous for you here in the city," she said to him as the others watched on.

Zoe then came into the fray. "Why do you have to smuggle us out? Why can't we just leave? No one knows who we are," she said somewhat frantically.

"I'm afraid that's not an option, Zoe," Ayla said to her. Before she could ask why, Ayla continued, "Maybe you'll be able to walk out of here without any problem, but what if you're stopped and questioned? Or worse they take you somewhere and

235

torture you? I just don't think I can handle knowing that more of my friends are in danger because they know me," she said to them referring to, of course, Raj being captured and Malik and Juliette being gunned down in Chicago. What she told them was mostly true; however, she also couldn't risk the entire revolution on not knowing, when pressed or threatened, that Gabe and Zoe could keep what they know a secret.

"So, what are we going to do?" Gabe asked.

"For now, you'll just stay here, out of sight," Ayla said to them.

The team ate their dinner and shared a few laughs and tears. Each member was there for a different reason. Ruiz, Couchman, Frank, and Jake would all tell you that they were there to finish what they started, but in reality, they each had their own stories to tell. They were all around the same age as Ayla and would have been young adults during the government crackdown on C.A.T. and the fighting that followed.

Couchman was a car enthusiast. He loved working on classic cars with his dad and was planning on becoming a mechanic when he finished high school. He was eighteen when the military showed up to his school and burned down the auto-body shop and arrested his teacher for speaking the truth about the human rights violations that were happening. He later would hear about how his teacher was executed and that was when he decided to join the resistance.

Ruiz, like Miles, was a career military man who had bounced around the country from base to base bringing his family with him. He was married with two small kids and had already had war experience as a young twenty-something army specialist. When he was called into New York City from Fort Hood, he left his family behind. Ruiz was actually sent there to fight against the revolution but decided to abandon the fight when the government decided to use lethal force on its own citizens. By the time he finally made it back to Fort Hood, his family had vanished along with the other families of soldiers who joined the revolution. In the years after the war ended, he tried finding them but sadly was unsuccessful.

Everyone knew Jake was into computers and he helped the revolution by being a part of the technical side of the war. Part of why Ayla was attracted to him was his nerdy intelligence. What people didn't know was that before the country descended into chaos, he was actually a very successful PC gamer. As a young man, he was on the cusp of becoming a sponsored professional gamer. He loved building his own PC's for his friends and family, and even sold some out of his parent's garage. At some point, the United States Government decided that the use of personal computers was a threat to their power and control; a tool to spread information and to organize protests. After the government shut down the major social media outlets, they came after anyone that was linked to the spreading of antigovernment messages, which Jake had started doing at some point. They tracked his IP address to his parents' house. Once they realized what was happening, Jake's parents rushed him out the back door and told him to run and hide. The last he saw of them was when they were forced into the back of the camouflaged army truck and driven away. Afraid to return home, Jake joined the revolution to continue his fight.

Frank Tidwell, who remained quite mysterious to the team, was kind of a loner and an avid outdoorsman. He had a house and several acres of wooded land in Northern California where he lived with his two chocolate labs. When he wasn't out exploring his own property, he usually was out on a hunting trip at the popular destinations across the country. He was an avid fan of the Second Amendment and when the United States government suspended the right to bear arms, that's when he decided enough was enough.

Dinner lasted longer than it normally did. Each team member knew they'd have to say goodbye to Frank when it was over and although they all assumed they would see him again in a few days, in the back of their minds they all knew there was a real possibility that he might not make it there. All it would take is one city enforcer to think he looked suspicious. But all good things must end and as the conversations slowed and the laughs died down, Frank began gearing up for his long journey back to Miles and the rest of the team, deep in the Angeles Forest.

Frank slid his backpack over his shoulders and looked out the window. "I suppose it's dark enough for me to get going," he said as he looked back to the others. They all said their goodbyes and Ayla shook his hand and wished him luck.

She followed him out the door and closed it behind her. The two of them stood on the landing of the stairs that led to the upstairs apartment. She wanted to run through the plan one more time before she sent him on his way. "What's your name?" she asked him.

"My name is Robert Foster, I'm from a small settlement in Yosemite."

"Yosemite?" she asked him.

"I used to love going there and I heard there are a lot of small communities in the National Parks doing well," he said to her.

"Okay, Rob, what are you doing in Los Angeles?" she asked him

"I'm looking for my daughter, she ran off about a month ago with her boyfriend and I came to get her back," he said.

"Well, I don't see her, where is she?" she asked as if she was interrogating him.

To her surprise, Frank's eyes began to well up and his chin quivered slightly and he spoke as if he had experienced real loss, "She... She made it very clear she wants nothing to do with her family." Wiping away his tears he again looked Ayla in the eye.

"Damn, Frank. You're good," she said somberly as she put her hand on his shoulder," maybe you should have been an actor. Good luck. We'll see you in a few days." He nodded and headed down the stairs.

She watched him descend the stairway and disappear down the dimly lit streets of the market area. She wondered where all that emotion came from. Was he just a good actor? She asked herself, or was that pain real? Those questions would all have to wait as the mission was all that really mattered. She waited on the landing for a few more minutes and then went back inside to join the others.

After the excitement of Frank's departure, Zoe and Gabe went to their room for the night, and Couchman and Ruiz went to their bedroom that they had claimed earlier. Ellie was gathering her things to leave, which prompted Ayla to ask her if she had a safe place for the night. "My place isn't too far from here," she said.

"Maybe you should just stay here with us from now on," Ayla suggested. "Things are starting to heat up here and I would really feel better if I knew where everyone was."

"What about all of my things?" she asked.

"We still have some time. We'll make a trip over there during the day where we can hide out in the open with everyone. We'll get your essentials and then you can stay here until we make our move to JPL." Ayla could tell that Ellie didn't want to leave. After all, she had been here in the city living alone with just her mysterious grandfather, who was now gone. The small group had become pretty close and Ellie fit in just right with them.

"Okay, thanks, General." Ellie said with a smile. She went into the same bedroom as Couchman and Ruiz, where Couchman graciously gave up his cot and slept on the floor. This finally gave Jake and Ayla the alone time they both desired but could only express through eye contact throughout the evening. They once again pressed their mattresses together and quietly embraced each other.

The next morning, Ayla awoke lying on Jake's shirtless chest, her light-colored hair brushed his face slightly which in turn, woke him up as well. "Good morning," he said to her.

"Good morning," she replied as she stretched up to kiss him which caused her bare shoulders to peak out from under their blanket.

This was followed by a third voice. "Good Morning!" The voice, which belonged to Couchman, startled both Jake and Ayla. They both looked up and were greeted by the rest of the team staring at them in the kitchen. It would seem that in their passionate evening, they either both forgot where they were and who they were with, or didn't care. They were met with a mixture of reactions. Ellie was laughing, Gabe and Zoe had shocked expressions, and Couchman had a smile on his face that no one knew he was capable of making. Ayla pulled the blanket up over her shoulders and then over her head in embarrassment. Ellie, feeling sympathetic but still laughing, decided to help out the red-faced couple. "Okay, as I am technically second in command here, I order everyone with clothes on to exit the kitchen area," she said with fits of laughter.

"Oh come on, you're no fun," Couchman said as Ellie

pushed the group out of the kitchen to give the General and Jake some privacy.

After putting themselves together, Jake and Ayla joined the others in the living room area. "Hey guys," Couchman said in a sly manner.

"Okay, you've had your fun," Ayla said to him. She continued to address the group. "We're all adults here. Please can we keep this between us here and our little team?" The group could sense both her embarrassment and her urgency and they all nodded in agreement.

After a short pause, Couchman raised his hand. "Yes?" Ayla asked him with a hint of annoyance in her voice.

"What about Frank? He's on the team, can I tell him?" he asked like a kid who just learned a secret from his friend.

"Frank already knows," Jake answered for the general and Ayla gave him a look. "Well, he sort of knows," he said as Couchman slumped in his chair looking deflated.

Ayla wasn't quite sure how to feel about how everything transpired so she decided to focus on the mission in the hopes to move past her humiliating moment. She looked back toward the group and once again addressed them as a unit, "Since we are all in agreement, we need to discuss what our next move is. If everything goes smoothly, Frank should get to the team sometime today. We'll have to assume it will take them a day to mobilize." She paused and thought for a moment. "I think we should leave at midnight tonight."

"I'm not sure that's such a good idea," Ellie said. Ayla waited for her to explain herself. "There are curfews around here, and patrols enforcing the rules. No one is ever out at night we'd stick out like a sore thumb," she concluded.

"Okay, Colonel Dumont, what do you purpose?" Ayla

decided to give her a chance to prove herself.

"Our best bet is to leave the same way you came here. Hide in the open. Blend in during the day," she said.

"You're the expert on Los Angeles so that's what we'll do," Ayla said. "We'll leave tomorrow morning when the market area starts to pick up. We can't travel in a group though. We should plot out a route on the map and leave two at a time. Ellie, you and Couchman can go first. Zoe and Gabe, you will wait ten minutes and then you'll leave, and Jake and I will go last. Ruiz, I want you to go with them," she said looking toward Gabe and Zoe. "It's too risky to go in a group of three so you'll leave just after they do, maybe a couple minutes and just trail them and make sure they're safe." Ruiz nodded. "In the meantime, Ellie you go back to your place and get the rest of your stuff."

Chapter 33

Getting the Gang Back Together

The next morning arrived and the team gathered up their belongings to head out to the rendezvous point. As they discussed the day prior, they left in small groups to hide in the open, with Jake and Ayla leaving last. Ayla watched each group leave and with each departure, her anxiety grew. Her unease was probably at its highest when she watched Gabe and Zoe leave. She knew they had the least amount of experience and was worried they might give the team away. After they left, she pulled Ruiz aside to talk to him privately. "I'm hoping you don't run into any problems. But if you do, they cannot give away what we're doing." She paused and looked Ruiz in the eyes.

He was a bit surprised by her sternness and he asked her "Just what are you trying to tell me? Are you asking me to do what I think you're asking me to do?"

"No!" Ayla said, shocked. "What kind of monster do you think I am? I'm just saying, do whatever you have to do. If something happens make a scene, start a riot, anything."

By the time they finished their chat, it was time for him to go. Jake, who had been watching Gabe and Zoe, pointed him in the right direction and wished him luck.

Now it was time for Jake and Ayla to wait their turn. "Are you ready?" Jake asked her.

She looked around the apartment one last time and looked at

him and said, "I should be asking you that question."

They picked up their snacks and walked out the door and headed in the same direction of the rest of the crew. They first walked through the busy market leaving the fish shop behind. They continued down the road passing the small shops and bakeries and past where the person was shot by the Los Angeles enforcers.

Once they made it out of the market, they again entered into the tent city where the scores of humans were struggling to survive. Then they came to the abandoned suburbs where forgotten homes were boarded up and overgrown with vegetation from neglect. Out in this part of Los Angeles, there weren't many people around. It was oddly quiet and peaceful. Jake and Ayla used this time on their walk to get to know each other more. They talked about their childhoods, who they were before things went south, and where they were stationed during the first war. Jake told her all about how his career as a professional gamer fell just short because the war. Ayla teased him as he tried to explain how professional gaming had evolved over the years.

Finally, they made it to the overpass where they were to stage their takeover of the incoming supply trucks. Jake pointed to the footprints that led through the mud underneath the bridge and said, "Look, the others must've passed through here." They followed the path under the bridge and continued on to the building it led to.

The abandoned warehouse was once the property of the Jet Propulsion Laboratory. It was a large building, with dark gray exterior walls that had many spots of rust and disrepair. It was still daylight out so they kept a watchful eye on their surroundings, making sure they weren't being watched. Ayla pushed open the old metal door, she was sure at some point it was in better working order but now it made a loud squealing sound as she opened it. They crept inside the large, mostly empty, warehouse. The light shined through the windows illuminating square patches on the dirty concrete floor. There were no signs of their friends until Ellie and Couchman propped their heads up from behind some old waste containers. "Where are the others?" Ayla asked them.

"You two are the first ones to come back," Ellie said.

"I knew something like this was going to happen. That's why I wanted them out of the picture. This is so infuriating," Ayla said as she placed her hands on her head out of frustration. "I take it you haven't heard from Ruiz either?" she asked the other two. Couchman shook his head indicating that they had not seen him. Ayla was the most noticeably upset member of the team; she paced around the open space as the four revolutionaries anxiously waited for the other three people to arrive. On the exterior, she mainly painted the picture that she was upset that the mission could have been jeopardized, but inside she was also worried about her friends and what may have happened to them.

After what seemed like hours, there finally was some action. Through the same metal door that Jake and Ayla entered, the sound of metal creaking and moving echoed in the empty space. As the door slowly opened, a sliver of light was laid out on the dark and dusty concrete floor. Not knowing who exactly was entering, the team drew their guns and aimed them toward the sound as they took defensive positions behind the waste containers. The first thing they saw was the end of a pistol. Whoever was coming in was being equally as cautious as the team inside. Finally, after a few suspenseful seconds, Ayla realized it was Ruiz. She still waited though to ensure he was alone and it was safe. Once Ruiz was able to see inside and realized there was no apparent danger, he holstered his gun and closed the door behind him. He turned around and saw his four friends standing there after they emerged from their hiding spots.

"Are you trying to give me a heart attack?" Ruiz asked as he was startled seeing them all standing there.

"Why are you so jumpy?" Ayla asked him. "And where are Gabe and Zoe? And where have you been?" Ayla flooded Ruiz with questions demanding to know what happened during his journey across the city.

"I followed them just like you said," Ruiz began to tell his story. "I followed them through the market, everything was going fine. When we got to tent city there was some guy preaching. There was a huge crowd of people, and they went right into it. I tried to keep up with them but the crowd got bigger and bigger and next thing I knew I lost them. I searched around for hours trying not to give myself away. I don't think they ever planned on meeting us here."

As she usually did when she was given news she wasn't prepared to hear, Ayla took a few moments to herself to absorb everything Ruiz had told her. "Well, I tried to tell them this would be the safest place," she paused again and looked at the four remaining teammates and continued on, "I guess we just hope they blend in and can get out of town on their own. We can't derail the plan for two civilians." Ayla tried to stay unemotional about her friends' departures, but she couldn't help but feel slightly irked that they lied to her and left so recklessly.

Jake could sense Ayla's uneasiness about the entire situation and decided to speak up to get her back on track. "So, what do we do now?" he asked her.

Ayla snapped back to reality and answered him promptly. "Now we wait and hope Frank was able to get to Miles and that they're on their way."

Couchman was next to speak up. "I don't want to sound pessimistic about our chances here, but are we really supposed to take over Los Angeles with just what we've got, because I don't like those odds."

Ayla knew this question would come eventually as it was a legitimate concern so she was prepared to answer. "I had the same questions that you have, Couchman. When I had my meeting with Dumont, he assured me that we will not be alone. Apparently, we're not the only group of rebels hiding out."

"If I may take the lead here, General, I think I can clear some things up," Ellie said to which Ayla gave her the green light to continue. "Once we're ready to have these other groups join us we need to send a signal to let them know."

"What kind of signal?" Ayla asked.

"Something big, something that lets them know the war is starting," Ellie said. Ayla was about to speak up but Ellie continued. "There's something else too. I have a contact that I can use to help coordinate everything. He's sort of a messenger for the other groups hiding out."

Ayla was a little perturbed at the fact that there was yet another thing she was not told. She tried to keep her cool though and continued as if it was not a big deal. "Okay, great," she said in response to her admission. She then laid out how she thought the rest of the day would look like. "Now, Miles, Frank, and everyone else should be back here tonight or tomorrow, I'm guessing. It's a big group so it will probably take some time. I want to treat this situation as if we could be compromised at any moment. We'll take turns with perimeter security, I'll go first and you can work it out amongst yourselves who relieves me. We brought some food with us that we can ration out but hopefully we won't be here for too long. The truck convoy comes in two days which doesn't give us a lot of time so we'll need to make sure all the details are tight. I'm going to go around and see where the best places are to get a good lay of the land. In the meantime, the rest of you get some rest."

Ayla left the rest of the group behind and made her way to the opposite end of the warehouse. She was happy to be alone at the moment as she needed a breather. The sound of her footsteps echoed through the large empty building as she approached a small door that led to the west end of the structure. This exit faced the highway where they were to seize the convoy truck. She unlocked the door from the inside and opened it just a crack, which again caused the orange setting sunlight to cascade upon the dirty warehouse floor. As she peered out through the opening, she could feel the warmth of the sun on her face. There was not much to see except for more abandoned homes and highways. She decided it was not worth it to go outside just yet, as it seemed too dangerous to be walking around when it was still daylight out. She closed the door back up and the sounds of the locks could be heard reverberating through the large empty building.

She spotted another door on the north side of the building and headed toward it to again do a brief inspection of the exterior surroundings. She unlocked it and again the light spilled onto the floor but not as dramatic as before due to the sun's position in the sky. This time, she could see some more abandoned buildings from the old jet propulsion laboratory. It was a desolate place and there were no signs of anyone having been there in quite some time. Further down along the wall, she spotted some metal stairs that led to a small area above the main floor. She walked up the stairs, running her hands along the old metal railing that was once painted yellow but now was chipped and scraped. She was now standing in the small enclosed space that had a few offices with their own doors. This area was above where the rest of her crew were resting. From here she could see out the windows on three of the four sides of the building, she also noticed a catwalk that spanned the length of the warehouse where she could walk and get a good view of the fourth side. Ayla decided this would be the best place to keep watch on the area while the rest of her teammates rested.

She did a quick walk around and looked out each of the windows and could see that all was quiet outside. She located a corner office that had windows on both the North and East sides of the building. The door was left slightly ajar from the last person who left the office and had a large frosted glass window on the upper half. Etched into the glass with black lettering was the name Judy Davenport. Underneath the name it said director. There was not much to this office; there was a chair knocked over on the floor behind a desk, and some random papers here and there. There was an empty filing cabinet with one of the drawers open. A couple of the windows in the office were able to be propped open which Ayla did thinking it would help with security. She grabbed the chair from the floor, placed it behind the desk and sat down and put her feet up.

This was the first time that Ayla had been alone in quite a while. She used this moment to sit and reflect upon just how far they had come since she met Miles in Chicago. So many things had happened and they had traveled so far, but yet she felt as though they hadn't accomplished anything. There had already been so many victims of collateral damage along the way. Malik and Juliette, killed by the same mayor who claimed to be on their side, also presumed dead now. His brother, Ryan Gould, gunned down by bandits. Raj and his friend Laura, kidnapped by her brother, of all people. Then there were Gabe and Zoe, who apparently had decided they were better off on their own.

Her thoughts were interrupted by a slight tapping on the door which slightly startled her. It was Jake coming to check on her. "Aren't you supposed to be resting, soldier?" she asked him with a smile.

"I couldn't sleep. I wanted to make sure you were okay." He said to her. "I'm glad I did though, you're the one that looks like you could use some rest."

"I'm pretty tired, I guess," she said to him. "Do you mind taking over for a bit?" she asked.

"Not at all, General," he said as he saluted her in jest. She explained to him her strategy using the windows and the catwalk that led to the other side of the building and told him to periodically take a walk around and check.

"Thanks, Jake," she said to him as she started to walk past him. He grabbed her arm and kissed her. No more words were said and their hands were the last thing to touch as she walked away down the stairs to get some rest, leaving him behind.

The first night in the abandoned jet propulsion warehouse went fairly smoothly. They rotated security duty as the others rested. They awoke the next day with the hope that the rest of their platoon would arrive. They split up the food that they had and ate a quick breakfast. The day dragged on with not much action as they rotated through watch duty and kept each other busy with more stories of their pasts.

After several hours of nothingness, it was again Ayla's turn to take watch duty. She ascended to the top floor and did her initial sweep of the perimeter and like before, she saw nothing. She took a seat in Judy Davenport's office and after several minutes of quiet, she heard footsteps coming from the east side of the building's open window. She anxiously got up and went to check. She slowly lifted her head up toward the window's opening to see if she could find what caused the sounds. Eventually, she spotted a man in the woods: it was Frank. He had made his way out and onto the jet propulsion property and he was alone. Ayla was able to get his attention by whistling as she had done in their trek from Las Vegas to Los Angeles. She motioned for him to head to the south side of the building and she met him at the front door.

She opened the side door that the team had entered through the day before and let him in. He looked tired and dirty but otherwise he appeared to be okay. "Frank!" she exclaimed as she hugged him catching him off guard, but he was also happy to see them again and hugged her back. "What's going on? Where's Miles?" she pressed him.

"They're all about a mile back, I volunteered to come first to find the best route and come up with a plan of how to get everyone here safely," Frank said slightly winded.

"Well, what do you think?" Ayla asked him.

"There are some spots where we're pretty exposed between here and there. But there's also nobody around except for us. I think if we came in small groups of five or so people we should probably be okay," Frank said.

"That will take all night won't it?" Couchman chimed in.

"You wanted my opinion, that's my opinion," Frank said in a tone that suggested he didn't appreciate being questioned after his two-day ordeal of traveling alone.

"Okay, Frank," Ayla said, "I'll let you take the lead on this. What do you need from us?"

"Some water, food, and a fifteen-minute break before I go back to get the rest," Frank said, to which Ayla motioned to Jake to help with his request. After getting a snack and some rest, Frank told Ayla his plan. "I'll head back and let Miles know that the coast is clear and that we'll be traveling in small groups. We have a map so everyone should be able to find which building we're at. It took me about twenty minutes so I think if we sent them in fifteen-minute intervals we should be good."

"What about the Humvee?" Ayla asked him, as it was integral to their next plan.

"It's with us. I guess we'll just have the last group drive it here," he said.

"I'd really like for you to stay up there, Frank, and be the one who brings the Humvee back," Ayla said to him.

He agreed and just like that, Frank was off again, headed back toward Miles and the rest of the team. The warehouse should have plenty of space for the two hundred-or-so revolutionaries that would be joining them soon. Based off of Ellie's knowledge of the city, they already had enough numbers to take over the Los Angeles enforcer barracks. According to her, there were only at most fifty to sixty enforcers who occupied the building at one time while the other hundred or so enforcers on the city's payroll would be out patrolling their jurisdictions. Ellie had guessed that a small percentage of those enforcers would abandon their posts or even try to join Ayla and her team. She did however stress that some would fight back and not go quietly.

After about forty-five minutes, the first group of revolutionaries had finally arrived at the warehouse including Miles. The two old friends were happy to see each other as Ayla gave him a hug and the two caught up about what they had been doing in the other's absence. Ayla told him about her meeting with Dumont and their stay in the apartment above the fish shop, while Miles told her about life on the truck trail depot in the

California wilderness.

It was well into the night and the warehouse was starting to fill up. By this time, Ayla's original team had been relieved of their lookout duties and had been replaced by lower-ranked soldiers. Ayla and Miles were still catching each other up and going over strategy and now they included all their trusted officers including Colonel Ellie, and Captains, Jake, Couchman, Ruiz and Hudson, their rescuer from the Las Vegas airport conflict. The only person missing was Frank, who would be coming in with the last group.

"General Lang?" Jake asked, "Do you have something for me?"

"You mean this?" Miles asked as he reached into his rucksack and pulled out the laptop that they had found up at the truck trail. He handed it to Jake, who smiled and immediately turned it on to continue exploring its contents.

Ayla, who had forgotten how cute he was when he got all nerdy, cracked a smile before getting back to business. "So first things first, we need some volunteers who are willing to act out our little charade."

"No, you don't, General," Couchman said, "Ruiz and I have already talked about it, we're going to do it. Frank's in too. We've already got our scene ready to play out." Ayla looked to Ruiz and he nodded his head in agreement.

"Okay, great, run me through it," she said to them.

Couchman and Ruiz began to describe the scene that the three soldiers had created. "So, we're going to go with a medical emergency like we talked about before. The Humvee will be parked across the middle of the road and we'll be tending to Frank, who's going to have a heart attack. When they get close, I'm going to flag them down while Ruiz tends to Frank. I'll distract the driver and Ruiz will be doing fake CPR to sell it and that's when you spring the attack."

The group paused following Couchman's description and Miles looked to Ayla to gauge her response. "Okay, I like it. It doesn't have to win any Oscars, just give us enough time to do our thing. There's a great spot out there where we could hide on an embankment, it's pretty steep and should keep us out of sight," she said. "Does anybody have any other thoughts or questions?" she asked.

Just then, Ellie raised her hand. "I do, what's an Oscar?"

The rest of the team laughed "You're showing your age, General," Miles said chuckling.

"You boys will need these," Miles said as he handed them the army uniforms that they had confiscated from their prisoners at the truck trail base.

"Oh yea, what happened to those guys?" Ayla asked Miles.

"Our friend who gave up all the information has decided to join the cause." Ayla looked at him skeptically. "Don't worry he knows next to nothing and I've got a special detail assigned to him, he has a shadow twenty-four-seven. Unfortunately, he didn't know much beyond what he was assigned to," Miles said.

"What about the other guy?" she asked.

"He wasn't so lucky," Miles said which got her attention. "He tried to run; we can't have anyone giving us away," Miles said unapologetically to which Ayla agreed. "When is this convoy coming?" he asked changing the subject

"According to Ellie, it's coming the day after tomorrow in the morning," she said to Miles.

"They're usually coming through around nine in the morning, give or take an hour. I'd say if we're all in place an hour before, we should be safe and can wait it out until they come,"

Ellie said joining the conversation.

"Let's make it seven, just to be safe," Miles said, to which they all agreed.

Just then the east-facing bay doors opened up with a loud creaking sound and a rumbling of a chain that a soldier was pulling hand over hand, to open the door. It was Frank arriving with the stolen army Humvee. "I guess everyone is here, you're up, General," Miles said.

Shortly after Frank turned off the engine and got out of the car, Ayla stood up on one of the old crates in preparation to address her team as a whole. It would be the first time she had the opportunity to do so since the airport. Out of her back pocket, she pulled out her revolutionary arm band and tied it around her left bicep displaying the symbols of their efforts. She still had her black hat on, the one she took from a young soldier out in the wilderness. She took it off and pitched it to the side, her bright white hair stood out against the dark backdrop of the warehouse. She stood there staring out at her platoon and despite being dimly lit by only a few flashlights, she could see their faces and how somewhere on their body, they too donned the symbols of the revolution. The regiment of soldiers in the warehouse began to notice her standing over them and a natural hush fell over the crowd as they prepared to hear their leader speak.

"First of all," she began to address them, "I want to thank each and every one of you for making it this far. I know you are all very determined. We all have our own stories here; we're all here for our own reasons. I'll tell you mine. You have to go all the way back to when this whole thing started," she paused for a moment and looked around at the crowd. Their eyes were fixed on her. They were almost all younger than her; most of them were children during the first revolution. She started up again; ready to tell her tale, which only a few knew.

"I was just a kid. My parents, they were trying to help people, people who were being mistreated by those sworn to protect us. They helped a lot of people. I was proud of them. They were starting to make a name for themselves around town, until one day, I watched as soldiers in a Humvee just like that one," she said as she pointed aggressively toward the Humvee that Frank had just driven into the warehouse not that long ago. "The army forced their way into our house, they dragged my parents to the street, put them on their knees, and shot them both in the back of the head," she said as she raised her voice passionately. "I was barely a teenager, my brother..." She paused briefly to gather herself. "My brother couldn't have been more than eight years old. I covered his eyes so he didn't have to see our parents being murdered."

She again looked around at her soldiers, she had their unwavering attention. Each of them fixated on her. "General Lang," she said motioning to her friend, "he took us in, trained us, and helped me become the woman I am today. Together, we joined up and gave the resistance everything we had. But as we all know we lost that fight. Many of you have similar stories, I'm sure. I know there are some of you out there who helped fight. I know there are some of you out there who were just trying to survive after the war. This time around will be different, this time it's not about the Constitution, it's not about the government abusing their power, this time it's about survival," she said again raising her voice at just the right time.

Now, the soldiers watching her were starting to react, some were nodding their heads, a few started to clap, and some chattering had picked up, "Just like you, there are thousands of us out there fighting to survive, and this time, we're bringing the fight to their front door. We're bringing the fight to their biggest and best city. The day after tomorrow, Los Angeles will be ours!" she yelled bringing her speech to a close. The soldiers cheered, high-fived each other and hugged. Some of them even threw their hands in the air.

Ayla gave them a chance to settle down before she concluded. "We've got one day to prepare and we are going to get it right. Tonight, you only have one order and that's to get some rest. Tomorrow we're going to split everyone up into different groups and work until the plan is foolproof. Thank you," she said as she finally stepped down from the crates, to which she was given an enthusiastic round of applause.

"That's why you're on the crates and I'm down here," Miles said to her with a smile. "Great speech," he said.

After her address, the commotion slowly died down. The soldiers were starting to turn in for the night as it was already very late. Luckily, they had a whole day tomorrow to prep for their mission. By now, they were making makeshift beds from their belongings using their backpacks as pillows. Ayla had spotted Jake to the left of her against the wall setting up a spot to get some rest; he laid his things down next to him saving her a spot.

Just then, Ellie approached Ayla and Miles. She motioned for them to follow her off to the side away from most people and when she felt comfortable, she started speaking to them softly "I'm going to meet one of my contacts tonight. He's my guy I told you about before, my liaison for all the other teams out there."

"You're just telling us this now?" Ayla asked her.

"I wanted to tell you but we all have a role to play in this war," she said sounding like her grandfather.

"Where is this happening? Please tell me you didn't tell him where we are," Ayla said bitterly.

Ellie looked insulted by the question. "Absolutely not," she said swiftly, which caused Ayla to give her a look and without saying anything, Ellie had already known her mistake, "I mean no, General, I didn't," she said a little more calmly. "I'm meeting him at an old high school a mile or two down the road. He knows we're in the area but I didn't tell him where we were exactly."

"What's the purpose of this meeting?" Ayla asked.

"They need to know the plan too. I think it's important we're all on the same page," Ellie said.

Ayla was now a little annoyed at all the back and forth, but had to admit that Ellie made a good point. She was also conscious of the fact that she couldn't be too upset with her as Ellie reminded her of herself when she was younger. She was also starting to understand why Miles had always tried to keep her in check during the war. "Okay fine, but nothing about the truck plan; just let them know about the barracks," she said.

"What do you need from us, Ellie?" Miles asked breaking up the discussion.

"Let me take one of the guys with me, just for an extra set of eyes," she said.

Ayla looked around, Frank was sleeping, and she knew she was being selfish but she wasn't going to send Jake. "Ruiz and Couchman are your choices. Go see who wants to volunteer," she said to her. Ayla watched as she walked away toward Couchman.

"Go get some rest, Ayla," Miles said to her.

She nodded and lay down in the spot next to Jake that he had saved for her. He reached out for her, which prompted her to shake her head. She was already the subject of her little apartment gossip chatter and she had no interest in being looked at in any way other than the leader of the platoon. She worried that showing any vulnerability or affection might make her appear weak. "Find anything else on that computer?" she asked him in an attempt to appear normal.

"Nothing new, really," Jake said to her. "Without their network connection, I can't access their intranet."

"Let's get some sleep," she said as she laid her head down on her backpack.

Chapter 34

The Plan

The next morning, the regiment of soldiers began their day just as they'd been doing for the past several weeks. They had a light breakfast that consisted of food they took from the truck trail base, small game that had hunted while stationed there, and water filled from creeks and rivers that they transported in anything they could find to hold it.

Ayla, Miles, and Ellie all convened for a private meeting in one of the upstairs offices of the abandoned JPL warehouse. "What did you find out?" Ayla asked her.

Ellie began to explain what she had learned from her midnight rendezvous at the abandoned high school. "The good news is that there are a lot more of us out there, all ready to follow your lead. He thinks there are about thirty to forty more groups of soldiers just like ours spread throughout Los Angeles."

"What does that give us? About ten thousand, maybe give or take a few," Ayla said answering her own question.

"He also said once we make our move on the enforcer barracks, we can expect a lot of civilian support, regular people joining the movement," Ellie said.

"That's definitely enough to take Los Angeles There's no way they have that many enforcers or army troops in the area. For now, I mean. There'll be more though eventually," Ayla said.

"Now, you said that was the good news. What's the bad

news?" Miles asked.

"The bad news is that we have no idea where these other troops are located in the city. There are a lot of abandoned places in the surrounding areas but they could be miles away. We have no idea of how and when they will arrive. All I know is that they'll be waiting for our signal once we take the barracks," Ellie said.

"Our signal?" Miles asked.

"Yea about that, we're going to have to figure out a way to show we've taken the barracks over, something big. It's something Dumont and I talked about. He wants to bring the fight here so not only will it signal our people to come and fight but also tells the Army 'Hey, come get us,'" Ayla said.

"What did you have in mind?" Miles asked her.

Ayla had secretly been plotting this for some time and knew the answer already. "Across the street is the governor's office. We're going to blow it up," she said bluntly.

"That will get the message across, I think," Miles said with smile.

"All right, Ellie, go get the captains please. It's time to get this plan in motion. Bring the map with you too," Ayla said.

For a brief moment, it was just Miles and Ayla alone in the upstairs office. "How are you feeling about all this, General?" Miles asked her

"I know we have the numbers to take the barracks. If what Ellie told us is true, I think we have the numbers to take Los Angeles. The only question left is: what is Dumont doing? Once we take the city, we won't stand a chance against the army. They'll send everything they have at us, just to prove a point. We know they won't hesitate to decimate the city. I mean they've already done that everywhere else. Our fates lie in the hands of Alexander Dumont," she said to him.

Before he could respond, Ellie had arrived back to the office with the others. "Okay, everyone let's get this thing moving. We have our actors and you're all ready to go right?" Ayla asked Frank, Ruiz, and Couchman, and they all nodded. "Okay, all of us here in this room are going to be responsible for a set group of soldiers." She began outlying her plan of attack by first describing how she wanted to position soldiers in different strategic locations along the highway where they planned to ambush the supply convoy making its way to Los Angeles. "So basically I want to have this convoy surrounded once it stops. That means I want two groups of soldiers lying in wait on the embankments, one on each side. Once we give the signal, these soldiers will storm the road and surround the entire convoy. Jake and Ellie, this will be your job: you will be the two on the ground leading the two teams," she said.

"What's the signal?" Jake asked.

"This is where it gets messy," she continued. "We need to take out the drivers. We're expecting one lead Humvee, one semi-truck type of transport vehicle and a Humvee following behind. We're going to have to follow your lead on this one, Couchman. As you approach the semi-truck driver's window don't get too close. Hudson, Miles, and I will be the shooters and that will be the signal. Once that happens, that's when you two surround them," she said looking toward Jake and Ellie. "Whoever is left alive we'll have to take prisoner." Ayla concluded by asking if there were any questions or concerns.

"I like it, solid plan," Miles said confidently.

Ayla continued, "Well, that's phase one. Phase two is getting to the barracks. Hopefully we're far enough out that the gunshots aren't heard by anyone and this goes smoothly. We'll match personnel in each vehicle. Meaning, if they have two men in Humvee A so will we. The only kink in that plan is that we are going to have a third Humvee so hopefully that doesn't raise any flags. The rest of us will hide in the trailer. If we need to make room in the back we can get rid of anything that isn't of value to us. We know, again from Ellie's research, that the headquarters are here," she said as she pointed to another spot on the map. "It's an old LAPD station, with a few additions. There's a blockade and only one entrance, manned by two guards. The plan is to get through the gate with no problems. From what Ellie has seen in the past, they usually let the convoy in without any extra checks. The truck backs into a loading dock around the back side of the station and that's going to be how we get in. Whoever is driving the truck will back in and stop just before getting to the garage bay. One important thing here is to not open the trailer doors until they open their garage doors. Once that happens, our driver opens the trailer up and our people storm out of there like hell and get into that unloading area. After that, it's on. We take the barracks and kill whoever stands in our way," Ayla said as she laid out the plan in great detail.

"What if we don't make it through the entrance blockade?" Ellie asked.

"The mission is to take the barracks. Driving through the gate will make it easy on us. But if we don't, the mission is still to take the barracks. We just start fighting from somewhere else," Ayla said. After pausing for any other questions, she continued. "We have no blue prints or plans of this building. Once we get in there, we're going to have to be through and sweep every corner of the place. Once we take control, we'll regroup and talk about the next phase." She rolled up the map and Ayla and her team went downstairs to join the rest of their soldiers. From there they began to divide them into their teams for the convoy ambush.

The sorting of soldiers and going over plans took the majority of the day. The officers all worked together on instructing the soldiers how the entire day should look. Toward the end of it all, Ayla once again took up her spot on the old crates to make another announcement while the soldiers were settling in and eating a light dinner. "All right, listen up everyone. I know it hasn't been easy, I know you're hungry, I know you're tired of sleeping on floors, tired of walking, and probably tired of this old warehouse," she said, which drew a few chuckles. "This is not going to be another speech to rally you up. If you weren't ready to fight, then you wouldn't still be here. But that's exactly what it is from here on out. Starting tomorrow, we go to war and believe me they won't go down without a fight. We must be prepared to kill and be killed. Look around you, think about your friends here today, and think about the people you left behind. Tomorrow you fight for them, you fight for each other, and you fight for yourself. Fight for the millions we've lost because of our so-called government's response to people wanting to be free," she paused and looked around at the crowd and continued in a more somber tone. "It's true we might not all make it. But someone once told me living in fear and poverty isn't really a life worth living," she said as she picked Zoe out of the crowd and nodded to her. She then concluded her speech, "Get some rest, everyone be ready at six a.m. Tomorrow we take this country back." The ending of this speech wasn't met with the usual wild cheering but more so with a quiet determination.

Chapter 35

Hostile Takeovers

It was finally here. The day Ayla had been waiting for since starting her journey back in Chicago with Miles. Really it's the day she had been waiting for since they lost all those years ago and were forced into hiding. "Let's wake them up," she said in a serious tone to all her officers. "Get your people up, get some food in them and get them ready to go. We'll take one team at a time and get them in position by the highway."

In minutes, every soldier in the warehouse was up and ready to go. Their weapons were locked and loaded, ruck sacks were on their backs, and they wore their revolutionary uniforms, displaying their iconic emblem proudly; there'd be no more hiding now.

She ordered Couchman, Ruiz, and Frank to leave first. They piled into the Humvee and once again the creaking bay doors of the warehouse opened up. There was no orange light spilling into the warehouse this time, as it was still dark out. Frank turned the ignition and the Humvee roared to life and as it began to exit the warehouse, cheers erupted with soldiers clapping their hands, whistling, and slapping the side of the big vehicle. The reaction was just what Ayla had hoped for as they sent their first team out into the field.

She gave them about ten minutes before she directed Ellie and Jake to lead their teams and get them into position. By the time Ayla, Miles, and Hudson made it outside, the sun was just beginning to rise. They followed the same route as the others, who had flattened the grass creating a visible pathway to the rendezvous point. As Ayla stepped away from the old JPL warehouse, she turned around and gave it one last look. Then with confidence in her stride, she continued down toward the road.

Just like they had laid out the day before, all the soldiers were in place on the embankments that surrounded the fake roadside emergency scene. Ayla, Hudson and Miles would have to set up somewhere where they were hidden, but had a clear shot at the drivers. Before she left to find her shooting position, she searched out Jake who had his eyes already locked onto her from his position on the sloped roadside. They connected for a few seconds and no words were needed as they both knew what the other wanted to say in that moment.

They finally got everyone in place and had about an hour to spare until the convoy would be traveling down the highway. The three shooters gathered near their hiding spots to discuss their plan. "All right, we'll follow your lead Miles. You take out the truck driver and Hudson as soon as you hear that shot, you take out your driver." After her instructions, they all found places to camp out with good visibility, far enough away to not be seen but close enough to get a good shot.

The sun had now risen enough in the sky that the dimly lit landscape had become a sunny California morning. Ayla could feel the warmth on her back as her shadow was cast down in front of her. She looked around taking it all in. To her right was Miles, who met eyes with her and gave her a reaffirming head nod. She looked further down and saw Hudson, who was doing one last inspection of his rifle. She gazed down onto the highway and saw

266

her soldiers, all waiting to strike. The moment was starting to sink in for her. This was it, she thought to herself. Thoughts of all those she was fighting for started to enter her mind. Images of her mom and dad, Raj, all the people she witnessed living in misery in Chicago and Los Angeles and all the places in between. Even her Brother, despite the fact she still wanted to shoot him.

Her thoughts were interrupted as she could hear a rumbling in the distance. "They're early," she said aloud. She placed her fingers in her mouth and whistled loud and hard so all could hear her. She didn't need to say anything else as everyone knew that the moment was upon them. She watched as Frank lay down on the highway in front of the Humvee. His Army uniform was unbuttoned and Ruiz hovered over him as if he was giving him CPR. Couchman did his best to stand near them looking concerned with his hands over his head. Ayla, Miles, and Hudson all crept down a little further in an effort to stay hidden.

As the convoy grew closer, the roaring of the semi-truck grew louder. As it approached, you could hear the driver down shifting and the sounds of the engine slowing. Couchman started his show as Ruiz was pumping on Frank's chest. He began waving his arms frantically trying to signal the convoy to stop and help. They came to a rolling stop perfectly in front of where Ayla, Miles, and Hudson were hiding, aiming their rifles at the drivers of each vehicle. There were three vehicles just as they were expecting; one semi sandwiched between two Humvees. The driver of the semi rolled down his window and yelled to Couchman who was jogging toward them. "What's going on?" the driver asked.

Before Couchman was close enough to respond, the plan went into full swing by Miles taking his shot followed almost immediately by Ayla and Hudson. The shots were so perfectly timed that it sounded like one loud bang that echoed through the empty roadway. The targets were hit just as synchronous as the shots were fired. All three drivers were killed immediately and just like clockwork, the rest of Ayla's soldiers poured up onto the highway from their concealed hiding positions along the road's embankments, executing the perfect ambush. They yelled and screamed with passion as they climbed the hill and raced toward their targets with their guns drawn.

The remaining United States service members had no choice but to surrender. They were outnumbered significantly and none of them were seemingly ready to die for the supply convoy. Ayla, Miles, and Hudson made their way down to the newly acquired vehicles. "What do you want to do with them?" Couchman asked her referencing the prisoners.

"Restrain them and put them in the back with us. We'll have to sort them out later after we take the barracks. We don't have much time; they'll be expecting the truck soon," she said as Couchman nodded and motioned to some soldiers to take care of the prisoners that were corralled and sitting on the side of the road. As they started to tie them up, Ayla gave her next order. "Okay, let's open her and see what we're working with." Ruiz went to the back of the semi and began to open the large swinging metal doors. While he opened them, Ayla gave an important task to a soldier standing next to her: to clean the blood off the vehicles.

Inside they found a large variety of items. There were a few cases that had standard issued enforcer gear such as uniforms, shoes, and bullet proof vests. They also found a few cases with weapons. "This stuff will help," Miles said casually as he tossed the uniforms to Ayla and Ellie who were watching the action. After they emptied the cases, they disposed of the empty boxes off the side of the embankment, out of sight. Next, toward the front of the trailer were some more crates, which, to everyone's delight, were filled with some military issued ready to eat meals. The food was distributed and again the empty crates were tossed to the side to make room for all the soldiers.

"All right everyone, pile in, we don't have time to sit around and eat, let's go," Ayla said as the soldiers began cramming into the back of the trailer. "It's going to be tight so squeeze in," she said to them.

"So who's going in which car?" Miles asked her.

"I want you and Hudson to drive the first one, Couchman and Ruiz in the semi, Frank and Jake in the next Humvee, and Ellie, you and I will be in the last Humvee. I don't think they'll be expecting any women drivers so we'll try not to draw their attention." After the war, the United States banned most women from joining the military in an effort to rebuild the population.

Miles, Ayla, Ellie, and Jake all changed into their new uniforms they took from their prisoners and the dead bodies. Before entering into their respective rides, she addressed them all again. "Okay, this is where it could get messy. We have some Intel but we really don't know what we're getting into. Hopefully they see us coming and just let us in, no questions asked, but if not, you two are going to have to improvise," she said looking at Miles and Hudson who nodded showing their understanding. "If they don't let us through, we'll have to fight our way in. If things go down before we enter the gate, you two, open up that trailer so everyone can get out and we're at full strength," she said looking toward Frank and Jake who also nodded.

As they all entered their vehicles, Ayla walked past the semi and slapped the side of it with her hands and proceeded to the back which was packed full of soldiers, but still open. "Okay, people, be ready for anything, we'll see you at the barracks. Remember, when these doors open, don't hesitate, good luck," she said as she closed the doors on the semi-truck concealing the soldiers inside. She and Ellie entered the last Humvee and Ayla stuck the key into the ignition and the powerful engine came to life. Not much longer after that, the other two Humvees and the semi-truck started up and the convoy embarked on their journey to the Los Angeles City Enforcer Barracks.

Ayla was at the wheel and accelerated up behind the truck. They cruised along the desolate highway with the windows cracked about halfway allowing some of the fresh air to blow their hair around as they both gazed out at the abandoned suburbs. Of course Ellie's long blonde hair was fluttering around considerably more than Ayla's white pixie haircut. At the beginning of her adventure, it was long, dark, and free flowing; now it was short and light. She often forgot about the change and had to take a second look when she caught a glimpse of her reflection in the rear view mirror.

"Can I ask you a question?" Ellie asked breaking the silence of their ride.

"Um, sure, go ahead," Ayla answered her.

"What was it like? You know before all this happened?" she asked innocently.

Ayla hesitated and took her eyes off the road briefly to see Ellie was genuinely interested. She decided to indulge her. "What do you want to know?"

"I don't know, tell me about when you were a kid, anything," Ellie said.

Ayla, who hardly ever talked about her childhood, was a little reluctant to answer but decided to anyways. "I grew up near Buffalo, New York. Do you know where that is?" she asked her, to which Ellie shook her head no. "It's up north, near Canada. It's by Niagara Falls and Lake Erie," she said waiting to see if she had any idea where she was talking about.

"Sounds cold," Ellie said.

"We definitely had snow," she said laughing. "Where to start?" she asked rhetorically. "I mean we had a pretty normal childhood, I think, beside the whole martial law thing that happened. We went to school, played sports," she paused trying to think of what else to say. "I used to go to my friend's house and have sleepovers, play with Barbies," to which Ellie interrupted her with laughter.

"General Vural, the legend, played with dolls?" she said as more laughter poured out.

"Hey, do you want to know or not?" Ayla said smiling.

"Okay, I'm sorry, continue, please," Ellie said trying to contain herself.

"My parents had season tickets to the Sabres; they were a hockey team. We used to go to games all the time; it was so fun. We'd get all sorts of junk food like popcorn, cotton candy, and hot dogs," Ayla paused for a moment and continued but the narration took a more somber tone. "My dad used to cheer so loud but I think he really just did it for me and my brother. They were great parents," she said getting a little choked up.

"I can see why you lead us the way you do. Sounds like something worth fighting for," Ellie said sympathetically. Ayla nodded in agreement again trying to hide her emotion. Ellie, sensing her feelings, tried to change the topic. "So you and Jake, huh?" Ayla wasn't so enthusiastic about discussing that topic and gave Ellie a look, which prompted her to ask, "Too far?"

"Too far," Ayla affirmed although she did appreciate the effort on Ellie's behalf. It was nice to talk to someone on a personal level. It was something Ayla didn't get to do very often. She couldn't help but crack a small smile, which Ellie noticed but decided to just keep her mouth shut about Jake.

Deciding to change the topic after several seconds of silence, Ellie decided to ask about something else, "What do you think will happen if we win?"

"You mean 'when' we win," Ayla said with confidence.

"Yea, when we win," Ellie corrected herself.

She thought about it for a minute before responding, "I'd like to think that we can go back to the way it was but I don't know if that's possible. I suppose the first thing we'll need to do is pick someone to lead us," she said.

"Like you," Ellie suggested.

Not knowing quite what to say, Ayla looked at her before looking back at the empty highway. "I don't know, maybe... Depends, I guess."

"What would you do?" Ellie asked her.

Ayla hadn't ever really thought that far ahead and she didn't have an answer for her. "I don't know. What would you do?" she asked her the same question back.

Ellie didn't take nearly as long as Ayla to answer, almost as if she had thought about it previously. "I think there should still be a president, like there was before," she said, to which Ayla nodded in agreement and then to her surprise, Ellie continued on. "But I don't think we can have the same representative system like we had before. The house and the senate, governors, cabinet members, I think there were just too many people in the way of getting things done."

Ayla, who very much disagreed with what she said, decided to play devil's advocate and inquire more, "What do you propose instead of that? Do you want to bring back the monarchy?" she

272

asked her.

"Oh don't get me wrong," Ellie said. "I think they had the right idea. I just think it could be simplified, or scaled back a bit. Our population isn't nearly what it used to be so we could divide the country into a few regions and each region could vote for a President. Kind of like the old Electoral College but every vote is equal. Or each region elects its own leaders and they rule by committee. There are lots of possibilities," she said enthusiastically.

"How do you know all of this stuff?" Ayla asked her thinking back about how she didn't know about old movies but knows about governments and how they work.

"My grandpa taught me. He made me read a lot," Ellie said.

"Ah right, Dumont. Well, maybe I'll just have to keep you on as special advisor to President Vural," Ayla said as they both shared a laugh.

"All I know is that we can't let what happened before happen again. People need rights and they shouldn't fear their government. Every voice deserves to be heard," Ellie said passionately.

"That's something we both can agree upon," Ayla said.

As Ayla got to know her more and more, Ellie was starting to grow on her. She was a natural born leader, was obviously very book smart, she had proven to be brave on several occasions, and she was genuinely a nice person to talk to. With this realization, Ayla decided to give her more responsibilities. "I have another job for you," she said to her.

"What do you need?" Ellie asked.

"I want you to plan out how we're going to take out the governor's office. Figure the best way to get that signal out there for everyone to see. Can you do that?"

"Oh yeah, I can definitely do that," she said with enthusiasm as she pulled out a small journal from her pack and began to brainstorm the request.

After Ellie was given her new task, there wasn't much conversation to be had as she was fully engaged in her new mission. Several minutes went by and she finally picked her head up and said, "There's the barracks, straight ahead."

Chapter 36

The Signal

"All right, moment of truth," Ayla said aloud as the vehicles approached the gates. The convoy started to slow down, and as the Humvee's brakes squealed, the air hissed from the semi as it rolled to a stop. Ayla looked out in front of the convoy and could see a uniformed enforcer at the gate. After a brief moment of suspense, it was as if he recognized the drivers and waved them through. The arm of the security gate moved up and one by one, the convoy vehicles accelerated through the barricade entrance.

As Ayla and Ellie drove past, they both pulled their hats down low and casually waved at the guard who returned the gesture without hesitation. Ayla followed Jake's Humvee as the semi pulled up to the docking bay doors. They parked near the unloading area and watched as Couchman positioned the big rig to be backed into the open bay doors.

The occupants of the three Humvees all exited their vehicles and stood as cool and nonchalant as they could with their guns slung over their shoulders secretly ready to engage. The beeping of the semi-truck commenced as Couchman did his best to slowly back the rig in place. When he was within ten feet of the loading bay, he yelled out the window, "Hey open her up."

This was the moment they had been preparing for. Ayla's heartrate rose and she could feel the adrenaline pumping. Jake and Ruiz both approached the back of the semi truck's rear doors which were pointing directly at the open garage door of the barracks loading dock. There were two enforcers waiting at the door to greet the semi-truck and unload its contents. They had no idea what was in store for them. Ayla began to ready herself. She clicked the safety off on her gun and as she looked around, she realized that the plan so far was working perfectly. No one seemed to suspect them. The guards at the gate were chatting looking on at the truck. The enforcers at the bay doors were waiting impatiently to receive the load. There were a couple of guards stationed at lookout points that were dutifully looking out away from the barracks.

Jake and Ruiz unlocked their swinging truck doors and gave themselves a look, and simultaneously they quickly opened them. What followed, to the shock of the enforcers at the bay doors, was a siege of two hundred plus revolutionaries who came out shooting. They instantly took out both enforcers at the door with multiple shots fired. Ayla immediately focused her attention on the guards who were at the front gate. She shot them both before they even readied their weapons. Meanwhile, Miles and Hudson took out the guards who were in the lookout towers. The enforcers had no idea what hit them.

"Into the bay doors!" Ayla commanded her troops. As several more enforcers came running into the loading garage area. Her team took them out before they knew what they were running toward. Ayla worked her way into the lead. She gave one last order. "This is our moment! Let's Go!" she yelled as she led the charge into the corridors of the barracks.

The revolutionaries filled the hallways of the building like a tsunami wave. They checked every room, the basement, and even the bathrooms. They either killed or captured every last enforcer and overtook the barracks in a matter of minutes. The enforcers had no chance and were totally unprepared to fight them off. Some were even shot while eating their lunches trying to draw their weapons with a mouth full of food.

Most of the people who were out and about in the surrounding area had scattered and hid at the sound of gunfire, making the space feel abandoned and desolate. Word was sure to spread to the enforcers who were out on duty but the assumption was they would have either abandoned their posts and blended in to the general population, or fled north seeking refuge with their employer, the United States government.

After the dust settled, Ayla and Miles regrouped with their officers. They paid respect to their losses which were minimal, went over what went right and what went wrong, and what the next steps were. Ayla's first command was for Hudson. "We need to establish a secure perimeter. Hudson?" He came attentively. "I need you to be in charge of this facilities security and do it ASAP."

"Yes, ma'am," he saluted her and immediately got to work on securing the site.

"Okay. Ellie, you said that we have to signal the others that are waiting for us. Did you have a plan for that?" Ayla asked her.

Ellie loved it when Ayla gave her the spotlight. Not because she liked being the center of attention but it was two women leading at the center of what historically had always been a man's world. It was her chance to put her own mark on the war and to further establish her as a leader. With that, she embraced the opportunity and laid out her plan for taking over the governor's office. "Now I have two ideas here, option A is we take two small teams in and start on the bottom floor. We work our way up and evacuate any civilians, and take out anyone that stands in our way. Once we reach the roof, we set explosives and blow the top off, signaling to the other teams that it's time to move." She waited to gauge everyone's response. They all looked to Ayla to see what she thought.

After a brief pause, Ayla realized they were waiting on her and spoke up.

"Okay, what's option B?" she asked her.

Ellie continued, "Option B is less dangerous for us. But could result in some collateral damage and isn't a hundred percent guaranteed that it will make a signal large enough for everyone to see. But this is an enforcer's barracks, and they do have an armory. I know that they have a rocket launcher down there from my sources," she paused as everyone waited for her to continue. "We could just shoot it from the street," she said, as she pretended to shoot an imaginary R.P.G.

Ayla was ready to respond quickly because upon hearing option two, she already knew that would be her choice. "We're going to do option B." To which Miles gave her a concerned look. "Don't worry, I think there's a way we can get people out and do option two. But I'm not sending anyone in there if I don't have to. Now, like Ellie said, this is an enforcer barracks, they deal with crowd control all the time, right? There's got to be a megaphone or something here we can use so the people across the street can hear us. We'll give them like five minutes to evacuate."

"Five minutes?" Jake asked skeptically. "What if someone is going to the bathroom or something?" he asked sincerely.

"Okay, fine, ten minutes," Ayla said sarcastically to appease Jake's concerns. "If they aren't out in ten minutes, then that's their problem. I'm sure the people working there aren't all innocent anyways," she said unapologetically. "All right, next mission, Ellie, find the RPG, Jake, you find a way to get our voices heard." She chose Ellie because her previous knowledge of the barracks might give her a leg up here, and she chose Jake for the second task because she hoped that if there was nothing readily available, he might be able to rig something up due to his acuity for technology. She wrapped up her instructions by raising her voice for those around her to hear, "The rest of you, turn this place upside down, look for anything we can use, weapons, information, anything you think could be useful, hold onto it and give it to one of the captains. Oh, and one more thing; way to kick ass!" She concluded her speech and was met with thunderous cheers as they rummaged through every nook and cranny of the barracks.

As the commotion from her address died down, Jake and Ellie went off to complete their tasks. It was hard for her to just treat Jake like everyone else. She desperately wanted to grab him and celebrate the small victory, maybe even steal a kiss or better yet, find a quiet place in the barracks, but she knew she couldn't. Right now, the only thing that mattered above all else was completing the mission; and then on to the next one. "What do you want to do with our newest prisoners?" Miles asked her.

"I don't know. I was thinking we just toss them in the cells here and sort them out later. What do you think?" she asked Miles.

"I think that sounds like the easiest thing to do. Whoever's going to clean this mess up can decide what to do with them," he said, showing his lifelong mentality of a soldier by implying he had no desire to be a part of what will happen after all is said and done.

"What? So no President Lang?" Ayla said to him half joking.

"I already told you, I'm too old for all that stuff," he shouted to her as he walked away to go take care of their captives.

Shortly thereafter, Ellie returned with not one, but two rocket launchers. She excitedly displayed them to Ayla. "There's a whole bunch more stuff down there; guns, grenades, riot gear, and this!" she said as she pulled out a large hunting knife with the enthusiasm of a kid on Christmas.

"That thing is bigger than your arm. What are you going to do with that?" Ayla said jokingly.

"I don't know. But I'm keeping it," Ellie said as she placed it back in the sheath on her hip.

"Found a megaphone," Jake said out of nowhere as he accidentally pulled the trigger letting out a loud, high-pitched burst of sound causing everyone around to cringe and cover their ears. "Sorry, everybody." Jake said slightly embarrassed.

Right on cue following Jake's arrival, Hudson returned to inform Ayla that the barracks were now secure and patrols and lookouts were in place. Once Miles had returned, she had all of her platoon leaders and they were ready to go outside to begin the next phase of the revolution, blowing up the governor's office to send a signal to the rest of the troops lying in wait to join Ayla and the others.

Ayla led the way and opened the front doors to the barracks. They were just like your stereotypical police station glass doors but the doorways were inscribed with the words *Los Angeles Enforcers* and had the emblem which they all shared across the country; a clenched fist holding an American flag. It was now midday and as they walked down the stairs, the warm Southern California air was felt immediately. Many of the soldiers inside the barracks took notice of the action happening and they followed their leaders out to the sunshine. There was now a large gathering of them observing Ayla and her team. There were also a growing number of civilians who had begun to gather outside the perimeter of the barracks. Some were clamoring to join, while others were merely curious.

"What about all these people?" Couchman asked.

"Just leave them for now," Miles said. "They'll sort themselves out once the real fighting begins."

"Hand me that megaphone, Jake." She extended her hand as she kept her focus on the looming city hall building directly in front of her. "Who the hell is the governor here anyways, Ellie?"

"Uh, Reed. Thomas Reed," she said after a second of thinking.

Ayla looked around at her team and caught Jake's eyes to which he gave her a reaffirming nod. She then turned her attention to the city hall building. It was a tall, narrow structure that had about twenty floors. She held the megaphone up to her mouth and began to give her ten-minute warning. "Attention Governor Reed and anyone else who is still inside the building, my name is General Ayla Vural of the resistance. Los Angeles is now our city. You have exactly ten minutes to evacuate this building before it becomes a flaming beacon of freedom. You can choose to walk free or stay and die. The choice is yours and the clock starts now." She handed the megaphone back to Jake as Miles checked his watch to note the time.

Moments later, members of the governor's staff and other employees of the city began to exit the building. Some of them were in disbelief until they laid eyes on the large group of rebels who had turned the enforcer barracks into their new headquarters. They slowly trickled out until a robust man wearing a suit and tie came bumbling out. He had thinning hair which he had combed over and sported a large bushy mustache. He examined the rebels until he spotted Ayla and locked eyes with her. "Was that you on the megaphone?" he yelled to her from across the street as Ayla nodded to answer him. "What's this all about?" he yelled to her again.

Ayla again signaled Jake for the megaphone. "Is everyone out of the building, Tom?" she said aggressively as the megaphone made her voice echo through the empty streets.

"Yes, but…" he tried to ask again but before he finished his sentence, he stopped talking, and watched as Ayla handed the megaphone back to Jake and in turn she grabbed the rocket launcher from Ellie. The governor looked on in a state of confused shock as Ayla, without hesitation, placed the rocket launcher on her shoulder, took aim at the top floor of his building, and pushed down the trigger. What followed was a plume of smoke that sent the rocket whistling upward leaving a trail of exhaust in its wake. The governor and everyone else watched as it propelled itself rapidly toward his office. Seconds later it collided with the top floor with a booming explosion that sent flames and black smoke high into the sky. The rebels and the governor could feel the heat from the explosion twenty floors down as debris and glass came raining down on the sidewalks below. The rebels cheered and celebrated in front of the barracks. Ayla stared up at the flaming tower and without looking away, she said to Ellie who was standing at her side, "Do you think they'll see that signal, Ellie?"

"Oh yea, General, you'll have your army in no time," Ellie said as she too stared up at the flames.

"So much for ten minutes ay, General?" Miles asked her as he watched the tower burn in the midday sun.

"The moment felt right," she said casually as another explosion erupted from the building. Miles looked at her and just shook his head as he had become accustomed to her impulsive decision making.

Governor Reed took one last look at the rebels before fleeing with the rest of the buildings' occupants.

Chapter 37

If You Burn It, They Will Come

The building had been burning for quite some time now and as it did, it filled the afternoon sky with a pillar of black smoke. So much so that it had cast a shadow over the barracks. After an hour or so of this, the security team notified Hudson that there was a large group of people headed in their direction. Ayla and the others went to see for themselves, and after looking through the binoculars, she handed them off to Ellie. "Must be five hundred at least. Recognize anyone?" she asked her.

"Yep, right on time too," she said as she handed the binoculars off to Miles. "That's Mateo. My contact I met with that night at JPL. I think we're going to have to expand our perimeter, it's about to get crowded," she said with a smile.

"All right team, Ellie, you and your guy Mateo are going to be in charge of getting a head count and coming up with a way to keep track of all the new people coming in, we'll need to keep tabs on everyone. Couchman and Ruiz, I want you two to work on expanding the barricades so we have space for everyone. Frank, I want you to help Hudson on securing the base as it gets bigger. The bigger we get, the more manpower we need for perimeter security. Jake, I want you to be in charge of inventory on any new and incoming tech and supplies and anything else we dig up. Miles and I will oversee the operation and start planning our next move. Anything comes up that needs our attention, come get us and we will go from there. Any questions?" she asked the group and once she was confident they were clear, she sent them off to perform their duties.

Miles and Ayla sat down together at a long table down in the small lunch room of the barracks. Ayla rolled out the map to plan the next move her growing army would take. "It's pretty obvious that Dumont intends to use us as bait. I still don't know what he has planned but I'm telling you now I have no intention of being a pawn in his chess game and getting a bunch of people killed," she said to him as the activity swirled around them.

"I agree, if we stay here we're sitting ducks but we don't have much time," Miles said. "If I had to guess, the army will probably find out about us pretty quickly so we only have a few days to act," he concluded.

"I've been thinking a lot about it, I think we need to set up base camp here," she said as she pointed to an area north of where they were.

Miles grinned and looked closer at the map, "I like the idea, it gives us the high ground and we'll be able to see them coming," he said.

"Plus look here," she said as she pointed at the area again. "This curve will act as a natural funnel. We can squeeze them all into one place."

"What's travel looking like?" he asked her as he continued to analyze the map.

"It's almost ten miles from here. So our vehicles can get there no problem as long as the roads are clear. Walkers might take four or five hours if I had to guess. Not counting any breaks," she said.

"You're also assuming we don't run into any rouge enforcers out there," Miles said.

"I'm thinking once they see how many of us there are, they'll turn and run," she said confidently.

"Okay, I like it, I'm on board. I've always wanted to see the Hollywood sign, what's left of it I guess," he said.

Once all the remaining troops arrived at the barracks, Ayla's plan was to transplant her army. She knew based on what Dumont said that the United States would be coming to take back the city and what better way to fend them off than to pick one of the highest points in the area. It was large enough that they could spread out their numbers, and high enough to spot them miles away, all while forcing the enemy into a compromising position.

Ayla and Miles decided to split up and make their rounds on their ever-expanding resistance headquarters. The groups of resistance fighters were coming in droves from all around the country. They all had received similar instructions to hide out in various locations in and around southern California until they were signaled to fall in. Ayla first touched base with Ellie and met her JPL contact Mateo. Ellie had informed her that in just the time that she had sent her away they had already received five different groups of resistance fighters and their numbers had almost quadrupled. Ayla also informed Mateo that he would be the liaison for all the incoming groups of resistance fighters and that he would report directly to Ellie.

She met up with Frank and Hudson who had provided her with the details of the security plan. They had assigned different groups different responsibilities and even set up a rotating schedule for the lookout personnel. She also informed them they needed to begin thinking about convoy security as they would be on the move again soon. She asked them to provide her with plans for using on foot transportation, motor vehicle transportation, or a combination of both and what they believed would be the easiest and safest option. Although she wasn't ready to give up information on where they would be headed, she promised they would find out more tonight as she planned to meet with her officers again later in the evening.

Her next stop was to get to Jake. She found him in the basement where all the weapons had been stored. He was seated at a long metal table which was covered in various communications equipment, two laptops, and other items that Ayla didn't recognize. He sat tinkering with some mechanical device, occasionally jotting down notes with the pencil he held behind his ear. He was surrounded by a few helpers he had chosen to assist him in organizing things. Ayla just watched him for a moment. His brown hair was falling down in from of his glasses which caused him to tuck it off to the side. Doing so made him realize she was watching him.

"Oh hey," he said with a smile which Ayla returned to him. "I've got some really neat stuff, some guys from Texas brought some two-way radios, and we also got two more laptops…" he continued to talk as Ayla grabbed him and pushed him behind a metal rack full of enforcer uniforms, hidden away from his helpers. He was so excited about everything he was finding, he was still going on about it until Ayla kissed him. This of course shut him up as they shared a romantic moment hiding in the basement of the temporary resistance headquarters.

"I had to get one in while I could," she said to him.

"You know I think they have some cots over there," he said to her pressing his luck.

"Normally I would say gross but it does look better than what we used above the fish shop," she said with a grimace on her face which caused him to get even more excited. To his dismay though, she quickly assured him that in fact that would not be happening. "From here on out, I don't think we will get many more of these moments," she said as she rested her head on his chest.

"Just don't forget about me when you're leading the charge," he said.

"Never," she said as she kissed him one more time. After an extended embrace, they separated and she got back to business. "Listen; bring your list tonight when we meet back up, cafeteria about seven, okay?"

He nodded and she began to walk away but not before he reached out and grabbed her hand, "Hey, be careful okay."

"Always," she said as she set out to find Couchman and Ruiz.

She found the pair outside. She had ordered them to help expand the base using crowd control barricades but when she located them, they were simply chatting and staring across at the smoldering smoke. "What's going on boys? Thought we were making space here?" she asked them.

"Yea we are or we did," Couchman said as he pointed to the edge of the perimeter but kept his eyes on the black smoke. The sun was beginning to set which provided the skyline with a luminous orange glow. The black smoke rising in the setting sun was picturesque and Ayla joined the men taking in the beautiful chaos they had created.

After a few moments, Ruiz broke the silence. "That was pretty badass, General," he said to her as they continued to stare at the scene.

"Thanks, Ruiz," she said sincerely. "I hate to break up this moment but we've got work to do. Go see if you can help out somewhere all right, guys. Meet back at the cafeteria at seven, okay?" she said to them as she walked away. The pair still didn't move so she raised her voice slightly, "Come on, let's go." They finally listened to her and split up looking for a way to contribute.

The hour had finally come and Ayla and Miles were waiting for the arrival of their platoon leaders. They soon trickled in one by one along with those who led the arriving groups of resistance fighters. The area was packed full of both familiar and unfamiliar faces. Ayla started it off after she looked around the room and saw a lot of new people. "Ellie, what are our numbers looking like?"

"So far, we've had thirteen different groups come, the smallest was around fifty and the largest was about five hundred. Right now if I had to guess I'd say we're just over three thousand," she said.

After hearing about her disappointing numbers, Ayla was now confident that moving to Mount Lee, otherwise known as the location of the Hollywood sign, was the right choice. "Are we expecting more?" she asked Ellie and Mateo.

"I think we can expect to double our numbers by morning. After that, I'm not sure what to expect," Ellie said.

Ayla turned her back on the rest of her team and spoke so only Miles could hear her, "Six thousand unorganized troops against the U.S. army? Is Dumont trying to kill us?" she said. Miles just raised his eyebrows because deep down he too was questioning what they were getting themselves into.

"Okay, clear the room. Get everybody out except for group leaders and my people," Ayla commanded and when nothing happened she raised her voice again. "Now let's go people move!" She said as everyone scrambled to force all the non-essential people out of the cafeteria. After a few chaotic minutes, the only people left in the room were Ayla's team and the thirteen new group leaders who had come to join Ayla's army.

"All right, what I am about to discuss stays here. This is need-to-know information so if someone in your crew has a question you tell them to just fall in line. Once Ellie and Mateo are satisfied we have everyone here, we're going to move again." This garnered some muttered concerns amongst her new members.

"This seems pretty safe here, why move?" one new member asked aloud to the group.

"We're sitting ducks here." Ayla said as she approached the young soldier. "You want to be stuck in this building when the U.S. Government sends ten thousand troops to kill us all where we stand?"

"Ten thousand?" he asked with a slight tremble.

"Maybe more," she said as she turned back around. "That's why we're going to move to the highest point in the area. We're going to Hollywood," she said, trying not to sound clichéd as she pointed to Mount Lee on the map.

"You can't be serious?" Ellie said.

"It's our best shot," Ayla said. "We're going to be outnumbered, there's no doubt about it. If we get the high ground, use some creativity, maybe we have a chance at doing this."

Another new member raised his hand to ask a question and Ayla motioned for him to speak. "I don't want to be a downer here but this seems like a suicide mission. Why fight at all if we are so outnumbered?" he asked

"Fair question; all I can say is that there are bigger things at play here. We are just a small cog in a big machine. We're playing a role that hopefully will end up as a victory for the resistance," Ayla said, which to her knowledge was true, she just had no idea what the machine was. She had been asked to trust Dumont, which was becoming more and more difficult, but she gave him her word. She continued on, "I know it's hard to blindly go all in here, but I need all of you to have faith that there is a plan. When the time comes and we're face to face with the enemy and I ask all those soldiers out there to put their lives on the line, they're going to look to you to see how you react. I'll need your confidence, without that we've already lost."

A lot of the new people started to nod their head and absorb what she was conveying. Ayla had a great way of motivating people. She knew how to speak to them, when to be excited, serious, calm, or show empathy. Some of this she learned from Miles but most of it was just her natural leadership skills.

After she was confident the new people had her back she sent them all away with an assignment. "We have some really smart and creative people here. I want you all to be thinking about ways we can make this location work to our advantage. How can we make six thousand troops feel like twenty thousand troops? Don't tell anyone yet but think about who your best minds are and be ready to bring them into the frey."

She thanked all of them before ending the meeting. Afterwards, she took some time to chat with some of the new leaders and got a feel for who they were and where they came from. Most of the groups came from the southwest region of the country but there were some that had come from all over. There were a few resistance groups from random settlements throughout the Midwest much like Pikesville, one group came all the way from Florida, and there were of course a few from Los Angeles. Their members, however, were from all over the country. The first war spread people out across the land and when it was all over, they didn't have the means to get back to their homes. Most survivors, like Ayla, just settled wherever they could find a place that made them feel safe.

After the conversations started to die down, the newcomers returned to their groups who had all started to make camps outside within the perimeter of the enforcer barracks. "What's the plan now?" Jake asked Ayla off to the side.

"Can you find us a place to sleep and get some food for us?" she asked him.

"What are you going to do?" he asked without answering her.

"I'm going to make some rounds and try to talk to some of the new people; I don't want to be a total stranger when things hit the fan out there," she said.

"All right, but I'm going to come find you if it gets too late. Generals need rest too," he said to her.

Touched by his concern for her, she smiled and kissed his cheek. "I won't be too late," she said as she turned and exited the cafeteria.

By the time she made it outside, the sun had set and darkness had descended across the camp. Besides a handful of areas that had access to electricity, Los Angeles was mostly illuminated only by the moonlight. Luckily for her army, the barracks and the surrounding buildings had power. That didn't stop the now nearly four thousand troops from setting up camp fires which were spread throughout the area. Ayla was able to stop and meet many soldiers and hear their stories of why they joined. Everyone had a similar tale, just different names and locations. Their stories only fueled Ayla's desire to get justice for every single one of them.

Outside the camp, the civilian population was also growing. Word was spreading fast through the city that the enforcers had been taken down and that revolutionaries were forming an army. Many ordinary people trying to survive in Los Angeles had now come in hopes of joining the rebellion. Maybe we'll have the numbers after all, she thought to herself as she gazed out at the expanding crowd.

Just when she was about to turn back to the barracks to find Jake, someone began shouting her name. "Ayla! Ayla!" The voice screamed. She could see someone running toward her but as she had ventured a ways from the main building, she only had the orange light from the fires to see. She clutched her pistol that was hidden in her waist as a precaution. "Ayla!" The voice called again.

As the calls came nearer, she began to recognize the voice. "Raj?" she screamed with excitement as she started to run toward him. "Raj!" again she yelled his name. The two met in the middle of the packed army camp. As they came together they both stared at each other in disbelief before hugging. "How is this possible?" she asked as she squeezed him.

"I can't believe it's you," he said finally as they separated.

"Look at you!" she said as she took a step back. He was decked out in black pants and a black shirt which displayed the insignia of the revolution. He was bigger now. When he was taken by Evan, they forced him to train as a soldier and as a result he was in top shape. "You're huge!" she said.

"Look at me? Look at you! You're in charge of all this?" he said as he looked around.

"Pretty crazy, right?" she said to him, to which he just nodded with wide, excited eyes. "How did you get here? What happened?" she asked

The two found a place to sit and chat and Raj told his story. "It's kind of a blur, but I know one thing, your brother is… Not a good person," he said to her, to which she kind of nodded admitting that she knew he was right. "He brought us to this

292

place, I'm not even sure where we were, but it felt like an old army base, it was like a training facility for kids. They made us exercise all the time and basically tried to brainwash us to be loyal soldiers. Most of us weren't having it though. I'm not even sure how long I was there for but eventually a resistance group came and freed us. They basically said we could go back to wherever we came from or join them. Once I heard where they were headed I figured that would be my best shot at finding you."

"I'm so glad you did. What about Laura?" she asked concerned.

"She's here with me," he said excitedly.

"Oh?" Ayla asked him.

"Yea," he said back to her smiling. Without either one of them saying, it was obvious that the two were an item.

"What about my brother, anything on him?" she asked him.

"I never saw him again after he left us there," he said.

"You know, I kind of have a boyfriend too," she said changing the subject to which Raj looked at her in a surprising yet happy way. "But keep it on the DL; I don't want him knowing that yet," she said as they shared a laugh.

"Do you want to come inside?" she asked him

"Um, no I should probably get back to my team, and Laura. She worries about me," he said.

The two old friends hugged it out one more time and for now, went their separate ways. Upon returning to the barracks she found Jake who had managed to procure a private area where they could eat and talk candidly. She told him all about the people she met and of course her reunion with Raj. Eventually, after a long eventful day, they fell asleep.

Chapter 38

Hollywood Bound

The next morning Ayla and Jake got up and made their way to the cafeteria. There, Ayla was given an update on what went on through the night from Hudson in terms of security. Other than a few minor altercations from both inside and outside the fence, he didn't have much to say. Ellie's report on the other hand was much more interesting. "What kind of numbers did we get over night?" Ayla asked her.

"They were about what we thought they were going to be, right around six thousand," she said hesitantly. Ayla had a feeling there was more to tell so she asked if there was anything else to report. "I'm not really sure how to explain it to you. You better come take a look for yourself," Ellie told her.

Ayla and the rest of the leadership team made their way outside to see what Ellie was unable to explain. At first there was nothing unexpected; Ayla could see with her own eyes that there were a lot more soldiers within the perimeter of their headquarters. There were smoldering campfires, some soldiers were up and starting their day, while others were still sleeping under the slowly rising sun.

Her observations on her soldiers were interrupted when Ellie spoke up, "They just all kept coming all night long."

"Who?" Ayla asked as Ellie pointed out beyond the fence.

Ayla finally saw what she was referring to; thousands and

thousands of people had filled the streets surrounding the old enforcer's barracks. It wasn't just people looking to fight; there were families, women, and children. Some looked like they had brought everything they owned with them. It was a new tent city. There were even older folks who came holding their grandchildren, pointing toward her army telling stories. The people of Los Angeles came in droves to surround the first sign of hope in years.

"How many are there?" Ayla asked as she stood up on a bench to take a longer look.

"We lost count around four in the morning. But we're pretty confident it's upwards of ten thousand, maybe more," Ellie said.

"Ten thousand?" Ayla asked again, astonished.

"A lot of them want to fight. Some said they just had to come, that they were hopeful. They heard stories of a war hero coming back to save them and they needed to come see," Ellie said as Ayla looked down at her.

"I need to talk to them," Ayla said as she looked back out at the crowd. "All of them."

The team made their way to the roof of the enforcer's barracks and Miles handed Ayla the same megaphone that she had used to speak to Governor Reed.

"This is a big crowd Miles," she said as he made the handoff.

"Ayla, I truly mean this. You are our leader and I believe in you. We all do," he said as he looked around at the rest of the team who all nodded in agreement. "Whatever you say, I know it will be the right thing, and the people will listen."

She took his vote of confidence and the rest of her team's support and stood on the edge of the building's roof, megaphone in hand. The soldiers down below had already noticed the root top gathering and began to huddle around the building in anticipation. Some pointed up toward Ayla saying "Look that's her." "That's the general" as other excited conversations took place. The people outside the perimeter began to take notice too and soon the eyes of thousands were upon her, waiting to hear their leader speak.

Ayla took a deep breath and pressed the trigger on the megaphone and began her speech. "Hello everyone." Her voice echoed through the crowd. "My name is General Ayla Vural and like most of you, I've come a long way to be here today. I want to thank you all for your dedication, patriotism, and sacrifice. I had the chance to speak to some of you last night and hearing your stories is an inspiration to all of us up here. I know the last several years have been tough. We've lost loved ones, seen our liberties stripped away, we've seen our neighbors starve in the street. I am here to tell you that ends now!" she said loudly and confident, as some claps and cheers rang out from the crowd, she then continued, "For those who remember the old days, and for those who have only ever known this way of life, I have one promise for you. That if you can summon all the bravery and courage you have and fight alongside me, I promise you we'll have the chance to bring this country back to its former glory. I ask that you put your faith in the leaders you followed here as I have asked them to put their faith in me, and together we can tear the oppressors down and build a new!" She shouted loudly which was met with applause from her army. As they cheered her, she spotted Raj in the crowd who looked as determined as ever.

Once the applause died down she spoke again. "To all those outside our walls." She began to address the thousands of civilians who had gathered around them, "I see you and I hear you. Thank you for coming and helping us remember why we're here. The children here will remember this day as the day everything changed for the better. I know there are some of you out there that want to fight. I can't promise you a weapon, but I can promise you an opportunity. We'll be moving on soon from this place and if you want to join, this is your chance. To all of the moms and dads and grandmas and grandpas out there, go home, keep your families safe and live to enjoy the coming days of freedom. Everyone else, gather your things and ready yourselves, we're on the move in two hours."

She concluded her speech unceremoniously and as she stepped down from the rooftop ledge, the soldiers below her began to scramble around getting prepared to embark on another journey. Ayla and her leaders huddled around her on the rooftop to get their next set of instructions. "We're going to send a team ahead in one of the Humvees to get a lay of the land and make sure there is nothing unexpected. Frank and Ruiz, I want you two to handle this. Use the map and find the quickest and easiest route to the top of the hill. When you get back you'll lead the convoy. Couchman, you'll be next in the semi. We'll load it up and use it for extra weapons and supplies we take from the barracks. Get a team and get it loaded. Jake and Hudson, you'll follow Couchman in another Humvee, you'll be the pace car, make sure we don't get too far ahead of the walkers. Ellie, Miles, and I will be in the other Humvee. We'll go on ahead and get our base of operations setup. Everyone clear? Any questions?" she asked.

"What about the other vehicles? There are a couple trucks and another Humvee," Hudson asked.

"I'll leave that to you and Jake to designate who gets to have those," she said as he nodded in to affirm his orders. "Anything else?" she asked and when no other questions were posed she sent them on their way to begin the next, albeit short, trip to the Hollywood sign.

Frank and Ruiz immediately gathered their personal items, along with the map that Ayla had been using, and loaded themselves into a Humvee to find the best route to the Hollywood sign. You never knew what you could run into when you ventured out in post-war America. In many places roads were destroyed, buildings could be collapsed blocking the way, and bandits were always a concern, although not usually in the cities. Having them chart the way gave Ayla peace of mind that they wouldn't run into any unforeseen problems that would impede her goal of reaching their destination quickly and without incident.

As everyone scrambled to prepare the mass exodus, Ayla, Miles, and Ellie started to load up their Humvee. Jake approached Ayla and pulled her aside. "Hey, you know what's up there, right? On top of that mountain?" he asked her.

"Big white letters that spell Hollywood?" she said jokingly.

"Yes, but there used to be a big radio tower. I think I could broadcast from there. Get even more people to help our cause," he said slyly.

"Do people even use radios any more?" she asked him.

"Oh yea, that hasn't gone anywhere. If they've got a radio turned on, I can have them hear us," he said.

"Hey, Miles, Jake's riding with us now, can you tell Hudson he's on his own," she said as she turned back to Jake. "This is great. This could be really big for us," she said to him. Although Ayla really did think it could help them recruit more people, she also thought about Alexander Dumont and what her real mission had been from the start, to draw out the troops from the capital and bring the fight to Los Angeles. What better way to announce her hostile intentions to the United States government than to broadcast it directly into their homes. This would also help guarantee that she would be able to bring the army right where she wanted them: the horseshoe-shaped valley at the base of Mount Lee.

About an hour later, Frank and Ruiz returned. They gave the map to Ayla and showed her what they believed to be the best route to the top. They reported that the way was clear, that there wasn't an enforcer in sight, and that there was no sign of the army yet. After some final exchanges between her and her officers who would be leading the convoy. Ayla, Miles, Jake, and Ellie all hopped into a Humvee to make the drive to the iconic landmark.

On their way out of the barracks, they were met with soldiers applauding their exit and once on the street the sea of civilians parted forming a center lane down the road. Here, they were able to get a better look at the people they were fighting for, who stood around them and cheered. Most were skinny and frail with tattered clothing. The years of living in squalor took their toll on the people of Los Angeles. It was no wonder they flocked to the first sign of hope. Some clapped, others reached out to try to touch the passing vehicle, and some prayed as they drove by.

They soon left the scene of the barracks and began to make their way through the mostly abandoned streets. Their drive was very similar to what they saw when they first arrived in the city. For the first half of the trip, it was a very urban landscape, with empty businesses and buildings crammed together, block after block. That soon transformed into more of what used to be residential areas followed by the winding uphill road that led to the top of the mountain. They could see the Hollywood sign and it surprisingly hadn't suffered the same fate as other unattended structures. It stood out boldly against the backdrop of the green mountain landscape. Here the terrain was similar to what the team saw at the Mount Ludkin truck trail, their former headquarters in the Angeles National Forest. The drive took about thirty minutes and was the easiest leg of Ayla's long journey going all the way back to Chicago. The convoy of the thousands of revolutionaries and civilians turned soldiers, would take about four hours before they started to arrive. Walking on foot mostly uphill is a tall task with such a large group.

Ayla and her team finally reached the summit. Jake was right about the radio tower, it stood tall at the peak of the mountain and it appeared the surrounding structures were still in good shape. "I don't see how this will work to our advantage," Jake said as he stared out toward the back side of the Hollywood sign.

"Turn around, Jake," Ayla said to him.

"Oh, that makes more sense now," he said as he stared down toward the horseshoe valley that the back side of the mountain formed. "That looks like a cemetery down there," he said.

"It's about to get a lot more crowded," Miles said as Ayla and Ellie rolled their eyes at his poor attempt at humor. "What?" he asked as they walked away.

They made their way inside the building directly under the radio tower by smashing a padlock with the butt of a rifle. Once inside they located what appeared to be the main control area of the communication equipment. "All right, Jake, this is your time to shine," Ayla said to him.

"As long as there's still power I should be able to do this." He found an old fuse box and wiped away the cobwebs. "Here goes nothing," he said as he threw the large switch to the on position. After a brief moment of nothing they could hear the station slowly come back to life with a low electrical humming sound filling the air. "We're in business!" Jake said excitedly.

"Just give me a few minutes to get everything set," he said as he pulled out the laptop and connected it to the radio stations outlets.

In the meantime, Ellie, Miles, and Ayla all went back outside to reevaluate their plan. "This is perfect, Ayla," Miles said. "We can literally cover this mountainside and rain down fire into that valley."

They continued to talk strategy as they looked out at the cityscape. Because there were no more cars packing the highways, and no more factories polluting the air, the infamous smog of Los Angeles no longer existed. The team could see for miles including the still smoldering governor's office. "All right, I'm ready to broadcast," Jake yelled from the door of the radio tower, interrupting the conversation.

They walked swiftly toward the building and followed Jake inside to where he had the broadcast all set up and ready to go. "So what do I do?" Ayla asked him.

"Just tell me when you're ready and I'll fire this baby up. All you have to do is hold this button and talk into here," he said showing her an old desk microphone.

"What are you going to say?" Miles asked her.

"I don't know. I usually just improvise," she said as she nodded toward Jake who did some typing and clicking on his laptop and pointed at her when it was time to talk. She pulled up a chair, sat down, took a deep breath, and started her broadcast. "My fellow citizens of the once great United States of America; my name is General Ayla Vural of the Resistance. I am broadcasting this to you live from the Hollywood sign to tell you that the Greater Los Angeles area is no longer under the thumb of the United States Government. We have liberated this city. If you wish to come and help us restore the American way of life that many of us once knew, then please join us, we will be waiting for you. Again, coming to you from Hollywood, I repeat Los

Angeles is free. To those that oppose us, the president and his gang of oligarchs, I say this to you; Los Angeles is the first of many cities that we will liberate from your oppression. If you stand in our way, everything you know and love will cease to be and you will suffer the consequences that all dictatorships eventually face, the guns of the people they tyrannize. This is the resistance." She released the button from the microphone and leaned back into her chair.

"That was awesome," Jake said wide eyed.

"I agree, that was really good," Ellie said.

"How far did that broadcast go Jake?" Miles asked.

"Technically it could go on forever, it just depends on who has a radio on and how strong of a receiver it has," he said.

"Let's just hope someone in the capital was listening," Ayla said.

The four-person team had some time to kill before the convoy would start to arrive. They explored the radio tower and the surrounding buildings and plotted out strategic locations on the hillside that would help their chances in the upcoming conflict, all while taking in the scenic views from the top of the mountain.

A few hours had passed since they first arrived and they could finally hear the faint rumbling of the semi-truck and its unmistakable sounds of downshifting as it tried to climb the steep roads that led to the top of Mount Lee. Soon after, the now two-mile long convoy began to arrive at their new headquarters. Leading the way as planned was Frank and Ruiz followed by Couchman in the semi.

As more and more of the convoy arrived, Ayla and Miles directed each resistance group to occupy different sections of the hillside. Before long, the slopes were littered with armed resistance fighters ready to take on anything. It also worked out conveniently for Raj's group: they got the highest and centermost position on the mountain.

As for her army of civilians, she appointed a few leaders based on their own natural following within the group. Many of them came with their own weapons that included kitchen knives, homemade items similar to axes, and some even managed to procure a firearm. Ayla reluctantly decided they would be the first wave of attack. She stationed them all at the base of the mountain. Her rationale in doing so was that it would force the United States to either take aim at the charging civilian army or focus more on the hillside shooters who held the upper hand. Whatever they chose, Ayla felt it was a good strategy and gave them their best chance for victory.

By the end of the night, the entire convoy had arrived. Ayla and her leadership team had taken up residency in the radio broadcast building. Meanwhile outside, for the first time in its history, the back side of Mount Lee was more of a spectacle than the front. Thousands of resistance fighters had made makeshift camp sites and orange glowing fires dotted the landscape.

Chapter 39

The Night Before

In the coming days, Ayla's army grew slightly due to her radio broadcast but, all in all, her efforts only added a few thousand more civilians who joined the army at the base of the mountain. Overall, Ayla and Miles were pleased at the amount of support they had gathered over the course of their journey. When they started this mission in Chicago there was only a half dozen people in their convoy. The two of them had watched their numbers grow from six, to two hundred or so, and now the resistance army was well over twelve thousand soldiers. Most of them had seen action. Much like Ayla's team, they had all ran into some form of conflict with enforcers or army troops during their voyages.

After several days of occupation, things finally started to heat up. Some advanced scouts that Ayla had sent up North, had returned and reported that the Army was indeed on approach toward Los Angeles. It was developing just how Ayla and Dumont had hoped for. The scouts reported an army nearly twice the size of their own, which was what they had expected. They were set to arrive in one day's time. In preparation for the upcoming fight, Ayla called an emergency meeting with her team, all the leaders of the resistance group, and the leaders of the civilian army group. She hoped to give them one more rally speech, and inform them of what they should anticipate in terms of firepower.

It was night-time again on top of Resistance Hill. That's what the soldiers all started calling their new hideout and the name seemed to stick. There wasn't much room inside the small buildings that made up the radio tower facility, so they had the meeting outside in what was once the parking lot. The pavement was cracked and had some small shrubs growing where cars used to park. You could still see some of the painted yellow lines but most had faded in the hot California sun. Although the buildings still had some working electrical systems, the parking lot lights had gone out of service long ago, so the team had to build a campfire for suitable light. Ayla and her team were joined by the now twenty-seven other leaders. They all wore their own style of resistance uniform but there was one thing they all had in common; somewhere on their attire, the original red shield with the coiled yellow snake could be seen. Except, of course, the leaders of the civilian army who, due to lack of resources, showed their unity by tying red or black bans around their arms.

Once she was satisfied all were present and accounted for, Ayla began her meeting. "I'm sure all of you have heard that we're less than a day away from the arrival of the army. I know there have been some whispers that there's twenty thousand troops headed this way. Well, that number is wrong," she said as some of them breathed a sigh of relief. "There is probably more like thirty thousand," she said, which caused some chattering to pick up, but Ayla continued on. "This is what we expected and why we're here. This mountain is going to make us feel like we're fifty thousand strong. When tomorrow comes, this is what you can expect to see. It's going to be mostly ground troops. We know that most of the Humvees had been rigged to run on solar power, this tells us that their fuel supply is limited. Meaning the likelihood of airships or ground assault vehicles is very small. This doesn't mean they won't have any heavy artillery weapons or anything like that. They're going to bring the heat but again that's why we have the high ground." She looked around at the group as the orange fire reflected off their faces and began to pick up the intensity in hopes of providing some motivation. "We are going to rain hellfire down on them until they turn around and run home or until each and every one of them is dead."

"Now are there any questions before we send you on your way?" Miles chimed in.

Several leaders raised their hands and they called on them one by one from left to right. "Where are y'all going to be when all this happens?" the first man asked.

"Oh I'll be right beside you. I wouldn't miss this chance for anything. We all will be," Ayla said as she looked at her officers.

"Let's say hypothetically this doesn't go the way you want it to. What then?" the next man asked.

"Then we'll either be dead, captured, or on the run again and I don't know about you, but I don't plan on being captured or running. However, I will reiterate there are more things at play here then just our fight. It's important we play our role," she said to him.

One of the few female leaders besides Ayla and Ellie asked the next question. "What happens next? If we win I mean," she said.

Not wanting to give too much away Ayla answered with a pretty generic response, "Then we'll be one step closer to freedom."

After all their questions were answered, Ayla sent them off with some closing remarks. "Remember your role here. I need all of you, to get all of them ready to fight for their lives, remind them of why they're here and what the alternative is. Remind them that fighting for their freedom is worth risking their lives because a life deprived of opportunity is no life worth living. Good luck and God's speed. We'll see you out there."

Eventually all the leaders made their way back to their groups. Over the course of the next hour or so, Ayla could hear the reactions of the different addresses going on simultaneously. One group cheered, while another clapped. Even further down the mountain she could hear the civilian army yelling in excitement. As she gazed down on the orange spotted slopes, she was confident that her message was being conveyed throughout her army.

Once all the excitement died down, her team made their way back into the facilities of the radio tower. Jake once again had prepared a spot for him and Ayla. As he led her to their own secluded sleeping arrangement Ayla, out of the corner of her eye, saw Ellie leading Couchman by the hand off to their own private area. Ayla just laughed, which prompted Jake to ask her what was so funny. "Nothing, nothing at all," she said not wanting to call out her fellow woman.

Jake eventually brought her down the stairs in what must have been at some point a storage room. He had a makeshift bed made up out of the supplies he brought and illuminated the room with a little flashlight standing up on end. "It's as close to a candlelight dinner as you're going to get," he said to her smiling as he pulled two MRE's out of his backpack.

Ayla, who had never had anyone ever treat her like this, just looked at the room with her jaw slightly open but with a definite smile on her face. "When did you do all this?" she asked him.

"Well, not all of us are leading an army. I had some time to sneak away while you and Miles were doing your thing," he said.

"This is really nice Jake, thank you," she said sincerely.

He looked her in the eyes and spoke from his heart. "We don't know what's going to happen tomorrow and if it is our last night, I want to spend it with you," he said, to which she just stared up at him for a moment and then they kissed passionately and just held each other. Eventually they settled in and ate their food, talked for a while, and then shared a night together as if it was their last.

Chapter 40

The Battle of Mount Lee

The next morning, Ayla and Jake were up before the sunrise and outside they could hear some commotion. They exited their makeshift bedroom and found soldiers scurrying about exchanging guns and ammo. Ayla looked around for a moment and found Miles standing near the edge of the parking lot staring off toward the direction of the oncoming Army. "What's going on?" she asked him.

He nodded his head in the same direction he was staring and said, "They're coming."

Ayla looked outward and didn't see anything at first but then she saw it, headlights way off in the distance making their way up the winding road that led to the cemetery at the base of the mountain. "Somebody find Hudson for me," Ayla shouted.

Shortly thereafter, Hudson came running from the radio tower still getting his uniform in order. "Yes, ma' am?" he asked her.

"I have a big ask for you." He nodded awaiting her orders. "I need you to lead the civilian army down there. They need someone that can set an example for them and more importantly they need someone to show them when to charge. It needs to be perfect," she said to him.

Hudson was a true soldier and a true believer in the cause, and although for a brief second you could tell he knew the danger involved was great, he was willing to do whatever it took to help win the war, no matter the cost. "You can count on me, General," he said to her with confidence.

"Take whoever you need. If there's anyone that you want to bring along who has what it takes, bring them," she said.

"I have a few men who would love to get up close and personal with the enemy," he said. She shook his hand and sent him down to the base of the mountain knowing that he might not make it back.

"I'm going to need to get down there too," she said to Miles as Jake looked at her with concern. "All we have is that megaphone, I need to get close enough so those bastards can hear me."

By now, the rest of her team had joined them looking out toward the oncoming threat. "If you're going, we're all going," Jake said, as he looked around at the others who gave their support to his declaration.

"Well there you have it, looks like it's a party," Miles said.

"All right meet me back here in like thirty minutes, and we'll all go down together," she said. She turned and headed back to her make shift room and Jake followed her. Once they got back to where they slept, she picked up his bag, handed it to him, and said to him, "I need you to understand that I have to go to a different place today," she said as Jake tried to open his mouth to speak. "Alone," she said again as she pushed his bag into his chest and pushed him out the door.

Seconds later, to Ayla's surprise, the door swung back open. It was Jake. "You don't get to do that yet," he said to her. She tried to speak but this time it was Jake who interrupted her. "I know you're the general today and are in charge of an army, but I want Ayla for just a few more seconds," he said and to her own surprise she stayed quiet and let him continue. "This whole time, living in this hell hole, I searched for purpose. Then one day I found it. It wasn't the idea of freedom, or killing U.S. soldiers, it was you. You're my purpose, Ayla, and if that means fighting a war and dying for you then that's what I'll do." He paused for a moment but then gained the confidence he needed. "I love you, Ayla, and if we survive this I'm going to marry you." He finished his profession and the two just stood there for a moment. Ayla was speechless and Jake couldn't take the silence any more. "Okay, you can be general again now," he said as he turned and walked away.

"Wait, Jake!" she yelled to him and chased him down. "I love you too!" she said as they embraced and kissed each other one last time before the big confrontation. "Now, get out of here, you're making me soft," she said jokingly.

Ayla returned to her room alone. It reminded her of the tenement house back in Chicago. The walls were metal with rusty orange blemishes, the light above her flickered intermittingly, and the space was cramped. She took off the bulky sweatshirt she had been wearing and underneath she was sporting a fitted, black, short sleeve shirt. She reached down and tightened her laces on her boots and then pulled the black band with the symbol of the resistance out of her bag. She tied it on her arm and placed her black hat over her shimmering, short white hair. She took it upon herself to take some of the supplies at the enforcer barracks. She had a protective vest that she wore over the top of her shirt. She then strapped a utility belt around her waist. This had a holster for her pistol and had some other small compartments but they were unfortunately empty. Her pants were also black and form fitting. Her last piece of attire was the most important, the automatic rifle that she acquired from the enforcer armory. She hoisted it over her shoulder and considered herself almost ready. She took a few more minutes to mentally prepare herself. This was the moment she had been waiting for; the culmination of Dumont's planning and her leadership efforts coming together. She was finally ready to step out and lead her army.

She made her way out to her team who were all waiting for her at the top of the mountain. They were all dressed similarly with their weapons at their sides. Miles had her megaphone and the group started making their way down the mountainside. As they passed the different resistance groups stationed at various points, they all looked to Ayla. She was fearless in the face of danger as the United States Army started to set up their base of operations in the cemetery. She could feel their eyes on her but in this moment she was laser focused on her enemy. This was done intentionally, she was trying to appear unfazed and determined in the hopes of instilling confidence in her army.

Once they got about halfway down the mountain, they were satisfied that the megaphone would be loud enough that her enemies could hear her. It took quite a while, but eventually, it appeared that the entirety of whatever forces they brought had all arrived at the cemetery. It was a sea of green army uniforms and Humvees that seemed endless as it extended below the horizon of Ayla's sight. To everyone's delight, the Humvees were all they had for vehicles as there were no tanks or any other heavy machinery in sight. Eventually, a group of four men came to the front of their encampment.

They too had a megaphone. "Where is Ayla Vural?" the first man asked as his voice echoed through the speaker.

Ayla grabbed the megaphone from Miles and held it up to her mouth. "That's General Vural to you," she said.

"What do you want, General?" he asked sarcastically.

"I have what I want. A city free from the U.S. A new

sovereign land and you are not welcome here!" she shot back.

Just then, Miles leaned over to her. "Is that who I think it is?" he asked as he stared at the four men.

She grabbed the binoculars and focused in on the men's faces. To her surprise, Miles was right. One of the men standing to the right of the man with the megaphone was none other than her own brother Evan. "That son of a..." she was cut off by the man's next message to the resistance.

"This is your one chance, give yourself up, tell your people here to go home and we'll only kill you for treason. End this pitiful charade," he said.

Ayla was about to raise the megaphone to reply but before she could, a single gunshot was fired from behind her and in an instant, Evan Vural's body crumpled as his blood sprayed all over the face of the man next to him. Ayla had a feeling she knew where the gunshot came from and as she turned around to look, her prediction was proven true as she saw Raj standing there, still aiming down the sight of his gun. He stood there for moment, staring at his victim and then he looked toward Ayla. There wasn't time for her to process the fact that Raj killed her brother or anything else for that matter because the response from the United States was swift. Gun fire started cascading up from the cemetery. She yelled as loud as she could in the megaphone "Fire!" and Ayla's war had begun.

The United States was forced to fight a two-front war as the army of civilian soldiers, led by Hudson, charged them, engaging in hand-to-hand combat, while Ayla and the rest of the mountainside resistance fighters took aim and fired repeatedly down onto them. "Don't let up!" Ayla yelled as she reloaded her weapon. Her plan was working. Although they were outnumbered they were winning and all was going according to plan.

Midway through the firefight, something started to happen.

Despite the seemingly endless gunfire there was a deep rumbling sound growing louder. Soon it sounded like a thunderstorm, louder than she had ever heard. It was so loud it started to drown out the sounds of the thousands of gunshots going off. As the deafening sound drew closer, it seemed that others had noticed too as the gunfire began to die down. Soon, those who were still standing on each side had stopped what they were doing and all looked to the sky as the roar became almost unbearable. Then through the clouds, Ayla saw it, a giant bomber aircraft followed by hundreds of fighter jets. Then, more and more filled the sky, some so low they could feel the rumbling in their chests. "What the hell is going on!" Miles yelled to her.

Ayla grabbed her binoculars and looked to the sky. She was able to focus in on some of the lower flying jets and caught the unmistakable green, white and red colors of a flag painted on the belly of one of the aircrafts. She looked to Miles and yelled back to him. "It's the Mexicans!" she yelled. Then it dawned on her. She thought back to the cryptic letter she found in Dumont's basement. "MP!" she yelled. Miles gave her a confusing look as the thunder from the fighter jets continued. "MP, Mexican President!" She then put two and two together and grabbed the Megaphone and started sprinting toward the base of the mountain followed by Jake and Miles. She pulled the trigger when she was close enough and yelled, "Hudson! Get out of—" Before she could finish the jets fired their missiles into the ground war happening down at the cemetery. A relentless barrage of fire and explosions rained down on both the United States Army and Ayla's civilian volunteers. The blast was so intense it sent Ayla, Jake, Miles, and the other soldiers near the explosion flying through the air in the opposite direction.

As they came to and pulled themselves up from the ground they saw the once-green grass had been tuned into a scorched, black field with fire and smoke. The charred remains of thousands of soldiers, from both sides, littered the battlefield. The Mexican Air Force kept on flying north and as the rumbling from the jet engines dissipated it was replaced by the cheers of resistance fighters who had claimed victory in the wake of the successful air assault from the Mexicans.

The rest of the United States Army that survived had little choice but to retreat. They scattered and presumably hid in the abandoned city or left altogether.

"Where are they going?" Jake asked as Couchman and Ellie joined them at the base of the mountain.

"They're going to the capital. That was Dumont's plan all along. Draw the army out so the Mexicans could attack the capital with no one there to defend it," she said. "Frank and Ruiz?" she asked Ellie.

"They didn't make it," she said sadly.

They all took a moment for their departed friends until Ayla broke the silence, "They were good soldiers and better friends. I wish I could have thanked them for everything they did."

"Now what?" Couchman asked.

"Now we wait. Dumont had a plan and for now we are going to see what happens," she said. "We'll stay here for the night. Tend to the wounded and take care of the dead the best we can," she said as she looked around at all the bodies.

She looked at what remained of her team. They all had suffered some minor injuries, scrapes and bruises, nothing serious though. They were dirty and tired, but alive. "Take a few minutes and take care of yourselves but I want to have another meeting tonight with the team leaders so spread the word; same time and place," she said as she wiped blood away from her mouth with the back of her hand.

They all made their way back up the mountain toward the radio tower. On their way there they were greeted by celebrating soldiers. They wanted to shake hands with their leaders and Ayla and the others obliged and joined in, playing the part of happy victors. For the most part their happiness was genuine, but for Ayla, she knew that there was more to the puzzle. So many thoughts were running through her head. She wondered what Dumont's plan was for the capital, and what he was going to do next, and how the hell he got the Mexicans to agree to do this.

She continued to climb and think, occasionally shaking the hand of an admiring soldier, until she heard her name. "Ayla!"

She looked to the direction from which it came and saw Raj jogging toward her along the slanted mountainside. She wasn't really sure how to react. On one hand, her brother had not only betrayed her and the resistance but he also held her friend at gunpoint and threatened to kill him. But on the other hand, it was still her brother and any chance she had at reconciling with him was stolen from her.

Raj finally made his way to her panting from his short sprint. She waited and allowed him to explain himself. "I'm sorry, Ayla. I had to and I knew you couldn't. I couldn't stop myself after what he did to me, and to Laura," he said as his eyes met hers. He didn't have to say it but she could tell that something bad had happened to them. He started to lose control, his eyes welled up and he started to stutter, "I...I... jus... just couldn't. He did things to us, Ayla, in the woods. Don't make me say it," he said to her. Ayla grabbed him and hugged him. "It's okay. We can talk later," she said to him sending him on his way.

Chapter 41

The Aftermath

Later that evening, Ayla had her meeting with the surviving group leaders. Thanks to the bombardment from the Mexican Air Force, Ayla's army suffered minimal casualties. Unfortunately, the same could not be said for the civilian fraction of her forces. Most of the volunteers that joined up in Los Angeles had lost their lives. This too of course included Hudson and his few select soldiers he brought with him to lead them.

By the time the meeting commenced, the mountainside looked similar to what it was the night before, sporadic fires and makeshift camps dotted the terrain, only this time, at the base of the mountain there was a smoldering battlefield. Ayla held her meeting in the same parking lot. They surrounded the same fire pit and Ayla laid out what would happen next, even though she herself was not sure what to expect. What she did know was that she needed to give them some sort of guidance to relay the message to the thousands of soldiers who were technically still under her command, despite not currently having a mission.

"First of all, congratulations, we came here with the goal of winning and we did it," she said as they gave themselves a modest round of applause and then she continued, "Also, thank you for believing that you are a part of something bigger. I hope what you saw earlier today reinforces the faith you have in the organization of this resistance." They all listened on intently as she went on, "The second prong of this attack is probably obvious to you now. The Mexicans were passing through en route to the capital where they're assisting the take over and removal of the current U.S. governing body." They all clapped again, this time with more enthusiasm. Ayla of course never knew this was Dumont's actual plan but it was obvious now, so in order to save face, she pretended she was in on it the whole time.

"What now?" One of the resistance leaders asked.

"They'll complete their mission and we'll wait for them here. We'll confer and discuss the state of the capital and what we need to do next. Any other questions?" she asked and after none were asked, she sent them off to relay her message to their soldiers.

Meanwhile, it had been a long day for everyone, including Ayla's team which was now down to just Jake, Ayla, Miles, Ellie, and Couchman. They all returned to the radio tower and gathered in the large open area where Ayla sent out her original broadcast and that's where things got heated. "Let me ask you something, General," Miles said aggressively as he confronted Ayla. "Did you really send all those people out there to die like that?"

This really set Ayla off. She thought Miles knew her better than to ask that question. "Are you kidding right now? You saw me run down there; I tried to get them out of there. I had no idea the Mexicans were even coming!" she fired back at him. Before he could issue a retort she continued on, "I can't believe you'd even ask me that, don't you think I feel bad enough already," she started to go after him and Jake grabbed her to keep them separated.

"Okay, okay you're right. Sorry," Miles said putting his hands up as he could see Ayla was clearly upset at both him and the fact that all those people were killed in an instance.

Eventually, they both calmed down and cooler heads prevailed.

"What did Dumont tell you exactly?" Jake asked in an attempt to bring back a normal conversation.

"Nothing. I mean originally he wanted us to draw them out, which we did. It was my idea to come here though, so I'm not sure how he knew we were going to be here even," she said.

"Radio broadcasts work both ways. If it traveled all the way north to the capital then chances are it made its way south to Mexico," Jake said.

"That answers that mystery," Miles said.

"So it was my fault. I led them straight here," Ayla said.

"No, Ayla, we'd all be dead if we fought them in the streets. They would have overwhelmed us," Ellie said trying to make her feel less guilty.

"Let's just get some rest. It's been a long, eventful day. We can figure things out tomorrow, we're all emotional right now," Couchman said, which surprised the others as he rarely spoke up and gave his honest opinion.

"He's right. I'm sorry, Ayla. I know better," Miles said apologizing to her again. This time she welcomed it.

The night seemed to drag on. The team ate some food, talked about the day and the friends they had lost. They even managed to share some laughs. Eventually, they all went to their sleeping areas including Jake and Ayla. Jake fell asleep pretty quickly which was understandable considering the day they had. Ayla, however, lay awake and stared at the ceiling. There was something she couldn't get off her mind and that was the rest of the letter she had found in Dumont's desk. At some point she lost the paper she scribbled notes on, but it didn't matter, she remembered it clearly and kept trying to decode its meaning.

MP had to mean Mexican President. RGHT, what does that

mean? she asked herself. *Rio Grande? What's the H for? Does T stand for Texas?* She racked her brain over and over again, but she never settled on anything that made sense. Eventually, she too drifted off to sleep.

The next day, Ayla was awoken to a deep whooshing sound. She lay in bed for a moment until the sound grew louder and then she realized what it was. She sprang out of bed and the unmistakable sound of a helicopter on approach became louder and louder. She gathered her things including her rifle and ran outside before Jake even knew what was happening.

She exited the building and she could see three helicopters descending from the sky. As they came in for a landing, some soldiers readied their weapons, to which Ayla raised her hand signaling them to stand down. As the trio came closer, the dirt and dust swirled and the bushes that crept up through the cracks of the asphalt, whipped back and forth. They finally landed and you could hear the whirling of engines powering down. Ayla ducked low and covered her head and eyes from the debris field of small particles buzzing around her. Through the flying dirt, she once again spotted the Mexican flag painted on the sides of the helicopters. Eventually, Miles, Jake, Ellie and Coachmen joined her outside.

The green metal doors slid open and two uniformed soldiers came out first followed by two older men. Ayla and Ellie both recognized the first gentleman immediately: it was Alexander Dumont. He was wearing a perfectly clean white suit with a matching fedora, and shiny dress shoes. He was followed by a less conspicuously dressed man in a standard black suit and tie. This man, Ayla was sure, must have been part of the Mexican government. Ellie soon rushed by Ayla and ran to her grandfather. At first the uniformed officers stopped her but he assured them it was ok and they had a quick hug under the still-rotating helicopter blades.

Alexander and his companion finally approached Ayla and her team and he spoke first, "Somewhere we can talk?" He yelled over the still-loud helicopter. Ayla motioned for him to follow them into the radio tower building.

They had all reached their destination and Ayla's team was standing on one side of the room opposite of Alexander Dumont and his small entourage. Ayla just waited for him to begin; after all, this was mostly his plan. "Ayla...General, congratulations you orchestrated your side of the plan to perfection, above and beyond," he said clapping his hands together.

"You look ridiculous, you know that right?" Ayla told him sharply.

He shrugged his shoulders. "I like this suit," he said as he looked down at his coat. "Anyways, I'm sure you're wondering who this is," he said as he motioned toward the man in the black suit.

The man in black stepped forward, "Hello, General, me llamo Vice President Enrique Hernandez, and on behalf of El Presidente and the people of Mexico, we wish to congratulate you on such a historic victory," he said genuinely, which Ayla nodded to acknowledge his praise. In this moment, she again thought of the cryptic letter, it had been signed "H" Could Hernandez be H? She asked herself.

"Enrique and I go way back. He's how I was able to get the Mexicans to help us," Dumont said.

"Before we get any further, let me ask a question. Who made the order to shoot the missiles?" Ayla asked pointedly.

"Well, me," Dumont said

"Grandpa, how could you?" Ellie asked in shock.

"There were lots of our people down there. Good soldiers and volunteers, fighting because I made them believe you had a plan for them!" Ayla said angrily.

"I did have a plan, a damn good one too. You of all people know, Ayla, that winning a war comes at a price," Dumont said.

"What was the price for the people living in the capital?" Ayla asked him.

"There is no capital, not any more ," he said bluntly.

"All those people, you just killed them? Women and children too?" she asked.

"Oh, grow up. This is what you wanted. The capital is gone, your enemies dead. Thanks to me. Now you can start all over," he said back to her.

"Oh, so I'm supposed to believe you did this for the good of the country, that you don't want anything out of this?" she asked him.

"I already told you, I'm too old for this. I finally can retire. H here tells me that Cancun is beautiful," he said confirming her suspicions about who H was.

She couldn't contain herself any longer. "What does 'RGHT' mean? I saw the letter, in your desk," she said.

Dumont looked back at the Vice President then back to Ayla as if he wasn't quite ready to share the information. He hesitated briefly but decided to tell her anyways as it seemed the cat was out of the bag. "Have you ever heard of Guadalupe Hidalgo?" he asked her.

"The name rings a bell, who is he?" she asked.

"Not who, but what. I'll give you a brief history lesson. Back in the mid eighteen hundreds, the United States and Mexico were at war. The U.S. defeated the Mexicans and signed the Treaty of Guadalupe Hidalgo. This, of course, forced Mexico to hand over

525,000 square miles of land to the U.S. This land becomes Arizona, California, Colorado, Nevada, and so on, you get the idea," he said to her.

Ayla waited for him to get to his point. "R-G-H-T. 'Repeal of Guadalupe Hidalgo Treaty,'" he said.

"You didn't," Ellie said

"What does that mean?" Jake asked.

"It means you're standing in Mexico, Jake," Ayla said as her gaze was still focused on Dumont. "You gave away half the country!" she said to him.

"Like I said, victory comes with a cost," he said, unashamed.

At this point, the Vice President of Mexico spoke up in an attempt to calm the situation. "Listen, I know, this is shocking for you, but we have been working on this for a long time. It is not a bad thing. Mexico has stepped up in the absence of the U.S. We've become a global leader, not just in our economy, but in all facets. We have advances in modern medicine, technology, and we are only growing stronger every day," he said.

"How is that supposed to help us?" she asked.

"The people who live here, who will become Mexican citizens, will have access to that world. They will have the same rights as every other Mexican citizen," he said.

"What about the rest of OUR country?" she asked.

"I am making a pledge to you right now that our government and the people of Mexico will help you rebuild. We want to work with you to start to restore the United States so it can work toward what it used to be. The President wants to work directly with you Ayla," he said enthusiastically.

"This is happening, Ayla, the deal is done. I think it's pretty generous. You've seen what they can do. They could take over the whole country but they aren't because we made an agreement," Dumont piped in.

"We already have troops on the ground working to make things safe, starting at the southern border. We're working with the Red Cross to get help to those who need it most," the Vice President said.

"We remain independent?" she asked.

"Always, you have my word," the Vice President said. "The President would like to meet you; he very much wants to work with you to help your people," he said.

Ayla thought for a moment. She thought of all the horrible things she saw as a young girl, the training with Miles, the battles she fought in. She had flashes of her life in hiding in Chicago, the tenement houses, and then reliving it all again in her most recent journey. She looked back at Jake who was watching her process things. "No," she said as she looked him in the eyes. She thought of the last exchange they had together and how they told each other how they felt. Her whole life had been dictated by this conflict. It was at this moment where she decided she was finished.

"I don't understand, what do you mean, no?" Dumont said.

"My whole life, since I was thirteen years old, has been decided by war. It has taken so much from me. I'm ready to see what life is like without it," she said.

"This country needs someone to lead them, Ayla. It was supposed to be you," Dumont said.

"They have their leader," she said.

"Who?" the Vice President asked.

"Her," Ayla said pointing to Ellie.

This caught everyone by surprise including Ellie. "Ellie?" Dumont said, "She's just a kid."

"Hey, I am not," Ellie said as she approached Ayla, "What

are you doing?" she asked her in a hushed tone.

"Ellie, you're the smartest person I know. You're a natural born leader, brave, and you've got great ideas on how to go forward. Plus, don't you think it's about time a woman ran this place? Look what old men have done while they were in charge," Ayla said to her. "It's a no-brainer. Plus, she's got the right name for the job." No one else in the room objected and even though Alexander Dumont was taken aback by her nomination, he secretly enjoyed the fact that someone with his last name would be the next President.

Ellie smiled and hugged her, "Thank you. I won't ever forget this," she whispered to her.

"Okay, Madam President, are you ready to go?" H said to her as he grabbed her hand.

"Yes, well, Interim Madam President. Oh and he's coming too," she said as she pointed to Couchman which prompted a smile from Ayla, who knew their secret.

They all said their goodbyes and Jake, Ayla, and Miles all watched as the trio of helicopters ascended in the air with a flurry of wind and noise.

Epilogue

The doorbell rang, and a little boy came running down the stairs to open the door. "Hi, honey. Where's your mom?" Zoe asked as she held the hand of her now-four-year-old daughter.

"Mom!" the boy yelled, "Aunt Zoe is here."

"Be right down Zoe!" Ayla yelled from upstairs.

"Go play with Frankie, sweetie," Zoe said as the two children ran off to play. Zoe could feel the cold air from the air conditioner kick on overhead so she closed the door behind her. Just as the door closed, Ayla came down the stairs. Her long brown hair had finally returned, although for now she had it in a ponytail; her newest addition loved to pull and chew on it while Ayla carried her around the house. It was Ayla and Jake's second child they had adopted since finding a home after the battle atop Resistance Hill. There were so many children in need from the war torn United States and Jake and Ayla so badly wanted to start a family, it worked out perfectly.

"Where are the boys?" Ayla asked as she grabbed her sunglasses from the fireplace mantle. They were sitting next to a picture of Jake, Ayla and their two children. There was also a picture from their wedding day and next to that in a black frame, was the crumpled and wrinkled picture of her family that she unearthed years ago in Chicago.

"Oh, they're out in the greenhouse. I think Miles is talking their ear off again about the good old days," Zoe said, to which Ayla rolled her eyes.

"Do you know if they were able to get the corn planted yet?" Ayla asked her.

"Yea, I think Gabe handed it off to Raj and Laura," she said. Ayla and her team took advantage of their accomplishments and successes from four years ago. In recognition of their service and sacrifice to both nations, they were granted dual citizenship. They also were given a nice chunk of land in the Napa Valley, and after a few years of hard work, they built themselves a small communal living space. After things settled down, Gabe and Zoe were able to hunt down Ayla and along with her and Jake, Raj and Laura also lived there. Miles finally came around and got a place nearby as well. Ironically the heroes of the revolution all technically lived in Mexico, but none of them cared, as they were just happy to be alive and together.

The Mexicans kept good on their word. Shortly after the war, they sent out envoys and Red Cross teams across the country. They identified the greatest areas of need and intervened at the direction of Madame President Ellie Dumont, who was just reelected by the newly formed boroughs of the rebuilding United States.

Within their small little corner of the world, Ayla and Jake live comfortably with their two children. Gabe and Zoe still get to do the hunting and Raj and Laura help wherever they can. Miles started playing the old man card and likes to sit around and pretend he's too feeble to help. With Jake's technological prowess, they created a pretty advanced self-sustaining farm that grew vegetables and medicinal herbs and plants.

Life was finally good for Ayla; her whole existence since that fateful day in her front yard, years ago, had been filled with conflict. The only life she ever knew revolved around war and violence. Until one day, a nerdy soldier excited about a computer, made her realize she could have more. She was finally happy and at peace, Ayla's war had finally come to an end.